Murder Undeniable

Kat and Mouse Mystery Series

Anita Waller

First published in 2018 by Bloodhound Books

www.bloodhoundbooks.com

Print ISBN 978-1912604-99-9

Also By Anita Waller

Psychological thrillers
Beautiful
Angel
34 Days
Strategy
Captor
Game Players
Malignant

Supernatural
Winterscroft

Praise For Anita Waller

"a masterclass in suspense. This is Waller at her best" *Betsy Reavley – bestselling author of Murder at the Book Club and The Optician's Wife*

"a whirlwind of a read and a poignant one" *– Nicki's Book Blog*

"if you are after a book that deals with family, relationships and friendship that takes dark turns and twists that will hook you from the very beginning then you really do need to read this" *– Yvonne Me and My Books*

"Thanks for a great read Anita Waller! When is the next one out??" **Rebecca Burton – If Only I Could Read Faster**

"This book has lots of gasp out loud moments and plenty that will make you a little weepy too (it did for me anyway)." **Lorna Cassidy – On The Shelf Reviews**

"This is an engrossing read that I pretty much inhaled." **Philomena Callan – Cheekypee Reads And Reviews**

"Waller has an amazing skill to grab you and keep you interested until the very last page." **Eclectic Ramblings of Author Heather Osborne**

"WOW! ANITA HAS DONE IT AGAIN. What a bloody brilliant, outstanding, captivating story." **Gemma Myers – Between The Pages Book Club**

"This is a very gritty read...Add into the mix, the ruthlessness of the gangsters and you've got a cracking crime thriller." **Claire Knight – A Knight's Reads**

"It has twists and turns, shocks and honestly at times I had no idea what the end would be!" **Donna Maguire – Donnas Book Blog**

"A plot to keep you turning from beginning to end. I really enjoyed this . A captivating read ." **Nicki Murphy – Nicki's Book Blog**

"... a really well written, gripping book with plenty of twists for me!" **Donna Maguire – Donnas Book Blog**

"...building up to a tense, drama packed read. I was literally biting my nails by the end." **Lorna Cassidy – On The Shelf Reviews**

"The author really keeps you on the edge of your seat – the twists made me gasp and she sets the atmosphere absolutely perfectly." **Melisa Broadbent – Broadbean's Books**

"If you are looking for a crime thriller that is somewhat unnerving as it is every mothers worst nightmare, a fast paced page turner that keeps you guessing. Then I definitely recommend Captor!" **Dash Fan Book Reviews**

"Captor will have you gripped from the beginning and won't let you go until you have finished. It is a suspense filled crime thriller that will keep you guessing throughout." **Gemma Myers – Between The Pages Book Club**

Dedicated with love to my husband, Dave,
with gratitude for his patience and tea-making skills.
No teapots were hurt during the writing
of this book.

I would like to be there, were it but
to see how the cat jumps.

In WEK Anderson (ed), *Journals of Sir Walter Scott*
11 December 1826

Mountains will go into labour,
and a silly little mouse will be born.

Ars Poetica 1.139

Sweet is revenge – especially to women.

Don Juan (1819-24)
Canto1, st.117

1

8 May 2002

Caroline Phillips and Isla Norman sat on the ground behind the riverside wall; Caroline took out a packet of cigarettes and a lighter. 'Let's have one now before the lads get here,' she said, 'and then they can smoke their own instead of ours.'

Isla giggled. She was a giggly person by default, and at that moment her fascination for Oliver Merchant, with his blonde hair, slim body and piercing blue eyes, was making her even more giggly than usual.

'They said they'd come after football practice had finished, so they'll not be here yet.'

'I heard from Sarah last night. She said to wish Michael happy birthday, and she's sorry she's not here to take part.'

'She like her new school?' Caroline asked, dragging on the cigarette, and tucking her long brown hair behind her ears. Sarah Hodgson had been a close friend of both of them, and had suffered an enforced move to Essex following her father's promotion.

'She just said it was okay, sounded a bit quiet to me.'

Caroline laughed. 'Quiet? Sarah? What have they done to her?'

'Dunno. Maybe it's because it's another birthday here. We set this up between us, and she enjoyed four birthdays, including her own, then went to sunny Essex. Is Essex sunny?'

'No more than Derbyshire,' was Caroline's considered opinion.

Half an hour later, there was a crack of a football being hit against a wall, and the five lads they had been expecting came around the corner together. Peter Swift picked up the ball and they all crossed to join the girls. Each one took off their backpacks and removed two cans of lager.

The previous year, Anthony Jackson had been the first one of the group to become fifteen, and they had decided to meet by the river, take a can of lager each, and chill out together after school. It had been an excellent couple of hours, and that first birthday had led on to a promise to treat each birthday within the group of eight in the same way.

By the time the second birthday had arrived, Keith Lancaster's, the lager intake had doubled, and the girls had also brought snacks.

Each birthday had been a celebration of friends, and the only time all eight hadn't been there was when Sarah had moved away. Now they were seven, and Michael Damms was their honoured guest on this warm early May evening.

During the cold months, they had met twice in Oliver's garden, using the summer house, but the proximity to his parents tended to put a dampener on their conversations, and their drinking and smoking. It was much nicer down by the river; Michael's birthday was the 8th of May, and they would soon be meeting up again for Caroline's benefit on the 23rd of May.

Isla and Caroline produced crisps, peanuts and sausage rolls, and a general discussion was held that if they all chipped in one pound each for every birthday, the girls could get the food without having to dip into their own pockets.

They finished eating, and once again the cigarettes came out.

Only Peter refused to smoke. 'I've had some good news, so there'll be no more smoke going inside me.'

'What's that?' Anthony asked.

'It's top secret, I've said nothing at school in case I don't get accepted, but I'm going for a trial at Derby County.'

There was silence for a moment, then everybody clapped.

'That's brilliant,' Oliver said. 'You'll go to their academy if you're accepted?'

Peter nodded. 'Yep, and I'm not jeopardising that for the sake of a fag.'

They all toasted him with what remained in the bottom of their cans, and he blushed. He was the quiet one of the group, unused to the limelight.

Anthony took out a small plastic bag from the front pocket of his backpack. 'I didn't know whether to bring these or not,' he said, 'but this is a double celebration with Michael's birthday and Peter's news.' He offered the roll-up cigarettes around.

'What are they?' Caroline raised her eyebrows; her nervous reaction wasn't lost on the others.

'Joints,' Anthony laughed. 'They'll make you feel good. My treat to us for Michael's birthday.'

'Drugs?' Oliver said, reaching across and taking one. He lit it, and took a drag.

There was a slight pause, and then he said, 'Wow, happy sixteenth, Michael!'

The others, with the exception of Peter, all took one, and quietly sat with their backs to the stone wall, lost in the moment, not speaking, enjoying the new experience.

Darkness had fallen; Peter gathered up all the rubbish and filled two carrier bags. He left the others in their soporific marijuana induced haze and took the bags around to the wheelie bins at the back of the Co-op.

He smiled as he walked back to them; none of them looked capable, or even willing, to walk home. He could hear voices approaching where they were, although clearly on the other side of the stone wall, by the riverside itself. Peter dropped to his knees and held a finger to his lips. He didn't want anyone seeing his friends like this; if it were the police they could be in heaps of bother.

They all understood immediately; they too could hear the voices.

One man seemed to be crying, to be pleading for something. They heard 'please don't do this,' several times, and 'I'll get your money', followed by a small scream.

As the voices passed within three feet of their positions, they could tell that someone was being dragged, rather than walking unaided.

'Let's get him up the deeper stretch,' they heard the first man say, and Oliver turned around to Keith, mouthing 'Leon Rowe'. Keith dipped his head in agreement.

They remained behind the wall, not moving, until the voices faded slightly.

Keith spoke quietly. 'We say nothing of this. That was Leon Rowe and Brian King. Brian lives next door to us, and trust me I know his voice, and Leon's. Let's just pretend we never heard this. I feel sorry for that poor bugger, whoever he is.'

They felt suddenly sober.

'Can we go home?' Caroline's voice was quivery.

They picked up their bags, and Oliver carefully lifted his head above the wall. He could see the three men in the distance and, without speaking, waved the others to begin the walk home.

'Stick to the roads,' Anthony whispered. 'We don't want to be seen by anybody on the river path.'

It was as they were moving quietly away they heard the scream. It was dramatically cut short by a popping sound, almost immediately followed by a splash.

'We'll talk tomorrow,' Anthony said. He swung off to the right, accompanied by Oliver Merchant and Caroline Phillips. The others headed in the opposite direction.

Anthony and Oliver walked Caroline home first, and as she closed the garden gate she leaned over it. 'Those cigarettes, Anthony… can you get more of them?'

'As many as you want.'

She nodded. 'I want.'

'Me too,' Oliver joined in.

'Talk to me tomorrow in school,' Anthony said, and Caroline disappeared down the path.

Anthony Jackson's career began that night.

2

April 2017

Katerina Rowe's first impression of her husband had been he was the most handsome man she'd ever seen; his dark brown, almost-black, skin radiated health, laughter, and, let's face it, lusty sex appeal.

And she had pursued him just as ferociously as he had pursued her; she knew he loved the way her long blonde hair spread out on the pillow or hung into his eyes as they made love, her blue eyes not visible as she gave in to the pleasure of the moment. And he especially liked the time after when they simply lay in each other's arms, quietly satiated and content.

He had initially been shocked by her admission that she was still a virgin at thirty, but as he grew to know and love her, he also understood. God had come first in her life.

Deacon at the Parish Church of St Lawrence in the tiny village of Eyam, Derbyshire, had been her aim, and Leon Rowe had come into her life at the precise moment she had achieved that. One year later, they had married in the same church that had celebrated her christening.

And now it was fourth wedding anniversary time, with Leon Rowe still dealing drugs, still "arranging" do-it-yourself funerals, and still hiding it from his wife. His legitimate business, owning and running a string of pharmacies, was a cover for the darker business in his world; even his love for the ethereal beauty he had married couldn't make him give up the income he coveted and received.

Katerina stood in front of the mirror and twirled. It was strange to see herself without a clerical collar, and the red silk dress made her appear almost devilish. Leon stepped closer to her and wrapped his arms around her. They both looked in the mirror.

'Perfect,' he breathed, and leaned to kiss the neck that was unusually exposed. 'But it needs something else.' His hand went into his pocket, and produced, with a flourish, a small square black box. 'Happy anniversary, my love.'

She took the box and opened it. Inside was a glowing ruby pendant on a gold chain. 'Wow.' She didn't know what else to say. It took her breath away. Nestling in the box, it resembled a nugget of fire.

He took it from her and removed the jewellery. Fastening it around her neck, he smiled at the expression on her face.

She touched it lightly and shivered. 'Thank you… I'm a bit stuck for words. It's exquisite. And it goes perfectly with my dress.'

He laughed. 'And if you had settled on a blue dress for tonight, it would have been a sapphire.'

She leaned her back into his chest and looked into the mirror once more. 'And here's me thinking you're so clever. You spoil me, you know. I really don't need material things…'

'Maybe not, but I need to give you material things, occasionally. I love you, Katerina Rowe, so stop moaning. You taking a jacket? It's still really warm out.'

She shook her head. 'No, it's lovely to be able to go out without one, for a change. And we'll be in the taxi anyway.'

She picked up her bag, gold to match her shoes, and walked out of the room.

'Come on then, lazybones, let's get on our way. I'm ready for this steak.'

Enid Silvers was quiet. Victor, her husband, felt this was so unusual that it merited a comment.

'You okay?'

She looked up, startled out of her day-dreaming. 'I'm fine. Just… contemplating.'

'Contemplating what? The universe? The gas bill? Your belly button?'

'It's funny you should mention a belly button. I was sitting here imagining the patter of tiny feet from grandchildren. Do you think Katerina will ever give us one? She's thirty-five, her clock's ticking.'

'Does she want a baby?'

'I don't know. I daren't ask. I mean, who would have thought five years ago she would meet someone? I always thought she was married to the church, so her falling for Leon was a shock and a half. Should I ask her?'

Victor laughed. 'I wouldn't advise being blunt. Don't just say, "Are you planning on having kids?" She'll freak out. You'll have to be subtle, and you don't do subtle.'

'Victor!'

'Don't "Victor" me. You know exactly what I mean. Tread softly, take the wellie boots off. She's a gentle soul, is our Katerina, and I reckon she'll let us know soon enough. Your suggesting she might want a baby might just make her dig in her heels for another couple of years.'

Enid said nothing. What if there were a problem? Maybe they'd been trying, and it hadn't happened. Maybe that hunk of a man was infertile, or maybe Katerina had a problem. She was only a slip of a thing…

Enid would ask her, she could do subtle. Maybe.

The restaurant was busy, but Leon had specified the corner table and so they got it. The waiter held the chair out and Katerina sat down, grateful she didn't have to walk any further. Her everyday flat shoes that she wore during the week hadn't prepared her for the discomfort of strappy gold high heels, and she eased her feet so that the shoes were half on and half off.

'I've only walked fifty yards,' she whispered, 'and my feet don't like it.'

Leon grinned. 'I'll carry you back.'

'I might hold you to that.'

He picked up the menu and looked at his wife. 'You're beautiful.'

'Why thank you, kind sir. I might say the same about you.'

'Shall we just go home and go to bed?'

'What? When I've worn these shoes? Not likely.' And she looked down at her own menu.

The waiter watched them carefully; giving them his full attention, as if his job depended on it.

As soon as Leon Rowe laid down his menu and glanced across to him, the waiter moved.

'Are you ready to order, sir?'

'We are.'

He took copious notes as the couple explained how they wanted their steaks, then disappeared, genie-like, into the kitchen.

He reappeared seconds later with their champagne in a cooler and poured it for them.

The evening went perfectly. They laughed, held hands, behaved exactly as two people deeply in love should do, apart from the incessant business Leon needed to sort, via his mobile phone.

Leon had a problem; a trusted colleague had vanished, and he suspected another trusted colleague of causing the vanishing act. And the issue had arisen on his wedding anniversary, when he was out with his stunning wife, phone tucked securely into his pocket to stay there for two or three hours.

Katerina believed his explanation that some drugs had disappeared from one of the pharmacies, and it was the police keeping in touch with him. After all, he was an important man in the community, and it was his business.

They left the restaurant just before ten. The shoes were still a problem, and she kicked them off as they entered their front door.

'Hallelujah!' she yelled. 'Remind me never to wear them again. I'll stick them in the charity shop bag.'

'Wear your trainers next time.'

'Don't tempt me.'

He pulled her into his arms. 'Thank you. It's been such a lovely evening. Nightcap?'

'For a non-drinker, I seem to have drunk a lot,' she said thoughtfully. 'I'll just have a small amaretto, on ice.'

Leon moved to the drinks cabinet, took out two different bottles, then collected some ice. 'Lots of ice?'

Katerina nodded. 'You know me so well.' She closed her eyes, and let her head fall back on the sofa. She felt fat, full, and happy, a perfect evening.

Leon handed her the drink. 'Thank you for four wonderful years, my love.' They clinked glasses and she smiled.

'Been good, haven't they?'

'They have. They've been amazing.'

Katerina sipped at her drink, wondering how on earth she was going to manage the stairs. Her wobbly legs were nothing to do with the dodgy gold sandals, they were all to do with champagne, brandy and now amaretto. She hoped Tibby, their ginger tomcat, had already headed off out for the night; she wanted no disasters caused by falling over him as he twined himself around her legs.

Her lounge seemed to be full of flowers – Leon had presented her with two dozen glorious red roses, there had been a huge bunch from her parents, and an equally large bunch from Leon's parents in Canada. It had been a struggle finding enough containers for them all, and a large drinks jug had had to be utilised, Katerina thought, with pronounced effect.

When the delivery ordered in Canada had arrived, Leon had sat for a few minutes, just reading and stroking the accompanying card. She knew he missed his parents; she had met them for the first time at the wedding, but now, following a stroke, Alan was unable to travel. His face, once so like Leon's, was now twisted, making speech difficult, and one side of his body was paralysed. Sue never left his side.

Katerina vowed they would go to Canada and see them during the summer – surely Leon could take a couple of weeks off.

Leon sat by her side and swung her legs up onto his knees. He massaged her feet. 'Better?'

'Getting there. Can you clear a couple of weeks in August for us to go visit your mum and dad?'

'I'll try.'

'You'll do it.'

He smiled. Nobody argued with a drunken deacon.

'Leon, tell me about the phone calls.'

'What phone calls?'

'More the texts. You only had one phone call, and that certainly wasn't from the police, because you told whoever it was to keep it strictly to texts. What's going on?'

'I'd spoken to the police earlier. The texts were from my staff who were doing a complete stock check following a police request. It seems there's more missing than we had at first realised. Empty boxes that look like full ones, so they're counted as being sixteen tablets. It has to be one of my staff, but I've no clue as to who it is. The one who was texting me is a manager from one of the other shops. He's doing the stock check. I'm so sorry, did it spoil your night?'

She shook her head. 'No – sorry, I didn't realise it was this serious.'

'You want to see my phone?' He held his breath. *Say no. Say no.*

She laughed. 'Of course I don't. For a start, it's your business phone, and I wouldn't understand anything, but I wouldn't check your phone anyway. I'm not that paranoid, drunk or sober.'

'There was another issue that cropped up that I really couldn't deal with. Remember Gill, the assistant in the Eyam shop? She texted to say she won't be in tomorrow, she's had a fall and she can't put any weight on her ankle. I can't expect Neil to run the place on his own, so I'm going to have to spend ten minutes now trying to get a stand in.'

'I'll do it. How hard can it be?' She giggled. 'I'll go in with you in the morning. If there's any awkward customers, I can ask Neil.'

'You sure? That would give me tomorrow to sort it out properly.'

'I'm sure. It's only for a day, and won't affect anything at church. What time do we need to get up?'

'About seven. Sorry.'

She struggled to sit up. 'I think I'd better go to bed. You coming?'

Leon laughed. 'You think you can make it up those stairs on your own? I'll take you up, then come down and make sure everything's secure.'

He helped her to stand, and she giggled again as she fell against him. 'I think I was about eighteen last time I felt like this.'

After helping her up to the bedroom, Leon seated her on the stool at the dressing table. He left her to remove any remaining make-up, had a quick two-minute shower in the en-suite, then returned to the bedroom. She scooped up the cleansing wipes and dropped them in the waste bin, before just looking at herself in the mirror. She could see Leon reflected just over her left shoulder, wearing only a white towel and carrying a glass of water. He took her breath away; the water droplets glistening on his dark skin were like diamonds against black velvet.

'I thought you might need some water in the night,' he said, and kissed the top of her head.

The ruby around her neck glittered with amazing fire, deep deep red, even though the stone was a pink-red. She raised her right hand to touch it. It felt warm. She unfastened it and laid it on her dressing table. Such a beautiful stone.

She placed the water on her bedside table and snuggled down. 'I'm fine. It's probably that I've had more to drink than normal but my legs are very wobbly.' She giggled for a third time.

He kissed her lips. 'Okay, you sleep. I'm going downstairs for a bit, listen to some music and finish my nightcap. I love you, Kat.' He kissed her again.

'Love you too,' she said, and closed her eyes.

Kat waited until she could hear soft music from downstairs, then crept out of bed and across to the ruby pendant, glistening in its box. She tentatively lifted it out and stroked it, such an amazing gift, then placed it back in the box, before leaving it on her bedside table. It would join the diamond pendant, the diamond bracelet and the emerald earrings, all previous anniversary gifts, in her safe in the morning.

Sleep claimed her quickly, as she listened to the music of Beethoven flowing quietly up the stairs.

Leon nursed the glass of whisky, savouring both the smell and the taste of it. He had enjoyed the evening so much with his woman, the absolute love of his life.

He sipped at the whisky and felt his phone vibrate.

The text from Terry Vincent was simple. **Found PH. Says he buried GR in Ecclesall Woods. What do you want me to do?**

His response was equally simple. **Bury him too. Text when he's dead.**

He continued to sip at his drink, thinking about George Reynolds, the late George Reynolds it seemed. He'd have to do something about George's wife and kids; perhaps pop in one day to ask her where George was, and leave her some cash when she said she didn't know.

It was a bit of a relief that Paddy Halloran was about to be exterminated. And he didn't have a wife he needed to compensate. He'd been a loose cannon for a while, and killing George, one of his more reliable workers, had to be punished. It briefly gave Leon food for thought as he wondered how they had found out from Paddy that he had buried George in the woods…

He wondered where in Ecclesall Woods the two men resided; he hoped it was in one of the denser parts, maybe they wouldn't be found at all then. He made a mental note to ask Terry Vincent for the location, he wanted no surprises.

His glass was empty, and he considered topping it up again, killing a little more time before going to bed. He wanted Kat to be soundly asleep, getting fully rested. She had a long and unusual day ahead of her, in the shop. The music was soporific, and he knew if he did give her more time, he would be in danger of falling asleep downstairs; he didn't want that.

Leon carried the glass through to the kitchen and rinsed it before putting it in the dishwasher. He switched off the music, checked all the doors and windows, set the alarm, and climbed the stairs.

Pausing in the doorway of the bedroom, Leon looked at his sleeping wife. Taking off the white towel and putting it in the laundry bin, he couldn't stop the smile that spread across his face. He'd loved her from the first time he met her and wanted her by his side for always.

But how long would she stay if she knew what his other life was like? He reckoned just long enough to grab the cat, pick up her fully loaded suitcase and throw her house keys at him, before running to her car.

3

Beth Walters looked at herself in the long mirror. He'd requested that she look good, and she didn't think he'd be disappointed. She had piled her long curly dark-brown hair on top of her head, adding six inches of extra height to her already impressive sixty-eight inches; her high heels added a further three inches. The yellow silk dress swirled around her knees as she walked, and she knew he would be knocked out.

She smiled into the mirror, practising how she would appear to him the first time he saw her. She hadn't been out with this one before; she knew him as Anthony Parkson but guessed that wasn't the truth. Her clients rarely gave genuine names. The agency had vetted him before advising her of the name he wished to use.

Her clients never said the names weren't real, but she was no dummy. It didn't take a genius to work it out, and she thought it was quite funny when she called them by the name she had been given, and they didn't answer because they didn't realise she was speaking to them.

One more year. She had to get through her final year at Sheffield University and she could pack in what she laughingly termed "the escort business". It wasn't about escorting someone to an engagement, it was about the sex she occasionally had to perform afterwards.

That was the real earner. She had learned to distance her mind from what was happening to her body, and the agency always paired her with someone of at least equal height, and reasonable good looks. For two years, she had saved most of her earnings, living on the very minimum that she could.

After graduation she intended taking a year out and seeing the world. But that night, it was Anthony Parkson's turn to use her. Her phone pinged, telling her he had arrived and was waiting outside. She switched off her lamp, called to Jo and Millie, her housemates, and headed out the door, locking it behind her.

He was standing by his car, a long sleek black Jaguar. She felt a small frisson of excitement as she saw how good looking he was. This was, indeed, a bonus.

'You have the password?' she asked with a smile, as she walked up to him.

'Wensleydale.'

She held out her hand. 'Hi, Anthony. My name is Beth.'

He shook her hand and opened the car door. 'Let me help you in. It's a low-slung seat.'

She lowered herself carefully into the car and locked her seatbelt into place.

'Ready?'

She nodded. 'We're going to the Alhambra?'

'We are. I'm hosting a gathering of clients, potential new ones, and senior staff. They'll be a fair amount of mingling to do, but you're there primarily to look good on my arm. And you do,' he added. 'Look good, I mean.'

'Thank you. I received your instructions.'

He grinned. 'Sorry about that, but it would have been awkward if you'd turned up in denim or something.'

'I don't think I'll let you down. I have to check your receipt from the agency for my fees before we go in, and then we can enjoy the evening.'

'Of course. If you look in the glove compartment, you'll see it.'

She leaned forward, took out the piece of paper and quickly scanned it. It seemed an awful lot of money. She received half of it, the agency kept the other half. She quickly took a photograph of it with her phone and put it back in the glove compartment. 'I photo it so that I can check my monthly fee payment from the agency. They've never been wrong, but there's always a first time, and it will be the time when I forget to take the photograph.'

He nodded. 'Good business head as well as remarkably beautiful. What do you do in the real world, Beth?'

'I'm a student.'

Anthony smiled. She obviously didn't want to give away too much.

They chatted of inconsequential things and fifteen minutes later they pulled up outside the venue; a doorman stepped forward to take the keys and park the Jaguar. She almost envied the man; she wouldn't have minded driving that car. It put her little red Mini to shame.

They walked up the steps to the entrance which led into a magnificent hall. People were going up and down the glamorous stairway, all dressed immaculately. Beth didn't feel out of place. She knew she looked good, and she was pleased to take the arm he held out for her. One day, she promised herself, she would meet a man like him for real.

There was a heady smell of perfume in the air, expensive perfume. She excused herself to go to the bathroom before the meal started, and Anthony watched her walk up the stairs, along with at least ten other men all watching her.

His own eyes never left the stairs; smiling as she returned to him.

Shortly after, they went into the huge dining room, and the meal was served. She estimated there were around seventy people there, and it was clear that everyone knew Anthony. There was much laughter, drinking of wine and general good-natured banter, then Anthony rose to make a speech. He promised no business, told everybody they were there to enjoy the evening, and tomorrow was soon enough to get back to the serious undertaking of making money. His speech was received with a round of applause, and he sat down and took her hand.

'Glad that's over,' he whispered. 'I hate making speeches.'

'Nobody would have known that.' She smiled. 'You did fine, very professional, and it was just long enough.'

They were ushered to a side room after the meal while the room was cleared, and then everyone drifted back into the dining room, where a small jazz band had been hired to play for the evening. Beth loved it; the music was good, the ambience perfect.

He referred to her as "my friend" every time he introduced her to someone new, although in a couple of instances she recognised the men she was being acquainted with; they were men who, while screwing her, had explained they used escorts because they had no wife. These men were standing by the side of their wives, looking as if they were wondering where they had seen the beautiful woman before.

It was a good evening. By eleven, many had gone home, leaving a nucleus of about twenty who clearly wanted to party the night away, including Anthony.

Someone suggested they go clubbing, and taxis were ordered. Anthony took it upon himself to advise the receptionist that there would be half a dozen cars in their car park overnight, as they were heading into town. They would be collected when his friends were sober enough to drive.

The taxis arrived, and they were soon at Steel, the nightclub of choice for most of them.

Beth had been several times. It always made her feel uneasy. The drugs were dealt openly, the music certainly wasn't the wonderful jazz that had captivated her during the earlier part of the evening, and the lighting was so low it made seeing anything almost impossible.

She sat on a bar stool and looked around her. Anthony remained by her side.

He held up a hand and immediately the barman moved across to them. 'Beth?'

'I'll just have a Coke, thanks, Anthony.'

'One Coke, and I'll have one of my usual please.'

'Yes, sir.' The barman quickly dealt with their order, handing Beth her drink, and sliding what looked like a double malt to Anthony.

'Will I be taking you home later, or can I look forward to the whole evening together?'

'As long as you pay me direct and don't divulge anything to the agency, I can be available until tomorrow morning,' she said with a smile. 'And I do expect breakfast.'

He felt a stirring in his groin at her words, and he returned her smile. 'I can be very discrete. And I'm sure I can produce scrambled eggs.'

He sipped at the malt whisky and casually surveyed the room. The music was loud, bouncing off the walls in time to the strobe lighting whirling around the entire room. Bodies were packed like sardines on the small dance area. It was dark, difficult to see faces, and the rapid flickering movements of the strobe effect made it even harder. He didn't want to be there.

'Shall we go?'

'You can't,' Beth answered. 'You're here with your friends and business colleagues. You can't really abandon them.'

'They'll not even notice.' He grinned at her, an infectious smile.

She picked up her bag. 'Come on then. I'll go out first, you follow in a minute, and they won't think we're going.'

He nodded. 'You want a job as my secretary?'

'No, thanks.' She laughed. 'You couldn't afford me.'

Beth went out through the door they had entered just a few minutes earlier and waited on the steps until Anthony joined her. The bouncer stood to attention as he realised who she was waiting for, and he stepped to the pavement edge to get them a taxi, after speaking into a walkie-talkie.

A cab pulled up within seconds and Anthony held the door, helping her climb inside. She was glad it was a black cab; with her heels it wouldn't have been easy getting out of a car.

Beth leaned across towards Anthony, trying to get a look at the driver. As she had bent her head to climb into the back, she thought she had recognised him, but no amount of peering through the dividing window helped her remember why she thought she knew him.

She settled back, and Anthony took her hand.

'You've been amazing tonight,' he said, and raised her hand to his lips.

'Thank you. I enjoy functions like this evening's party. I've never seen so many designer dresses in one room. And I need to tell you that jazz combo was perfect for the occasion.'

'Thank you. I've known them years, usually book them because my friends expect them now, and would be annoyed if they didn't play. I have to tell you, none of the other women could hold a candle to you. You looked wonderful. Yellow suits you, and I was proud to have you by my side. In future, if it's okay with you, I'd like to book you direct for any business requirements I may have. I am quite happy to pay the agency rates, but you might as well have all of it instead of half.'

She smiled, not really sure how to respond. Nobody had suggested this to her before. 'Thank you,' was all she could manage to say.

Anthony pulled her a little closer, and she leaned against him.

'Where are we going?'

'I live in a village called Eyam. Do you know it?'

'I know of it, of course, our local famous plague village; the villagers do a well-dressing annually. My nan and I do a drive round of all the wells every year, and the residents are always keen to explain how it's done, and how much they love doing it.'

'Indeed they do. The church takes a very active interest in everything that goes on, and the well-dressing is a massive part of the church year.'

'Do you go to church?' Beth was curious to know more about this man.

He laughed. 'No, I don't. It's not that I don't believe, it's more that I don't believe enough.'

She smiled. Exactly her feelings on the matter.

'Your nan? Do you live with her?'

'I don't, no. I couldn't do this job and live with her; she wouldn't understand. When I started at uni I bought a small house with the money my parents left me. They both died within a year of each other, so I sold their house and moved in with my nan. I was only sixteen. The money was put into trust until I was eighteen, and so I invested it in my little house as soon as I found out I'd got in at uni. I live with a couple of other girls, and it works okay. I see Nan every weekend, couldn't manage without her. She feeds me.' Beth laughed. 'And I always have cakes and scones to take back with me, so she feeds my housemates as well. She's wonderful, I love her to bits. The well-dressing trip has been something we've always done. She used to take me until I passed my driving test, now I take her.'

Beth watched the streetlights flashing by, and then darkness as they went on Derbyshire roads that were, in the main, unlit. Talking about her nan had reinforced how much she loved her, and Beth vowed to go and see her within the next couple of days.

'We go through the village,' Anthony said, pointing at the sign that proclaimed Eyam, 'and my place is as you leave at the far end of the main road. Another five minutes, and we'll be there.'

There was a sudden lurch, followed by a bang as the tyre hit the kerb, and Beth started to slide off the leather seat. Anthony tried to hold on to her, but he too was sliding, and they ultimately ended up on the floor, a tangled heap of arms and legs.

The taxi completed the ninety-degree left turn, travelled at speed down a side road before taking another left turn and careering down an alleyway. It stopped with a screech of brakes, and Anthony, who was almost back onto his seat, shot forward once more and landed on Beth.

'What the fuck?' he yelled and watched as the window slid open a couple of inches. The driver pointed a gun at him.

'Get out, Jackson. You too, slag,' he said, and waved the gun at Beth.

Anthony climbed out, then helped Beth to get out. There was a trace of blood on her face; having been injured as she fell. He pulled her close to him and she hid her face in his shoulder.

The taxi driver had joined them, standing six feet behind them. He waved the gun in the direction of the dead end of the alleyway. There were a couple of large waste bins, some pallets and black bags full of rubbish, and Anthony and Beth walked towards them.

'My real name's Anthony Jackson,' he whispered to her.

She clung on to him and nodded. 'Beth Walters.'

He squeezed her hand. She looked so scared and he could do nothing to comfort her. She looked as frightened as he felt.

'You, slag,' the driver said. 'Walk down to the end.'

Fear was written all over her face. She turned to Anthony, but he knew he couldn't do anything with a gun trained on them. 'Do as he says, and trust me,' he said. He needed to get a dialogue going with the guy, find out what the fuck he wanted, and why he'd done this.

He watched Beth stagger as she stumbled against something, and then turn around as she reached the end. She could go no further.

She saw the driver raise the gun, wait for a moment as if deciding whether to go for it or not, and then she saw Anthony's head explode. She screamed and tried to run back towards him, but the gun turned in her direction. Beth knew she was so close to death, and she dropped to her knees, her legs unable to support her. 'Please… no,' she heard herself shriek, her throat tightening with fear.

Once more the gunman hesitated and then he seemed to shake his head before pulling the trigger.

The bullet hit her in the shoulder and she went down. Her yellow silk dress on the black bags of rubbish caused her to slide, but finally she stopped. The driver walked towards her and she stayed unmoving, sprawled on her back amidst the rubbish, her eyes tightly closed, her dress almost up to her breasts. If this was the end, she didn't want to see it coming.

She heard his footsteps getting nearer and terror enveloped her. He kicked her head, and still she made no sound. He lifted the gun by the barrel and brought it down on her forehead.

Blackness.

4

'It's time to get up.'

'No.' Katerina pulled a pillow over her head.

'Yes.' Leon removed the pillow, and she tried unsuccessfully to hold on to it.

'This is grounds for divorce,' she said to him, looking at him through the only eye she would allow to open. The other one was still asleep.

Leon pulled the duvet from her.

'What time is it anyway?'

'Seven.'

'The morning seven? Why would you do that to me?'

'You're going into the pharmacy with me. Have you forgotten our little chat from last night? You're a wimp, Katerina Rowe. Neil will be there from about eight, he's doing a stock check of sorts, making sure nothing went missing since yesterday, so he can take you through one or two things before we open at nine.'

'I'll drive down later.'

'No, you'll go with me. You'll not bother if I leave you to do it on your own. Come on, wench, get up.' He rolled her onto her side and smacked her bum.

'You're a brute.' She swung her feet towards the floor, leaving her head still in bed.

'All of you,' he said with a smile. He was used to her non-compliance with morning discussions. He was lucky she was speaking anything out loud. It took at least two coffees to motivate his beautiful woman.

One coffee already imbibed, and one in her hand, she settled into the passenger seat, still feeling grumpy.

'What on earth made you think I would want to get up at this ungodly hour? Do you know how much I had to drink last night?'

Leon smiled. She'd get over it, given time. About three weeks, he reckoned. He drove slowly down into the village, through the centre until he reached the shop.

'Neil hasn't arrived yet,' he said. 'His car's not here, but he won't be long.'

'He's probably still in bed,' was the sarcastic retort he received.

He parked outside the shop and helped Kat from the car.

'Come on, Grumpy. We'll walk round to the back door. If I raise the shutters and put a key anywhere near the front door, people will think we're open.'

Kat followed Leon around to the alleyway. At first she thought it was a bundle of rags. Then she felt Leon grab her arm and push her behind him.

'Don't take another step,' he said. 'There's blood…'

'Oh my Lord, it's a body.' She felt goosebumps move up her arms. 'We need to check if…'

'He's dead, Kat. He has very little left of his head.'

And then she saw the yellow dress. She dodged past Leon who was just taking out his phone and she ran towards the woman.

Leon shouted to her to stop, but she ignored him. This one still had a head. A very bloody head, but it was still on her shoulders and not splattered all over the floor.

The woman was lying on the black bags, her skirt still hiked up. Katerina reached towards her. 'Lord, help her, let her be alive,' she breathed, and placed a finger on the girl's neck.

There was a pulse; faint but a slight flicker still there.

'She's alive,' Katerina screamed to Leon. 'Get an ambulance!'

Leon hesitated, panicking slightly in case it had some connection to him. He couldn't tell who the man was, and he couldn't see the woman because his wife was in the way.

'Leon,' Katerina yelled again. 'Ambulance!'

999.

He quickly explained the circumstances, then passed the phone to Kat, who listened to what the operator was telling her to do. She carefully pulled the woman down from the piles of rubbish until she was lying flat, then got Leon to help turn her on her side. The beautiful silk dress was covered in blood, and the woman was clearly unconscious; she made no sounds. The operator continued to instruct Kat, reassuring her that the ambulance was on its way. Leon went to the beginning of the alleyway to meet it.

He guided it as it reversed down the narrow cul-de-sac, stopping it as it reached the body of the man.

They very quickly confirmed the man was dead, and assessed the woman as needing urgent treatment.

Within ten minutes of their arrival, she had been taken to a waiting air-ambulance, the pilot unable to land in the tiny village; they transferred her by taking her to the helicopter.

As a result her life was saved.

Kat's day in the shop was cancelled; the pharmacy had become a crime scene. Neil, Leon's pharmacist, had offered to stay at the shop although it was closed, in case the police needed anything, and Leon drove Kat back home. By then, she had definitely woken up.

The ambulance crew had told Kat the woman would be taken to the Northern General Hospital in Sheffield, so after Leon had returned her to their home she rang the hospital, explained her connection to the woman who she still had no name for, and asked if she had survived.

They wouldn't tell her anything.

Katerina couldn't get the woman's face out of her mind; she was beautiful, her dark hair turned an ugly shade of red.

Katerina saw the police car pull up outside and went to meet the two officers. After checking their credentials, she showed them through to the kitchen. Kat made drinks while they got out the paperwork necessary for her statement, and then she answered their questions.

The primary one was: did she know either of the victims.

'The man didn't have much of a head left,' she said quietly. 'Do you know who he is?'

'We do. We've identified him by his fingerprints. He's a business man by the name of Anthony Jackson. Have you heard of him?' PC Hannah Granger kept her eyes firmly fixed on Kat's face.

She searched through her memory and came up with nothing. 'I don't think so. What sort of business?'

'Pharmaceuticals.'

'Oh.'

'You know him?' PC Dave Irwin joined in the conversation.

'I don't even know of him, let alone know him. My husband is in the pharmaceutical industry; it just seemed strange that this poor dead man is in it too. Or was in it.'

'Is your husband here?'

'He's on his way.' As she spoke she heard the front door open. 'Leon? Is that you? We're in the kitchen.'

Leon walked through the house and bent to kiss his wife before acknowledging the police presence.

He switched on the kettle. 'Are you all okay for a drink?'

They held up their mugs, indicating they had drinks, but they suspended questions until he was also sitting at the table.

'Leon, that poor man was called Anthony Jackson. Did you know him?' Kat asked.

As curveballs go, it was a good one. Leon swallowed, thought about lying, then decided against it. 'Of Jackson Pharmaceuticals?'

'Yes, sir. Did you recognise him at the time?'

'He didn't have a face,' Leon said, unable to hide the sarcasm.

'No, of course he didn't. I do apologise. Did you know the lady?'

'I don't think so. Does she have a name?'

'According to her driving licence, she's called Bethan Walters.'

'And has she survived?' Kat interrupted, trying to stop an obvious shiver. 'I'd like to go and see her if that's okay.'

Hannah Granger went to answer. 'I don't think–'

'In my official capacity, of course,' Kat said firmly.

'Official capacity?'

'I'm Deacon at St Lawrence's, here in Eyam. I found her, she was in my parish, and I'd like to go and visit her.'

'We'll see that you are able to do that, Mrs… Ms… Rowe.'

'Reverend.' Kat smiled sweetly. 'It's Reverend Katerina Rowe when I'm on official business.'

Hannah made a note in her book. 'As soon as I find out where she is, I'll ring you. I know she was taken to the Northern General, but it depends on her injuries where she is now.'

Kat nodded. 'Thank you for that. I'll make sure I wear my clerical collar when I visit her, so that it's clear who I am, to your officers.'

Kat sat out in the garden and let her mind roam. They lived in a particularly quiet part of the village; no traffic noise, no close neighbours, and no sounds of children's voices raised as they played.

She knew beyond any doubt that she had to see Bethan Walters. She didn't know her, but she felt she was meant to have some sort of connection with her.

She smiled, inwardly laughing at herself. She had no beliefs when it came to anything a bit odd, she generally put everything down to coincidence. Maybe there would be answers if she talked to Ms Walters.

Kat lifted the arms on the sun lounger and let it go to a more comfortable position. The little stream that ran along the bottom of the garden was soporific, and she could feel her eyes closing.

She slept.

Leon watched her from the bedroom window, musing on just how lucky he had been to find her, at exactly the right point in his life. He had met her on a Tuesday, and by Thursday had been in love.

His life had revolved even then around drugs, money laundering, control of his men. And his women. He knew he would lose Kat if she ever discovered even the slightest thing about his illegal activities; he had told her he had a string of pharmacies, his legitimate life, but nothing of his imperfect world. And now something felt threatening.

He hadn't known Anthony Jackson well; there had been talk of him stepping up a league, but their paths rarely crossed. As if by mutual consent, they knew their own boundaries, although there had been a couple of incursions by Jackson onto Rowe territory, a couple of conversations in which development plans had been mentioned.

So why had Jackson died in the back alley leading to the rear of a Rowe Pharmacy? What had brought him there? Maybe the question should be who had brought him there? Leon had given no instructions, so it was somebody outside of his own circle of colleagues.

He and Kat had both made their statements, she denying any knowledge of either of the victims, he admitting to knowing Jackson, but only because he was in the same line of business. The police seemed to have been happy with that, but if Kat persisted in this ridiculous notion of checking on the woman, would she open some can of worms he didn't want opening?

He showered, changed into shorts and a T-shirt, then went downstairs to join his wife. She was awake.

'Isn't it lovely,' she said. 'The sound of that water, just perfect.'

'It's beautiful. Are you going out tonight, or do I get you all to myself?'

She laughed. 'Young Wives group, but I'll be back for half past eight. Then I'm all yours.'

'Good. It's been a rotten day. And how are you? Fully sober now?'

'I'm fine. A murder tends to do that, wipes out the alcohol.'

'I have a meeting tomorrow in London.' He broached the subject with caution. 'Would you like to go with me?'

'I can't. I have a meeting tomorrow as well. Nothing as glamorous as London, mine's in Nottingham. Are you staying overnight?'

'I think so. If it finishes early I'll head home, but if it's late I'll stay. I'll let you know when I ring you.'

She nodded. 'Don't worry about me, I'll be fine. I've to be in Nottingham for about half past nine, ready for a ten o'clock meeting, but hopefully it will all be over for midday. Ring any time after that.'

He kissed her. 'Okay. Now, are we eating before you go to Young Wives, or after?'

'I'm not hungry. Seeing Mr Jackson…'

'I know. I don't know what to say to help you. It was bad.'

'I'll maybe have a sandwich when I come back in.'

'Then I'll wait for you, do something for us. Then bed.'

'Oh, yes please.' She smiled.

'Hussy,' he responded. 'I meant we've both got an early start tomorrow, so needed an early bedtime. Mind you, your idea was better than mine…'

'Kiss me.' She held out her arms.

He willingly obliged.

Kat left home an hour later than her husband. She rang the hospital first to see how Bethan Walters was, and this time got a grudging, '*She had a comfortable night.*' She wondered if Beth herself would have echoed that.

Driving to Nottingham gave her time to reflect on the happenings of the previous day and she wondered what on earth had been so bad that one person had died, and the other one was critically injured.

She switched off the windscreen wipers as the rain seemed to have stopped, although she hoped her action wasn't temporary. Sunshine had been promised, and she was damned if she was going to settle for a murky grey day.

By the time she reached the hotel where the meeting was to take place, the sun had come out, and she was deeply regretting not bringing her sunglasses.

Throughout the entirety of the meeting, she struggled to follow what the speakers were saying. Sometimes her own small church seemed far distant from the bigger churches and cathedrals in the area, and she found many discussions to be irrelevant. Half way in, she decided she wasn't going straight home, she was going to the Northern General. She would brave the intricacies of Sheffield city centre, its ring road, and multiple incomprehensible roundabouts, and go find Bethan Walters.

The journey was as bad as she had feared, and when she finally reached the hospital, she had to drive around for half an hour trying to find a parking spot. By the time she reached the critical care ward, she was ready to deck anyone who said one word wrong to her.

There was a young officer sitting on a chair outside the room. He stood as she approached. 'Can I have your name please?'

'Reverend Katerina Rowe.' She touched her clerical collar for extra emphasis, ready for an argument.

'Thank you, ma'am,' he said, and held the door open for her. She felt quite deflated.

Bethan Walters was connected to several drips, her eyes closed, and a tube to help her breathing feeding like a snake down her throat. Her face was bruised quite spectacularly, but Kat rejoiced. It meant she had survived thus far.

Kat waited patiently; Bethan was having her blood pressure and temperature checked. The nurse finished and smiled at Kat.

'Prayers will help,' she said, and moved the blood pressure machine out of the way, allowing Kat to sit on a chair by the bed.

Beth had a bandage around her head, indicative of trauma to some degree, and scratches and dark blue bruising to her face. With the blood cleaned off, Kat could see how pretty the young woman was.

It was an automatic reaction to ask God for his help; Beth clearly needed it. Kat sat for two hours, holding Beth's hand, occasionally talking to her, telling her she was the woman who had found her, and her name was Kat. There was no response, and Kat knew she would be back every day until there was some recognition.

The doctor arrived, and despite Kat's questions, could tell her very little. They had operated on her head because she had a blood clot, and now it was a matter of waiting. They were sedating her, but when they stopped doing that it could be some time before she came out of the coma. Her injuries were severe, but she was in the best place.

Kat thanked him, and just before five, left to go home. She stood in the doorway and stared back at the still figure in the bed. 'Sleep tight, Beth,' Kat whispered. 'And God bless.'

She said goodnight to the constable, who said it would be someone different on the following day, so she needed her white collar again. She laughed. 'Thank you, I'll try to remember it.'

Leon rang as she was driving home, grumbling about the pharmaceutical business in general, and he was thinking of going into building a theme park because it would be much more fun.

She laughed. 'I'm sure it would. You're just pissed off because you can't get home tonight, and it's probably been a boring meeting.'

'It was about three new drugs that are coming out, all aimed at diabetes. They seem to be pretty powerful too, if the patter is anything to go by.'

'You'll be glad they're on the market if you ever get diabetes. Some drugs are good drugs, you know.'

'I know,' he grumbled. 'I just didn't think it would take all day. I thought we could…'

'We did, last night.'

'We can't do it two nights running? What are you saying, woman? Am I rationed?'

She giggled. 'You'll never know, will you. You're not coming home.'

She heard someone call his name, and he said he had to go. He was sharing a taxi to his hotel.

'Speak to you tomorrow. Love you,' she said, and disconnected.

It was only then that she realised she hadn't told him she had been to see Beth. Kat shrugged; maybe it was for the best.

It was quiet in the house. Katerina didn't bother sitting out in the garden; the promised sunshine hadn't warmed things up much, so she settled on the sofa with a book. She loved crime books that were solved by forensic evidence, and tonight she had decided Patricia Cornwell was the author to be reading.

Leon rang Katerina to say goodnight, sounding ever so slightly tipsy, and made her promise to double check the doors and windows were all secure before going to bed.

'I'm not afraid of being on my own,' she laughed. 'It's never bothered me. Now go to bed, and make sure your own door's locked. See you tomorrow, sweetheart.'

She switched on the late-night news, and caught the beginning of the local section. Leon's shop was clearly visible as the camera panned along the front of it, and then down the alleyway.

The presenter was asking for information, saying the police believed a taxi using false plates had brought the couple to the alleyway, before shooting the man. He then went on to say that the man lived in Eyam, although the woman's address was being withheld pending notification to next of kin.

Lived in Eyam? Katerina knew shock must be written on her face, and she closed her mouth with a snap.

This was only a small village, and she didn't know anyone by that name. She pulled her laptop towards her and entered "Anthony Jackson". She found very little; nothing to do with an inadequate search engine, a broken-down Internet, Google not understanding what she was asking, it was simply that Kat didn't do technology.

She could type her sermons, save them, and print them. Anything beyond that would never happen.

It was frustrating, but she would have to wait for Leon's return, and ask him to show her, once again, how to make it work for her.

She closed it down – she knew how to do that – and carried it back to the bookshelf. *One day*, she promised herself, as she did at least three times a week, *one day I will take a computer course. I'll get a certificate that will prove I'm not as thick as I appear to be.*

If computers could smile, her laptop would have done so.

She set the house alarm and went to bed.

5

K at was at the hospital by ten. She settled by the side of the still-comatose Beth. The nurse confirmed that Beth was holding her own, no better but no worse, and they were hopeful.

Just after eleven, an elderly lady was escorted into the room. She took one look at Kat with her white collar clearly visible, and her face drained of colour.

'Oh my god,' she said. 'Mouse, is she…?' She staggered as she tried to rush to Beth's bedside.

The nurse accompanying her reassured her. 'No, Mrs Lester. This lady is the one who found your granddaughter. This is Reverend Rowe.'

Kat stood and led the older woman to the chair. 'Please – sit down. There's been no change since I arrived about an hour ago. I've just been sitting and talking to her. I don't know whether she can hear or not, but they always say keep talking to people in a coma, so that's what we can do.'

Doris Lester reached across the bed and grasped Beth's hand. 'Oh, Mouse, sweetheart. What has he done to you?' She lifted her head to look at Kat. 'I've only just found out. I've been at my sister's house for a couple of days but had to come home early this morning for a doctor's appointment. There was a police car outside waiting for me.'

Kat reached across and held her hand. 'I'm so sorry, Mrs Lester. I've been praying…'

'Will she live?'

'They keep telling me she's holding her own, whatever that might mean. She's sedated, so won't be waking up until they can reduce what they're giving her. But I'll leave you with her. I'd like to keep dropping by if that's okay.'

'Of course.' Doris stared at her granddaughter. 'Look at her lovely face.'

'The bruises and scratches will heal,' Kat said gently. 'Here's my card. Ring me if you need me. Any time. You called her Mouse…?'

'She was tiny when she was born, about six weeks early. She looked like a little mouse, and we all took to calling her Mouse. It's stuck within the family, all her life. I call her Bethan when I tell her off.'

'That's lovely,' Kat smiled. 'You must love her very much.'

The elderly lady nodded, took the card, slipped it into her bag, and turned back to the bed. 'More than life itself,' she said. 'More than life itself.'

Kat slipped out and headed to her car. She drove slowly, deep in thought. It wouldn't be quite so easy once Leon was back home, and she knew her continued interest in Beth Walters would cause dissent between the two of them, but she had to continue to visit the desperately ill woman.

And it wasn't about it being part of her job, it wasn't about her being the one to be the first to help Beth, it wasn't about praying for her; it was a compulsion born of heaven knows what. She had to be there for her, and nobody was going to stop that.

Later that evening, she spoke at length with Leon. She told him about her hospital visits, about the unconscious woman's grandmother, she even told him about driving around and around the hospital grounds, desperately searching for a parking space.

He listened to it all, then sighed. 'You worry me, Katerina Rowe. Do you know this woman, this Bethan Walters?'

'Beth. Mouse.'

'Okay, Beth. Mouse? What's that about, and why have you taken it upon yourself to champion her?'

'She's badly injured, Leon. But I'm convinced she'll get better. And Mouse is what her family calls her. It's kind of nice, shows she's loved. I think Beth and Anthony must have been in that taxi they've caught on CCTV, thinking they were being driven to his house. Do you know where he lives?'

'What do you mean?'

'He lives in Eyam. According to the news, anyway. I don't know where, so he's not a churchgoer. You told the police you knew him. So do you know where his house is?'

'No idea. I don't really know him. I just know he's got a bit of a reputation for some not quite legal deals, and they're only rumours. I've never been in his company socially, he's kind of the opposition, if you like.'

'I tried to look him up on my laptop.'

'And?' He grinned as if he knew what was coming.

'I think I broke the Internet.'

'You can't break the Internet.'

'It didn't tell me anything. I assumed I'd broken something. I must learn this, Leon. I can't be so monumentally stupid.'

This time he laughed aloud. 'You're not stupid, look at the exams and qualifications you have, the degree you have. You're more than capable of cracking this. You just don't have the confidence to believe you can do it. You must listen to me. You cannot break anything. Well, you could if you threw the laptop out the window in temper, but there'll be no need for that. Come on, let's have a look. See if we can find where he lives. Lived.'

She opened the laptop, and he told her to type in Jackson's name. Leon then took her through several avenues that would lead her to the information she needed and revealed that Anthony Jackson had lived at the opposite end of Eyam to their own place, in a house situated in the middle of a field with an Eyam postal address, but nearer to the tiny hamlet of Bretton.

Kat looked at it pensively. 'So, they must have entered Eyam from our end, driven through the centre of the village, and to that alleyway. He killed him, knocked her unconscious, and disappeared. Wonder if he went back the same way. Or did he head out towards the Jackson house anyway? I feel as if I need to know this.'

'Why?' Leon frowned.

'I have no idea, but there's something so wrong about this whole thing, don't you think? I mean, this is a small village, nothing's happened here since the plague in 1666, and now we have a major police presence in the village, the alleyway is closed off and you can't access your shop's back door… Aren't you concerned? You can't even open the shop yet.'

'Of course I am, but not that concerned I want to track down this taxi driver. Who I suspect isn't a taxi driver, by the way. Taxi drivers don't tend to go around shooting their passengers.'

'But people don't have random black cabs, do they? Just on the off chance it might be needed for a crime one day. I could have understood more if it had been a car, but the cab had to have come from a genuine cab company. We need to find out which one.'

'What? We don't need to find out anything!'

'Sorry,' she mumbled. 'Guess I got carried away.'

Leon stared at her. 'Promise me you'll drop it, Kat. Don't go causing trouble. I don't want you ending up like this woman, this Beth.'

Her fingers were crossed as she said, 'I promise.'

'We're going to reduce her sedation today, see if she can come out of her coma on her own,' the nurse said quietly. 'The doctor is hopeful. She's young, fit, everything's on her side, so we'll monitor her until there's a change, and see what happens.'

'Does her nan know?'

'She does now. She'd gone home by the time the doctor took the decision last night, but I rang her earlier. She's on her way in.'

Kat nodded. That was good, Beth would need her nan there, when her eyes eventually opened.

Kat moved to sit by the bed, making sure there was a chair for Mrs Lester when she arrived, and took hold of Beth's hand.

'Hi, Beth, it's me again. Kat. May the Lord bless you.' She shuffled her chair a little closer, and grasped the cold hand again. She rubbed it between her own hands, trying to warm Beth.

'You need gloves on, Beth, your hands are cold. It's beautiful outside, lovely sunny weather. Your nan will be here shortly, so I won't be staying long today, I'll leave you with her. They're reducing your sedation so hopefully we'll meet properly soon.'

Kat felt a squeeze on her fingers and she gasped.

She turned around to the nurse. 'She squeezed my hand!'

The nurse moved across to the bed, and Kat got out of the way, almost falling over the chair leg in her panic to give the nurse the room she needed.

'Bethan. Can you hear me, sweetheart? Squeeze my fingers if you can.'

Kat saw the slim fingers move slightly, and the nurse raised Beth's eyelids and shone a light into them. The nurse reached across the back of the bed and pressed a bell. A doctor was there within seconds.

'It seems she's coming round, doctor,' the nurse said.

He repeated her actions with his torch, and smiled. 'Okay, Bethan. You seem to be waking up. It may take a while, but there will be someone here monitoring you.' He turned to the nurse. 'When she surfaces properly, press the bell. I'm just down the corridor doing some paperwork. Can we have a blood pressure and temperature check done right now please?'

The nurse nodded, and wheeled the machine across the room. Kat waited to one side while the professionals dealt with Beth.

Doris Lester came through the door like a whirlwind. 'Is she…?'

Kat laughed. 'She's certainly surfacing, Mrs Lester, but it's going to take some time. Would you like me to get out of your way?'

'No, I would not,' the elderly lady declared. 'You've been here for Mouse every day, stay as long as you want.'

They watched in silence until the nurse finished her checks, and then returned to the bedside.

Kat was getting to know Beth's nan quite well. They had talked at length about Beth, how bright she was, how she only had another year to do at the university and then she wanted to take a year out for travelling; Kat prayed both in church and out of it that there would be no permanent damage following the head injury she had seen as she tried to save the life of the young girl.

It was two hours later that they saw further signs of Beth's return to their world. Her eyes flickered, and she lifted her hand from the bedcover. The doctor was called again and this time he sat on the bed, by Beth's side.

'Bethan, can you hear me? Open your eyes, will you?'

They waited, intent on watching her for some further sign of movement. She reached up, eyes steadfastly closed, and pulled at the breathing tube down her throat.

'Hang on, Bethan, we'll remove it.' The doctor stood and eased the breathing tube out; she coughed. One eye opened and immediately closed.

'Come on, Bethan,' he said again. 'Try again.'

This time both eyes opened and stayed open for about five seconds. They closed once more.

'Your nan and your friend are here. Don't you want to see them?'

'Drink,' she mumbled, and the nurse poured water into a glass and held it to her lips. She took a small sip, still with her eyes closed.

It took over an hour to persuade her to open her eyes and keep them open. Her smile as she recognised her nan lit up the room.

'Nan,' she croaked, and Doris stepped forward to hug her.

'Dear girl, don't ever scare me like this again,' she murmured. 'I thought I'd lost you.'

Her eyes closed again, but only for a short time.

Kat touched her hand. 'Beth, I'm going to go home now I've seen you awake, and leave you with your nan.'

'Kat,' Beth murmured. 'Please tomorrow. Talk.'

Kat leaned over and kissed her head. 'I promise, tomorrow morning I'll return.'

Beth smiled, closed her eyes and drifted off to sleep once again, but this time everybody knew she would wake up when her body was rested.

Kat drove home in a much better frame of mind, happy that Beth had spoken.

Beth was in free fall. She was aware of people around her, telling her to open her eyes, to have a sip of water, on a scale of one to ten how was her pain. She wanted them to leave her alone.

And then the police arrived.

'Hello, Bethan. I'm DI Tessa Marsden. Can you hear me?'

Beth opened one eye.

'Good. It's important we find out exactly what you remember as quickly as possible.' The DI smiled at Beth. 'And I can read your thoughts. You're telling me to fuck off.'

Both of Beth's eyes opened. This policewoman really was a mind-reader.

'Can you speak, Beth?'

'A little.' Beth's voice was hoarse.

'Okay. Did you recognise the man who shot you?'

'No.'

'Were you heading for Mr Jackson's house?'

'Yes.'

'You were in a taxi?'

'Yes.'

'Thank you, you're doing well.'

A nurse was hovering, ready to jump in and put a stop to the questions but Marsden continued.

'Where did you get the cab?'

Beth paused for a moment to collect her thoughts. 'Steel.'

'The nightclub?'

Beth nodded.

'You called it yourself?'

Beth had a fleeting vision of a doorman on a walkie-talkie, and then seconds later, the cab appeared. 'Yes.' She couldn't be bothered with the true explanation.

'Was it the driver of the taxi who shot you?'

'Yes.'

Beth closed her eyes. She needed these people to go.

'Okay,' the nurse stepped in. 'That's enough. Come back when she's capable of talking.'

The DI nodded. 'Thank you. She can't remember much while she's so poorly anyway.' She leaned across and touched Beth's hand. 'Thank you, Bethan, we'll leave it for now.' Marsden left the room, stopping to speak to the officer outside the door.

The nurse wheeled the blood pressure machine towards the bed, and Beth opened her eyes. 'Thank you,' she said, 'that was getting boring.'

'Unfortunately, they'll be back, but I'll watch out for it happening. Can't you remember much about it?'

'Very little. I remember him shooting Anthony, and then turning the gun on me. I think he thought my injury was worse than it was. He walked over and kicked me in the face... oh!'

'Oh?'

'That's why I feel like I've gone ten rounds with Mohammed Ali. My cheek feels as though it's tightening and stiffening.'

'You've a corker of a bruise on the left side of your face, but there's no damage. It will get better, I promise.'

The nurse attached the machine, and then removed it a minute later with a smile. 'Even though you're pretty broken up and battered at the moment, your blood pressure is fine. You need any painkillers?'

'No, I'm good thanks. I need sleep.'

This time her eyes remained closed.

DI Marsden headed back to the station, frustrated by the lack of evidence. She needed to see if Steel had CCTV footage of the night in question; the only sighting they had of the taxi was when it had arrived at the alley. Luckily the pharmacy had installed two cameras, one on the front of the shop and one to cover activity in the alleyway.

Jackson's murder and Bethan Walters' attempted murder had been graphically clear, but the gunman's face had been covered by what Marsden thought was a balaclava. He wore a plain dark hoodie, black jeans, black shoes that looked to be trainers, and had nothing to distinguish him at all.

The plates on the taxi had been false, but Marsden could have put money on that anyway. This had clearly been planned.

So who had known the couple would be at Steel that night? Marsden needed Bethan Walters to get better very quickly and start providing some clarification. Preferably when no nurses were in attendance.

In the meantime, they would be interviewing Jackson's acquaintances, finding out a little more about Walters, maybe talking to Leon and Katerina Rowe again; it seemed that Reverend Rowe had been at the hospital every day since the shooting. Was it just part of her job and a feeling of responsibility because she had found her, or was there more to it?

Marsden pulled her keyboard towards her and made notes.

Leon was sleeping; Kat slid out of bed, careful not to disturb him, padded across to the dressing table and opened her safe. Leon had had the hidden compartment installed specifically to keep her valuables locked away securely, and she took out the ruby.

In the moonlight, the only illumination in the room, it gleamed. She loved the stone, and gently touched it.

She said a small prayer, put the box back in the safe and locked it.

She stood at the window for a while, looking down the garden towards the brook. Although she couldn't hear it, she knew it would be tinkling its way over the stones and rocks on its bed, a welcome sound at any time. The remembrance of that sound would have to soothe her.

The following day, after the early prayer meeting, she would head off to the hospital. She needed to talk to Beth, albeit carefully. She didn't want to set her recovery back in any way.

Beth knew there had been a change overnight. She felt different. The pain in her shoulder was no longer constant; it only hurt when she moved a little awkwardly, and her headache had massively diminished. She felt so much better, and could even manage a smile.

'Keep this up, Beth,' the doctor said, 'and we could be looking at letting you go home in a couple of days, provided there is someone there to look after you.'

'Yes, there is,' Beth said. 'I'm going to stay with my nan for a couple of weeks, just while I sort out my life. I have some decisions to make.'

'Then let's aim for Friday morning, provided at that point I think you'll be fit to leave us. In the meantime, rest, give all these cuts and bumps and wounds chance to heal. Deal?'

'Deal.'

6

Leon was in the office above his pharmacy in Eyam. It was strictly his office, kept locked at all times when he wasn't in it, and occasionally when he *was* in it.

There was a shipment coming in to Sheffield, and he was happy to leave all the details to Brian King. Friends since school days, they had gravitated into the dark side of Sheffield's underworld together.

Brian was different. He didn't have Leon's charisma, the distribution flair, he was the quiet partner. His ginger hair, only now beginning to tone down a little as he had hit his forties, was atop a pale face that held little colour. It was also atop a keen brain, a brain that dealt with knowledge. He knew exactly who had what, who owed what and who had to be dealt with.

Leon finished the paperwork and leaned back in his chair. He could hear two or three men's voices out in the alleyway, and he felt thankful that at last it could be cleaned. They had parked their truck at the entrance, and were filling it with every bit of rubbish that had been there on the night Jackson had died. Leon's instructions had been that he wanted to be able to eat his lunch off the floor out there, and he knew it would be steam cleaned to within an inch of its life. The blood was very visible, and he needed it gone.

Anthony Jackson had been a problem, now he wasn't; who the hell had taken the problem away? And the woman… who was she, and why did Kat feel she needed to be at her bedside every day? He felt a little out of control, and that wasn't normal for Leon Rowe.

He rang Brian's number and, as always, it was answered immediately.

'We need a meet.'

'When?'

'Soon. Very soon.'

There was a momentary hesitation while Brian checked his diary. 'Tomorrow morning? You want me there or are you coming here?' Brian was based at the distribution centre for the legitimate side of Leon's business empire.

'I'll be there for ten,' Leon said.

He disconnected and opened up his computer. He typed in Anthony Jackson and saw that there was an obituary, praising him for his charitable works, his loyalty to his friends and colleagues, their grief at his passing; nothing about the drugs he was bringing in and the insidious transgression into the Rowe dealership.

Jackson's funeral was scheduled for a week's time, and Leon thought he might go; it would be a respectful thing to do as the deceased had had his head blown away in the alleyway behind Rowe's Pharmacy.

Leon heard the noise of the steam cleaner and knew soon there would be no trace left of Jackson, other than this Beth Walters who Kat seemed to have taken under her wing.

Beth was awake and looking much more alert when Kat arrived.

'Okay to come in?'

'Of course. I can't smile at you though, it hurts.'

'You're looking tons better.'

'I feel it, but I keep falling asleep, no warning, one second I'm awake, the next I'm asleep.'

'That's fine. If you sleep, I'll go. Is your nan not here yet?'

'She's not coming today. She has a hospital appointment of her own, but it's a different hospital so I told her to leave it until tomorrow.'

Kat nodded. 'Then I'll stay a bit longer than I planned.'

'Good. I need to talk.'

'About?'

'About what happened.'

'Can you remember anything?'

'Bits. He told me his name was Anthony Parkson but he told me a different name when we got out of the cab. It was like… he wanted to be honest with me in case something bad happened. And it did.'

'His name was Anthony Jackson. Why did he tell you the wrong name?'

'Kat, I'm an escort and a part-time prostitute. I live in a world of wrong names. He knew I was Beth, but that was all. I told him my full name when he told me his. I don't think either of us expected to get out alive.'

'Did you see his face, the man who shot you?'

'The police asked me that, and I said no.'

'But?'

'I did. I saw it when we got in the taxi. I tried to have a better look because I thought I knew him, but I couldn't see him properly. When he shot us, he'd put on a balaclava.'

'Why did you say no when the police asked you?'

'I was scared. I'd only just surfaced, and they were here, wanting me to solve it for them. How long do you think I'll last if I give them a name?'

Kat paused, deep in thought.

'You've said nothing about what I do to earn money,' Beth continued.

'Do you earn a lot of money?'

'I do.'

'And are you normally safe?'

'I am. The clients are vetted by an agency, but obviously none of the escorts are on their books as hookers, we're all there to accompany the clients to posh dinners and suchlike. That's what I had done that evening, but I was heading back to Anthony's house to stay the night. He would have paid me separately for that.'

Beth closed her eyes for a moment.

'You're tired,' Kat said. 'Sleep for a while, we'll talk later.'

Beth nodded; her eyes remained closed.

Kat left the room to get a sandwich; she stopped by the officer outside the door.

'Would you like me to bring a coffee or something back for you?'

'Thank you, ma'am. That would be good.' He put his hand in his pocket to get some money but she stopped him. 'My treat. Are you here until Beth goes home?'

'We are.'

'Good. I'll get you that coffee.'

She returned a quarter of an hour later and handed over the coffee. 'All quiet?'

'Yes, ma'am. She only has you and her nan for visitors.'

'It'll get livelier,' Kat smiled. 'I understand Beth has two housemates who are itching to come to see her, but her nan has said no, not until she's stronger. She's getting stronger every day, so I reckon maybe tomorrow you'll be having extra visitors.'

'Are they pretty?'

Kat laughed. 'Never met them, but if they're anything like Beth, I'd say they're stunning.'

'Good. That'll liven things up.'

'You're cheeky,' Kat said, as she pushed through to Beth's room.

Beth was still sleeping, but restless. Her head kept moving from one side to the other and Kat hoped she wasn't experiencing a nightmare, one she couldn't get out of.

She watched the bruised and battered face as she ate her sandwich, wondering whether to wake her; she was clearly in a stressful situation. Eventually she gave in, and touched Beth's arm.

Her eyes flew open and the look of terror on her face was chilling.

'Beth, Beth – wake up,' Kat whispered softly, and Beth's huge eyes turned towards her.

'Oh God, Kat. It was so scary. He was making me clean up Anthony's brains and blood.'

'Who was, Beth?'

'The taxi driver. I know him.' She clutched on to Kat's hand. 'I just can't remember why, yet.'

Kat stood and reached for a glass of water. 'Have a sip of this. It'll help you calm down.'

Beth sipped at the water and then gave a huge shudder. 'I feel better now. It was just a nightmare.'

They sat quietly for a moment, and then Beth spoke quickly, as if she needed to get the words out before she lost her courage.

'I won't be doing it any more. It's going to have to come out if they ever find out who killed Anthony – the escort bit, I mean. And that's going to kill Nan. No amount of money is worth upsetting her.'

'Do your housemates know?'

'They know about the escort side, because they see me dressed up for the parties and stuff I go to, but they don't know I charge for the overnight stays.'

'Then why should it come out? If it ever does get to court, they can suggest what you were doing with Jackson, but all you have to say is that you just got on really well, you're both consenting adults, and you had jointly decided to spend the night together. That's not a crime, it's quite a natural thing to do. Nobody else is going to stand up in court and admit to sleeping with you for money, are they?'

'I still won't be doing it again. The money I've stashed away will have to be it, now. I was doing it to raise money for a year's trip around the world. No amount of money can erase seeing a man's head blown apart.'

'Will you be going to your nan's house when they say you can go home?'

Beth shook her head. 'Not an earthly. I've told them here that's where I'm going, but somebody left me for dead. They might try again, and I don't want Nan caught in the fallout from my stupidity. Likewise for the girls. I know it's my house, but I'll have to find somewhere else for the moment, somewhere else that nobody knows about. Can I tell you the location, Kat? You know… just in case.'

'You can come to me. We have plenty of spare room, and Leon won't mind. I can look after you until you're fully well, then you can make some decisions. Maybe put your house visibly up for sale, then buy another?'

'Stay with you? But that puts you in danger.'

'Nobody will know.'

'Oh, Reverend Rowe, you're pretty naïve.' Beth laughed. 'But thank you. I'll take you up on that offer provided your husband has the final say. It's not fair if I just arrive on your doorstep. And I'll tell Jo and Millie they'll have to find somewhere else. They won't like it, they won't like me, but they'll be safe away from the house. And staying with you will only be for as long as it takes me to get another home.'

'You'll be convalescent for a while, you're not going to bounce back from this quickly. And we have lots of security on the house, so your safety won't be an issue.'

'Thank you, Kat,' Beth said quietly. 'Thank you.'

Leon sat at his desk watching a re-run of the murder of Anthony Jackson. He didn't recognise anything about the man who had driven the taxi, not his clothes, his height, his stance. He didn't believe in coincidence; his alleyway had been chosen for this action, but why?

Jackson had been trying for some time to infiltrate his supply area, but not with any conviction. More chancing his arm than anything. They hadn't even bothered to warn him off, just ignored it. The Rowe/King partnership was solid and fair as long as there was no disruption to the financial side of their business.

Leon secretly admitted to it being something of a surprise that they lived in the same village, and if it hadn't been for Kat wanting to play Miss Marple, he wouldn't have known. Which brought him back in a roundabout way to his original thought – why kill him in the Rowe Pharmacy alleyway, and not his own home? Five more minutes and the taxi would have been on Jackson's driveway.

Was there some reason they didn't want him found for a while? And they must have known a pharmacy would have CCTV on all external doors. They certainly couldn't have known it would be himself and Kat who would make the gruesome discovery, so who would normally have made it?

Neil.

Was that a clue? How would Neil finding them help anybody? He was a very minor player in the darker side of the business, and a reluctant one at that. Blackmail kept him in line and if he'd found them, his first reaction would have been to ring Leon before sending for an ambulance. He did nothing without permission.

Leon was sure Neil wasn't in the mix.

Maybe the plan didn't involve anybody finding them quickly. Whoever wanted them dead knew of the alleyway; they wanted to make sure they were dead by leaving them overnight with no assistance. That had to be it. The alleyway was a perfect place to dump bodies.

Leon rubbed his eyes. It was bloody ridiculous. Maybe he needed to go to the hospital with Kat, see what this Beth woman had to say. Perhaps she could throw some light on why it had happened where it had, although he rather suspected she was an innocent in all of this. According to Kat, the girl had only met Jackson for the first time that night.

He stood and paced around the room, his mind churning. He needed more protection around him. Just for a short while, until things settled down and he felt more secure.

Kat handed Leon the poached eggs on toast, and sat down opposite him. 'I've something to tell you.'

'Is it serious?' he asked, trying to cope with the egg yolk going everywhere.

'Yes. I've asked Beth to come and stay with us for a few weeks when she gets out of hospital.'

He looked up. 'Oh, that is fairly serious.'

'I know, but she can't go home. She's worried that whoever thought he was leaving her for dead will still want her that way, so she can't go to her nan's house, that would put Mrs Lester in danger. Beth has her own house where she was living with two housemates before this happened, but she's now going to ask them to leave, to protect them, and she's putting it on the market. She intends buying a new one, so she could potentially be here until she finds that new one.'

Leon put down his knife and fork. 'Kat Rowe, if ever I'm in trouble, will you be my guardian angel?'

'That goes without saying.' She grinned. 'So you're not mad with me?'

'For looking after somebody? I should think not. When will she be coming? And are you happy with our security?'

'I should think she'll be here in two or three days. She's on the mend. And I think we're secure enough but you're the expert. Are we?'

'Can she handle a gun?' Leon's face was serious.

'I wouldn't have thought so. Luckily we don't have one.'

'Then she'd better learn quick. There will be a gun in this house if Beth Walters is in it. Deal-breaker, Kat.'

Kat let out a whoosh of air, and Leon returned to the problem of his rapidly cooling eggs on toast.

'But...' Kat could feel a stammer coming on. 'But where would we keep the damn thing?'

'Where will Beth be? In the sunshine room?' The guest room was yellow and lifted the spirits gloriously.

Kat nodded.

'Then it will be in the bedside cabinet by the side of her bed, in the drawer.'

Kat recognised defeat. 'Okay, but don't expect me to touch it.'

'You will both sit down with me and I will teach you how to use it safely, and you will touch it. You can't put your faith in a gun if you've never handled one. As I said, it's a deal-breaker. You're putting yourself at risk, Katerina, and I love you.'

His use of her full name told her just how serious he was, and she accepted defeat.

'I give in,' she said. 'But as soon as Beth leaves, the gun goes. Do you want to tell me how you know so much about guns?'

'The gun will go when she leaves. Brian and I used to go to a gun club at Bradwell in our early twenties, used to really enjoy it, but as the business grew we didn't have time for it any more. I learned a lot though, so I'll be passing some of that knowledge on to you two,' he said, dripping some egg on to his shirt. He sighed. 'And I'll put a clean shirt on when I've finished breakfast.'

'Erm… you might want to wash your chin as well.'

She stood and walked out of the kitchen feeling slightly shaky. Leon never laid down the law; normally she did pretty much what she wanted, and he would simply give a tolerant smile. But now it seemed he had put his foot down about them having his deal-breaking gun in the house.

A gun! The very thought scared her to bits. She couldn't see the need, nobody would know Beth was with them, in the little plague village of Eyam. She took her jacket from the cloakroom and returned to plant a kiss on her husband's head.

'I'm going for a quiet quarter of an hour in church, and then I'm off to the hospital. Don't forget to change your shirt.'

'I won't. Say a prayer for me.'

'I always do,' she retorted. 'You need all the help you can get.'

If only you knew, Kat, if only you knew. His thoughts followed her out of the door.

She drove to the church and was relieved to see it empty. She was normally happy to see other people there, but she needed her own time with God. She lit one of the small tea lights for Beth and sat down on the front pew.

Kat let her mind roam, drank in the peace of the sanctuary, and left twenty minutes later, feeling refreshed. Although they hadn't argued, she hated any sort of discord between her and Leon, and for him to be so insistent about an issue was unusual. She climbed into her car, and headed once again for Sheffield, hoping that Beth was getting somewhere near being discharged.

It was a long stressful journey followed by driving around and around an inadequate car park searching for a parking space, and she had the added strain of learning how to use a gun.

It never occurred to her to wonder where Leon was going to get the gun.

7

It was a different officer outside Beth's room, and Kat handed him a coffee. 'It's got milk in, and here's a couple of packets of sugar. You'll have to stir it with your pen,' she grinned at him.

'Thank you, ma'am. I don't take sugar anyway.' He returned her smile.

She went into the room, and Beth was sitting in the chair.

'Wow! That's progress! And no drips. You're feeling better?'

'I am, much better. They're talking about letting me go home Friday. Is it still okay for me to go with you?'

'Of course it is. We're putting you in what we call the sunshine room, so I'll leave you to guess what colour we decorated it. It's a lovely big room, and you take yourself off to it whenever you need to rest. There's a television in it if you need to watch some mindless daytime stuff. In fact you treat our home as your home.'

Beth visibly relaxed. 'That's a relief. I told the doctor I could go to yours, and I think that swung it. He'll confirm it Friday morning when I've had my blood pressure done, but it's looking good.'

Kat brought a plastic chair around and sat at Beth's side. 'I'll sit here until your nan comes. Does she know you're coming to me?'

Beth shook her head. 'Not yet. I'll tell her later. I've spoken to Millie and Jo though. That didn't go down well. I've told them I'm selling up, and there's no rush to leave until the sale goes through. But it's a disruption as they start their final year. They came to see me last night. It was a good visit, but I could tell they were worried. We've been together for a couple of years now. It did force me to make another decision though. I'm not going back to uni. Maybe sometime in the future I can complete the degree, but I'm a different person. I've had to grow up.'

'Whoosh. That's a massive decision to make. What will you do for a job?'

'I don't know. Maybe my own business. It occurred to me that if I rent a property, I'll have quite a lot of money. It gives me breathing space to work out what I want to do.' Beth looked down at her hands.

'I'm always here if you want to talk through ideas, thoughts, you can be sure of that.'

'Thank you, Kat. I feel especially close to you, and I can't say enough how grateful I am that it was you who saved me.'

'I didn't save you. The ambulance people did that. I simply found you and covered up your knickers.' She smiled.

'Covered up my knickers?'

'They were on full view. Your beautiful dress was somewhere around your neck when I found you.'

Beth blanched. 'Oh God, I wasn't…?'

'I don't think so. Your knickers were in place, as was your bra. I think you slid down the rubbish bags in your silk dress. They saw the taxi arrive, the two gunshots, and the taxi leave. He clearly thought he'd killed you. Every part of the attack was on CCTV, and at no time was there any sexual assault.'

Relief was obvious on Beth's face. 'The police came again to talk to me after you'd gone yesterday, but I think they've given up on me. I can't tell them anything. A DI Marsden left me with her card, in case anything does come back to me, but if it does I'll be more inclined to follow it up myself.'

'No.' Kat spoke firmly. 'We discuss everything. If you start with the vigilante stuff, I'll put you in the cellar and not the sunshine room.'

'You got a cellar?'

'No.'

'Okay. But if I remember anything, I promise I'll tell you. There's something so near to the edge of my memory…'

'Don't force it,' Kat said. 'It'll be there when you least expect it. And then we'll discuss talking to this policewoman.'

'You shouting at me?'

'I seem to be. You're turning out to be pretty feisty, Beth Walters. Pack it in. or I'll go back and blow out your candle.'

'What?'

'I had some time in church this morning, and I lit a candle for you. It can be blown out.'

Beth's peal of laughter reverberated around the room. 'Katerina Rowe, you're a star. I've never had a candle lit for me before today.'

'Tomorrow I might light three. You need all the help you can get,' Kat said with a grin. 'How did you know my name was Katerina?'

'Nan told me.'

'So shall we talk about your name? Mouse?'

Beth laughed. 'My family have always called me Mouse. I've seen my baby photos, and the name definitely fitted. It's kind of stuck.'

'It's lovely. Shows how loved you are. You have much family?'

'My mum's sister and her family live in Broadstairs… you know, Kent.'

Kat nodded.

'That's about it. There's just Nan and me in Sheffield now. It's fine, and Nan is going to live forever. She says so. And now I have you. I feel happily close to you. We're Kat and Mouse!' She grinned at Kat as she said the words.

'It's possibly survivor syndrome.'

'Survivor syndrome? What's that?'

'It's when you connect with the person who saved you.'

'You said you didn't save me, the ambulance men did.' Beth's face was triumphant.

'I saved your blushes. I saved you being ogled by every man there. Matching dress and knickers indeed.'

They dissolved into laughter just as the lady pushing the tea trolley opened the door.

Kat stood. 'I'll leave you in peace, Beth. Enjoy your cuppa, and God bless.'

She reached the door and Beth spoke. 'Kat… call me Mouse.'

Tessa Marsden read through the scant few statements they had collected. Leon Rowe, Katerina Rowe, and the victim herself, Bethan Walters. There was nothing to help in any of them. Marsden needed Bethan to gain some more memory, to give them just one little clue to follow, but so far there had been nothing.

The CCTV from outside Steel had showed them arriving in a taxi with two other passengers. They had been chatting and laughing, so they clearly knew each other. Half an hour later, Jackson and Walters were seen getting into another taxi and driving off, and that was it. If they could track down the two people, maybe they could shed some light on the subject.

Marsden picked up the large picture the tech lads had printed from the CCTV, and put it in a folder before leaving the office. 'Hannah! We're going out and you're driving.'

'We're going to Steel?' Hannah asked.

'We are if we can get through this bloody traffic,' her boss grumbled.

'Will it be open? It's only three o'clock.'

'Somebody will be there. They have to get ready for tonight, don't they?'

Hannah pulled up outside Steel some ten minutes later, hoping it wouldn't be a wasted journey. She sensed the DI was in a bad enough mood.

The side door was open, and they went through. It looked shabby without the glamorous lights of the evening. The cleaner was sweeping the floor in a somewhat lethargic manner, and when they asked him if anyone else was around, he indicated to a door with a movement of his head.

The door led to a corridor, which in turn revealed a door that said "Off ce" on it. Hannah wondered what had happened to the i, and why it hadn't been stuck back on.

Tessa knocked, and it was eventually opened.

'What?'

'Full of charm, Charlie.'

Charlie Earnshaw peered into the gloom of the corridor. 'DI Marsden, as I live and breathe. What do you want?'

'I need you to look at a picture, Charlie. Can we come in?'

She pushed on the door before he could stop her, and it opened to reveal a young girl, trying to get dressed as quickly as she had probably undressed earlier.

'You old enough, love?' Marsden asked drily.

'I'm eighteen.'

'Sit down. I need you to look at something. You too, Charlie.'

They both complied, both trying to fasten trousers at the same time. Hannah was trying desperately hard not to laugh.

Tessa Marsden took out the photograph and showed it to Charlie. 'Recognise them?'

He stared at it for a moment. 'Don't think so.'

'The picture's been taken from your CCTV footage.'

He looked again. 'I think I've seen them, but I don't know who they are. They're not regulars.'

The girl reached across and took the photograph. 'He's called Steve and she's called Ellie, but I can't tell you their surnames. They were here the other night when that feller was killed. They were in his group.'

'And you know that for definite?' Marsden tried not to let the shock show.

'For definite. Maybe I'm not the bimbo you initially thought, DI Marsden,' the girl said icily. 'I work the bar, and I listen. And I have a photographic memory.'

'Did you hear them say anything?'

'Not much – it was noisy. I heard them say it was a lot noisier than the Alhambra, but that was all.'

Marsden sat up a little straighter. 'What time was this?'

'After midnight. I can't be more precise than that.'

'So you think they'd been at the Alhambra before coming here?'

'Seemed like that. There was about fifteen or so people in their group, so I guessed they'd come on from somewhere else.'

Marsden stood. 'We'll need a statement from you…'

'Lily Kenworth. I'll come in to the station tomorrow morning, shall I?'

'Yes please. Ask for PC Hannah Granger here, will you? She'll look after you.'

Hannah Granger nodded and smiled.

Once seated in the car, Marsden turned to Hannah. 'Why didn't we know?'

'How could we? Bethan Walters can't remember anything, or she's simply not telling us anything, and Anthony Jackson is dead.'

'Right, let's go to the Alhambra.'

The receptionist smiled as the two police officers walked through the door. The smile disappeared when they said who they were, but Tessa was used to that reaction. It almost amused her. Almost.

'We're making enquiries about a Mr Anthony Jackson, who we believe was here with a party of friends…'

'Yes, he was,' the receptionist jumped in. 'Are you here for his car?'

Another mystery solved.

'For that, and for information,' Tessa said.

'Here's the key. All the others collected their cars the day after, but Mr Jackson didn't. Of course, he couldn't, could he?'

'And you didn't think to report to us that you had his car here?'

'The manager said to leave it until you turned up.'

Tessa picked up the key and looked at the receptionist. 'I'm going to look at this car. When I walk back in here I expect your manager to be waiting for me, with a list of Mr Jackson's guests if he has one. Understand?' Her tone was icy, and the receptionist nodded. There was a tiny hint of fear in her eyes.

Tessa and Hannah walked out to the car park and Tessa clicked the unlock button on the fob. The Jaguar's lights lit immediately, and they headed across the asphalt towards it.

'Some car,' Hannah said appreciatively.

'And he had the right girlfriend to accessorise it,' Tessa acknowledged. 'When she's not covered in bruises, I imagine she's a stunner.'

They both put on latex gloves, and Tessa opened the driver's door. Hannah moved to the passenger side and had a quick look around. She opened the glove box and emptied it.

'There's a car manual, a service book, a petrol receipt and an invoice of some sort.' Hannah opened up the piece of paper and read it.

'There's a turn up for the books,' she said. 'She wasn't his girlfriend. She was his escort.'

She passed the piece of paper across to her boss. 'I bet if we mention this invoice to Beth Walters we'd get a reaction. Funny how she hasn't mentioned it, isn't it?'

Tessa looked at the receipt, then put it in an evidence bag. 'What are we doing in this job, Hannah? She'll be earning twice as much as us.'

'Still rather have my job, boss. I can't be that nice to people, not for that long.' Hannah grinned.

They found nothing else in the car, so walked back inside the Alhambra to find the manager standing waiting for them.

'Did you know of Mr Jackson's death?' Marsden said before he could speak.

'I did.'

'And it didn't occur to you to ring and report his car was here, even though you knew it was?'

'I thought you would turn up for it eventually.'

'Not good enough. Not public spirited enough, sir. We'll conduct the next part of the interview at the station,' she said and turned to walk away. 'Follow me, sir.'

'What? Hang on a minute...'

'We've hung on for several days, sir. That's called withholding evidence.'

'Look, come into my office, and I'm sure we can sort this out.' Eric Firth looked ashen.

'Oh, you want to sort it out now, do you?' Tessa turned back to him. The bravado on his part, the cocky stance, had disappeared.

'Please, this way.'

They followed him behind the reception area, and to a door marked Manager. Hannah tried to hide her smile. The poor man had never stood a chance.

He showed Tessa to a chair, and then picked up a second one for Hannah.

'Now, what can I do for you?' he said, sitting down in his leather office chair; the loud farting noise from the leather clearly embarrassed him.

'Why was Anthony Jackson here?'

'He had booked our large function room for the night, for seventy people.'

'Seventy people?' Tessa tried to hide her surprise. Seventy people, and not one had come forward to say they had been with him. 'And you don't have a guest list?'

'I have a list of names, but only names, not addresses or companies or anything. We had to do a table plan for the meal.'

Tessa held out her hand.

'One minute. I need to print it.'

She waited while he found the file, and then the printer churned out the sheets. He reached across, stacked them tidily and handed them to her.

'Thank you,' she said. 'Now tell me about the evening.'

'It seemed to go very well. Mr Jackson gave a very short speech, thanking them for their support over the past year sort of thing, then everybody went into our smaller function room while we cleared the large one. He'd hired a jazz band, a very good one, for the evening and they played as soon as the guests headed back into the main room.'

'I need the name of that band.'

'I'm sorry, I can't help with that. They're apparently friends of Mr Jackson, he hired them. Several people had left by about eleven o'clock, and it really wound down soon after that. Around half a dozen people left their cars here overnight because they went on to somewhere else, and then picked them up the day after. We were just left with the Jaguar keys.'

Tessa looked at the key in her hand. 'It's just a car key.'

'Yes, he took his house key off, but left the car key here in case we needed to move it. They all did.'

Tessa stood. 'Thank you for your eventual cooperation, Mr Firth. We'll be back if we need to speak with you again. We'll move the car as soon as possible.'

The two women left the office, struggling to keep straight faces.

'Classic, boss, classic,' Hannah said, as they walked down the steps to reach their car.

'Think he knew anything else?'

'I would say not. He was so scared of being whisked off to the station, I don't think he'd have held anything back.'

'My feelings as well. We've hell of a job here though.' Tessa waved the printed sheets. 'Every one of these needs to be contacted, so we've to track down addresses. You want the job?'

Hannah laughed. 'No thanks, but I will if you insist.'

'No, you're okay.' Tessa smiled. 'I'll find somebody who's upset me, they can do it.'

8

'Welcome to our home,' Kat said as she led Mouse through the front door. 'I'll get your suitcase in a moment. Let me get you settled in first.'

They had called at Mouse's home to pick up some clothes, and Kat sensed that even that small but necessary activity had tired her friend.

Kat pushed open the lounge door. 'Go and make yourself comfortable, Mouse. I'll make us a drink that doesn't taste like hospital tea, then I'll show you your room.'

The lounge smelled of roses, and in the centre of the coffee table was a beautiful rose bowl filled with the flowers. Mouse sank into an armchair and laid back her head. The slight headache was always there, but they had assured her it would go eventually, when the swelling inside her brain diminished. She closed her eyes for a moment, letting the peace of the room envelop her.

Kat placed the tray on the coffee table and Mouse opened her eyes. 'Are the roses from your garden?'

'They are.' Kat smiled. 'The rose garden was well established when we moved in and I've no thoughts about changing it.'

She handed Mouse a tea, and they sat quietly for a couple of minutes.

'Did the drive here bring anything back to you?' Kat asked.

'No. There's something playing around in the back of my mind, but the drive didn't help. You didn't go by that alleyway, did you?'

'No, I deliberately avoided it.'

'Then in a couple of days we'll go there.'

'So what's playing around in your mind?'

'That I knew the driver, the man who killed Anthony.'

'How do you think you knew him? Was he a client you'd escorted?'

'Maybe. I don't think I slept with him; they seem to fix into your mind, but escorting jobs don't.'

Kat laughed. 'I have to admire you. I couldn't have done that job, not for a million pounds a night.'

'That's because you're a proper Christian…'

'No it's not, it's because I haven't the guts. Being a Christian doesn't make you blind to the delights of this world, you know – like Idris Elba and Tom Hardy.'

They grinned at each other, happy to be away from the sterility of the hospital.

'So when do I get to meet Mr Rowe?'

'He said he'd be home around four, but don't take that as an accurate guide. What he really means is sometime this afternoon or early evening. He's looking forward to meeting you.'

'And I him. Am I right thinking that you said he knew Anthony Jackson?'

'He didn't really know him, it was more that he knew *of* him. They're both in the same business, pharmaceuticals. Paths didn't really cross though. Leon's shops are spread all across Derbyshire and Nottinghamshire, whereas Jackson Pharmacies are more South Yorkshire and beyond. It's why we couldn't fathom him being killed in the alleyway of one of our shops.'

'Somebody trying to send you a message?' Mouse's face was serious.

'You mean you think Leon could be targeted?' Kat was frowning. 'Why would he be? It's a perfectly legitimate business, nothing in any way dodgy about it.'

'I don't know. They thought they'd killed me, and I'd never met Anthony before that night. I had no connection to him or any possibly nefarious goings-on. Is Leon a smart bloke?'

'Very smart.'

'Then he'll know he needs to be careful. In fact, I could stop the whole damn mess if I could just remember who that driver is.'

'Stop trying to force it,' Kat said gently. 'It will come when you least expect it. The thing is, even if the name does come to you, it might not be his real name if he were a client.'

'No, but it would be a start.'

Mouse put down her empty cup and closed her eyes. 'This feels so right, as if I've finally found somewhere I can be me. I promise to be out of your hair as soon as I find a place of my own, but for now I'm going to absorb this wonderful peace. And thank you for calling me Mouse, it sits so comfortably with me.'

Kat laughed. 'Then come for a little walk in the garden, then you'll really appreciate what sold this house to us in the first place.'

They went out through the patio doors and into the bright sunshine. The brook was definitely babbling, and the songs of the birds added to the tranquillity.

'Come and smell the rose garden,' Kat said. 'It's stunning.'

They walked around by the herb garden and into a sea of colour. Roses of every hue were present, and the perfume, hovering like a giant blanket in the air, was deliciously sweet.

'Oh my god, Kat, you can almost taste it.'

'Beautiful, isn't it? We moved in during December, and the original plan was to take them out to make this a vegetable garden, but we decided to wait and see what they were like. The vegetable garden was cancelled.'

'One day this is what I'll have.' Mouse looked pensively around. 'My little house in Sheffield, as you saw this morning, doesn't even have a garden, just a back yard.'

'Give it time, Mouse. You're very young. I didn't even leave home till I was thirty. I lived with Mum and Dad until Leon and I found each other.'

'That sounds so sweet.'

'Unexpected. My life was my church, but God moves in very mysterious ways, as you know now. He led us together.'

'Something led us together.'

DI Marsden faced her team, adding things to the board as she spoke. 'It now appears that Bethan Walters was his escort for the evening, at the grand do he'd organised at the Alhambra. We have a long list of people to work through, and I realise most of them will have nothing to add to the investigation, but some of them might and we don't know which ones are going to be the helpful ones. That means we have to interview and eliminate seventy people who we don't even have addresses for.' She cast her eyes around the room.

'Penny and Ray, split the list down the middle and find the addresses, will you. If you can find anything else about them, then do so.'

Penny and Ray looked sick; they now had proof that they'd upset the boss in some way and were on punishment duties.

'The car,' Tessa continued, 'is a black Jaguar, but it has been parked in the same place at the Alhambra since Mr Jackson and Miss Walters arrived there for the evening. We have checked it out, but I am not ordering a forensic examination of it unless we feel it necessary, because the car wasn't used after about seven on the night of the murder. They used taxis after that. One interesting thing came out of the car, a receipt for the escort services of Bethan Walters. The date on the receipt confirms Beth was his escort that night.'

Tessa stared around. 'Does anyone have anything to add? Have we got anything of interest that could be helpful in any way?'

'Was his house key on his car keys, boss? Is that why we couldn't get into his house?'

'No, he apparently took it off when he left the car key at the Alhambra. And it's not on the list of things we recovered from him, so somewhere there is a missing key. The killer didn't go near the body after he had shot him, we can see that from the CCTV, so where is that key? There's a lot of questions up here.' She pointed at the board. 'Let's start finding the answers. I want to know every damn last thing about Anthony Jackson, that has to be where the solutions are. Next briefing will be at eight tomorrow, don't be late. Penny and Ray, don't be late.'

That proved exactly what they had done to win the tedious job of address finding.

Tessa sat in her office, eyes almost closed, thinking. Beth's file wasn't very thick, and Tessa sat up, her eyes now open. She needed to know more about this woman; needed to penetrate the memory that couldn't seem to remember anything.

She had Katerina Rowe's address as well as Bethan Walters' own home address, but she knew the deacon had taken Beth to her home to recuperate.

Maybe Tessa going on her own would open Bethan up, not be quite so intimidating as turning up with Hannah.

She left the Chesterfield police station and headed towards Eyam.

'DI Marsden, good to see you.' Kat's smile was warm and welcoming; inside she was seething. Mouse had only been out of hospital a few hours. 'Come in. You want Beth, presumably?'

'Yes please. Is she here?'

'She is. She'll be here until she's well enough to move into her own place. She may be asleep, she went to her room for a rest. I'll go and check. Would you like to sit outside, or in the lounge?'

'Outside, it's such a lovely day.'

Kat took her through to the garden, then left her while she went to see if Mouse was awake.

She knocked gently on the bedroom door and Mouse opened it.

'I was just coming down. I heard the knock on the door and then Marsden's voice. I kind of guessed she wasn't here for you.'

'We're in the garden. Take your time, I'll tell her I had to wake you.'

'Thanks, I'll go splash my face and try to do something with my hair. It's the Worzel Gummidge effect at the moment.'

She headed for the bathroom, leaving Kat to go back downstairs.

Kat was concerned. Mouse looked drained, and certainly not as well as she had looked when they'd left hospital.

Joining Marsden in the garden, Kat sat in the chair next to her. 'This is beautiful, Reverend Rowe.'

'Please, I feel we're going to get to know each other quite well, call me Kat.'

Marsden nodded. 'Tessa. Is Bethan okay?'

'She looks washed out, but I'll take care of her. It's Beth, by the way. She's just trying to make herself look a bit more presentable and she'll be down. Can I offer you a drink?'

'Thank you. Cold water will be fine. After you've had a couple of coffees back at the station, water starts to taste like nectar.'

Kat smiled. 'I'll even throw some ice in the jug.' She headed back into the kitchen to see Leon helping himself to a glass of water.

'God, it's hot.' He bent to kiss his wife. 'Everything okay?'

'It's fine. DI Marsden is out in the garden, waiting for Beth. I'm just doing a jug of iced water.'

'Then I'll join you.' He kissed her again as she reached up to get a jug out of the cupboard. 'I'll put some shorts on first though. This damn suit's far too hot.'

He headed upstairs, and Kat tipped a load of ice into the jug. As she was filling it with water, it briefly occurred to her that Mouse didn't know Leon was home; Kat hoped Mouse was fully clothed.

Mouse stared into the bathroom mirror and gave one last tug of the brush through the curls. The bruises were turning a muddy shade of yellow, still sore when she touched her face, and she decided that pretty no longer described her, battered was a closer comparison.

She opened the bathroom door and saw the beautiful personage that was Leon Rowe for the first time.

Her twenty-year-old brain internally gasped.

His teeth seemed extra white against the blackness of his skin as he flashed a smile at her. He held out his hand. 'You must be Beth.'

'I am. And Kat never said a word about you other than your name. Hello, Leon.'

'It's very good to meet you.'

She laughed. 'And it's very good to meet you. I'm sorry if I looked shocked, Kat neglected to mention that lovely skin.'

'Don't worry about it. I don't think Kat realises I'm any different to anybody else of her acquaintance. You heading downstairs? Marsden's here.'

'I know. She woke me. I've just spent ten minutes trying to make myself look half presentable. I'll go down to Kat now.'

'Tell her I'll be five minutes.'

'No problem.'

Tessa and Kat were discussing herbs and their medicinal values when Mouse joined them.

'Water?' Kat passed a glass dripping with condensation to Mouse.

'Thank you. I need to take tablets.' She swallowed the painkillers and sat by Kat.

'I just came by for an informal chat really, Beth,' Tessa said. 'To see if anything had come back to you.'

'Nothing regarding the man who attacked us, I promise you, but we're going to go to the alleyway and see if that jolts my memory. The evening is coming back to me in little bites, but it only goes as far as the moment he shot me.'

'And did your memory forget that you escorted Anthony Jackson? You're not his girlfriend?'

'No, it didn't. But what difference does that make? I wasn't an escort girl at the point that he was killed. My escort duties finish at midnight, unless there is a prior arrangement for an extended function. There was no prior arrangement that night, because if that little group hadn't decided they wanted to go clubbing, it would all have been over just after eleven. I was on my own time as a friend, and a girl.'

Tessa nodded, deep in thought. 'What was he like?'

'He was very nice. Thoughtful, complimentary, funny. I really enjoyed his company. And good-looking up to the point that bullet blew away his face.' She felt tears prick her eyes.

'Let me take you back to the time where that small group decided to go clubbing. Did you know any of them?'

'Not really, I can't remember their names. Anthony ordered four taxis to take us to Steel, and then they left their car keys at reception. The men said they would be back for their cars when they were sober enough to drive.'

'What did Anthony do with his house key?'

Mouse looked surprised at the question. 'Erm, let me try to picture this. I can see us all milling around in the reception at Alhambra, deciding what to do.' She was quiet for a moment. 'He removed it from his key ring, handed the car key to the receptionist who tagged it with the registration number, and then he slipped his house key in his jacket pocket. Do you need it to get into his house?'

Tessa shook her head. 'No, we've already been in there. It was just curiosity really. It wasn't with his personal possessions. We have his wallet, his watch, his ring, but no house key. It just seemed strange, and I wondered if you'd put it in your bag or something to keep it safe for him.'

'No. I'm sure he put it in his right jacket pocket.'

'Another mystery then,' Marsden smiled. 'This damn case is full of them.'

Leon stepped between the patio doors and joined them. He once again bent to kiss his wife, who responded with a smile. He took every opportunity to kiss her.

'I've met Beth,' he said. 'It seems you neglected to mention the colour of my skin.'

'Colour of your skin?' Oh…' Kat held her hand to her mouth and burst out laughing. 'It's ebony, Mouse. No big deal.'

Mouse grinned in response.

'So, Beth, tell me if anything at all strange happened on that night.' Marsden attempted to bring the subject back around to the murder.

'I can't think of anything,' Mouse said. 'It was a perfectly normal evening, like a hundred others I've attended over the last two years. I recognised one or two of the men there, although don't bother asking me for their names because I wouldn't, and I couldn't, tell you. They don't use their real names with escorts. I didn't know Anthony's until we were forced into that alleyway. He told it to me when he realised things might not end well, and I told him my full name. It seemed the right thing to do.'

Marsden nodded, as if digesting Mouse's words. 'And what will you do now?'

'I'm pulling out of education for a start. I feel as if I've suddenly grown up. There'll be no more of the escort world. I want to work for myself, but I'm taking time to get over this before I make any decisions. I'm selling my house, going to sort that tomorrow if I feel up to it. My two housemates are looking for new rooms, not happily, but it's my decision. I'll miss them, but it's time to grow up.'

Marsden stood. 'Thank you, Beth. If anything does come back, please ring me. The clues on this case are a bit lacking, and to be honest, a return of your memory could be a massive breakthrough for us.'

'I'll see you to the door,' Leon said, also standing.

It was as Marsden was walking down the drive that she turned to him. 'You didn't know him… Anthony Jackson?'

He shook his head. 'Only his name really. He once attended a conference I was at, but we didn't speak. I just saw his name on the attendees list. I know we were in the same business, but that wouldn't give us a reason to be acquainted. Quite the opposite, actually.'

Marsden stared at him, holding eye contact. 'Yes, you're probably right.' The tingle in her spine told her something different.

9

There was a total absence of moonlight. Cloud cover was thick, and rain was promised for later in the night. He didn't want it raining yet; oh no, that wouldn't help at all.

He pressed the latch on the gate and slipped into the tarmacked back yard of the little house, so close to the Bramall Lane football ground. He had been told she had been released from the hospital, duly mended and spruced up, but he couldn't risk her memory coming alive with anything.

He knew she hadn't remembered who he was yet; his nurse girlfriend kept him well informed for a little bit of the ready supply of drugs he always had. She had provided him with the slag's address for a relatively small amount of cocaine. But he couldn't trust that Bethan Walters never would remember, so she had to be dealt with.

And it was all for the sake of the bigger picture. The day when he would have everything. With Anthony Jackson out of the way in such a spectacular fashion, life had looked good, but the slag had survived. Now she had to go, and properly this time.

The infiltration into Anthony Jackson's empire had already begun; he had met with his primary cohorts, had talks with them regarding bringing them across to him and forming one large organisation. They had been cautiously optimistic about it, because they were feeling rudderless. He had to strike now while they were mixed up and worried. But loose ends were no good.

And this loose end was about to be tied off.

He stood in the corner formed by the house wall and the dividing wall separating the yard from the neighbouring one; the darkest point. Inside his black balaclava he was sweating; it was a warm night that was about to get much warmer. He carefully lowered his backpack to the floor and removed the two bottles with the fabric sticking out of the top.

Walking silently to the back door, inspected earlier in the day, he placed the suction cup on the window glass nearest to the lock. The glasscutter scored around it, and a hard thump broke the circle away from the rest of the single-glazed panel.

The man reached his hand inside and turned the key. The door widened a few inches and stopped, so he re-closed it, removed the chain that was causing the problem and opened the door fully.

He stepped into the kitchen and listened for any sounds. Nothing, utter silence.

Quietly he went back to his corner outside, took the petrol can out of the backpack, then returned to sprinkle it on the stairs. He revisited the yard for the final equipment, the two petrol bombs.

Slipping back inside to stand at the bottom of the stairs, he lit the first one and threw it to the top of the stairs where it exploded, and everything erupted into a huge fireball. The noise it made was horrific and he moved back into the kitchen, lit the second one and smashed it at the bottom of the stairs.

Then he ran.

He didn't hang around to see the outcome; he guessed it might make the newspapers.

10

The fire service didn't recover the two bodies until the early hours of the day, so intense was the fire. News of the devastation reached Mouse when a friend rang her to find out if she was okay. They initially had crossed wires because Mouse thought she was asking following the shooting.

Kat immediately rang Tessa Marsden, who hadn't been told about it; she explained it came under Sheffield and not Chesterfield, but she would get back to them with any news.

Mouse felt sick. She knew she had been targeted; it was her house. Whoever had left her for dead wanted to really finish the job.

Ten minutes later, DI Marsden rang with the news that the fire had started around one in the morning, and two bodies had been recovered; both females, and both had died from smoke inhalation rather than burns.

'No,' Mouse moaned. 'This can't be. They've died because of me, because I did this bloody stupid job.'

Kat pulled her close and held her. There was nothing she could say.

Kat and Mouse stared at the smoke-blackened shell of the little house. It was an end-terrace property, and the fire service had been able to contain it sufficiently to stop it spreading to the adjoining house, but to Mouse's eyes it looked destroyed. Like her.

Three deaths since the night of the Alhambra function, and once the press published the names of the victims of this fire, whoever was doing it would know she hadn't been at home.

'I'm scared, Kat,' Mouse said quietly.

Kat took her hand. 'And I'm scared for you. I want us to go now, just to be on the safe side. I'm pretty anonymous because I've never lived and worked in Sheffield, so even if somebody is watching you they're not going to know who I am.'

'What shall I do about my car?'

'Where is it?'

'It's across the road on a side street. Couldn't park any closer the last time I was out in it.'

'Is it okay where it is? No parking restrictions?'

Mouse shook her head. 'No, it's fine.'

'Then we'll leave it for now. You're not fit to drive yet, your shoulder is still stiff, and you're still in varying degrees of pain.'

Mouse smiled. 'I'm trying to run before I can walk, aren't I?'

'You are. We'll come back in a few days when everything is moving a bit easier on you and get it then. Let's go home. You've an insurance company to ring. This needs fixing.'

11

He was angry. He'd been smiling when he saw the headlines, and the picture of the blackened house, but then he'd read the accompanying article and the smile had stopped.

The slag hadn't been there. Two other bints had, so he had a partial thrill knowing they would have been friends of the slag, but he felt as though it had all been a wasted effort.

Why the fuck hadn't he made sure she was dead before he left that alleyway? And where the hell was she now?

He slapped her across the face. Fran Drummond's head rocked back on her neck and she cried out. 'I don't know where she is. Perhaps she's gone to her nan's, that old woman who used to come and see her.'

'Christ almighty. What's the old tart's name? Stop pissing me about or I might have to hurt you.'

'Doris Lester, I think. I heard her say it a couple of times to the policeman sat at the door.' She was crying, he was scary when he was like this.

'Address?'

'No idea, but she caught the same bus as me one time, the 120, and got off at the Birley Hotel.'

'I'll fucking find her,' he growled. 'Get dressed, you're going home. And stop bloody crying, I can't stand it.'

'You hurt me,' she sobbed.

'I'll hurt you more if you don't shut up. Now let me think. And get out of here.'

She grabbed her clothes and ran for the bathroom. She tried splashing water on the redness in her cheek, but it had no effect – another door she would have to have walked into. She dressed quickly and silently opened the door. He was on his laptop, searching for Doris Lester, she guessed.

Fran let herself out the house without saying another word to him, clutching on to her bag that held the small amount of cocaine he had given her for the "seeing to" she had given him.

She tried not to think about the trouble she had just hefted on to the slight shoulders of Doris Lester.

12

'How could they know my address, Kat?' Mouse had been deep in thought on the journey back to Eyam. Nothing was making sense. 'The police knew it, and so did the hospital, but that's all.'

'If somebody wants to know an address, it's not difficult to find it, unless you're an idiot like me and can't work the Internet. I tried to find Jackson's address in Eyam and couldn't, but Leon did.'

'Can't work the Internet?'

'No, it stops working when I touch it.'

'Then it's a good job you've got me in your life,' Mouse responded with a grin. 'In fact, as soon as I'm up to doing a bit of online shopping, I need a new laptop. Mine was in the house.'

'Was there a lot of work on it?' Kat's troubled expression made Mouse laugh.

'Oh, you do cheer me up, Kat. Yes there was all the work from my uni course, and lots of personal stuff but it doesn't matter. It's all saved. As soon as I log in to my various accounts, it will all come tumbling back to earth out of a cloud.'

Kat nodded as though she understood. 'That's what Leon says.'

'And Leon's right. It's not difficult, but I do believe you need a mind that enjoys technology to benefit from it properly, and clearly you're not into it.'

'You're good at it then?'

'It's the thing I love most. And it's going to give us answers for this trouble I seem to have found myself in.'

'How?'

'Because I'm good. Or bad, depending how you look at it. I'm not telling you any more, not yet, because of who you are, that's not fair. So maybe this afternoon, if you don't mind, I'll borrow your laptop, buy one in your name so that it doesn't show me at your address, and transfer the money into your bank. Is that okay?'

'Of course. We've also got an appointment with my husband later.'

'What? With Leon?'

'Yes.' Kat tried to keep her face straight. 'At the kitchen table, around four o'clock.'

'He doesn't want me there.' Mouse's voice was flat.

'Rubbish. That's not it. I'm saying nothing more, and don't worry, he's absolutely fine about you staying with us.'

Kat watched the lights change to amber and put her foot down. She had been constantly watching her mirror all the way home, but there had been nothing to suggest anyone had followed them from the burnt-out house.

Tibby strolled to the car as they pulled onto the drive. Mouse bent down to stroke her and the cat rolled onto her back. 'Floozy,' Mouse remarked. 'Get up, cat, and I might feed you some treats.'

Kat turned to lock the car and looked startled. 'What? Feed me some treats? You have chocolate?'

'Wrong cat,' Mouse said with a grin, and pointed to the ginger tom now walking away, tail erect.

Kat shook her head. 'Come on, we need some lunch, and then you can shop for your laptop.'

Mouse tried to sleep but her mind was fully occupied. Kat had insisted she had an afternoon nap, but Kat's insistence came with no instructions regarding clearing her mind of extraneous matter. She was excited by the top-of-the-range laptop, and worried by the burnt-out house, but most of all she was devastated by Millie and Jo's deaths.

Millie had arrived in Sheffield from Newcastle, and Jo from Southampton, so it followed that their funerals would be held in their home cities. It hurt Mouse to think that she would never see them again, never have one of their late-night chats where they put the world and Sheffield University to rights, through the alcoholic haze created by several bottles of wine.

In the end, she gave up and went for a shower.

It was while she was in the shower that her mind went into overdrive.

She dressed quickly and ran downstairs, heading outside to find Kat. 'Kat, I have a worry.'

Kat looked up from the roses she was deadheading. 'What sort of worry?'

'My nan. If they found my address, what's to stop them finding hers? They'll know by now that I wasn't in my house, so what do you think the odds are that they'll go to my nan's next?'

'I think the odds are pretty high. Will she come here?'

Mouse stared at her. 'I didn't mean that. I'm imposing on your good nature enough. I meant I have to get her away from there to somewhere where they can't find her.'

'Here.' Kat was calm. 'Go and ring her, tell her your worries, and tell her to pack enough for a couple of weeks away. We can protect her. Come on, let's do it now.'

She dropped the secateurs on top of the dead flowers in the trug and gave Mouse a gentle push.

Ten minutes later, it was organised, despite Doris Lester's protestations that she could handle the little runt. It was only when it was explained that he might not be a little runt, he might be two or three very large runts, that she gave in.

'Only for two weeks, mind,' she said. 'Then I'm coming home.'

Doris looked around the room, decorated in the palest of green, with a small-flowered wallpaper on the main wall and thought how beautiful it was. The handmade quilt on the bed echoed the delicate colours used on the walls, and she couldn't help but compare it to the reds, yellows, purples and other assorted bright shades her granddaughter had used in her little house.

The little house that might be too far gone to rise from any ashes.

Doris wiped away a tear as she bent to put some clothes into the chest of drawers. Mouse seemed to have found a proper friend in Kat, and Doris was truly grateful. She sank into the armchair, soft and yielding and old, and picked up her book. She didn't want to go downstairs and disturb the girls, she would stay up here, maybe have a little nap.

Leon was home before four, and within a minute the three of them were sitting at the kitchen table, Mouse trying not to feel like a schoolgirl in front of the head.

Leon had placed a carrier bag on the table, and both women looked at it. Kat felt sick, Mouse felt curious.

'Okay,' he said. 'This is what it's all about.' He reached into the bag and took out the gun.

Mouse yelled, 'No!' and half stood, as if attempting to run.

'Sit down, Beth,' he said. 'You have no option but to accept this development. This gun will be put into your bedside drawer. I won't have you and Kat unprotected, and this is the best sort of protection I know. Have you ever fired a gun?'

Mouse slowly sat and shook her head. 'I'd never even seen one in real life before one put a bullet in me. What on earth do you expect me to do with that?'

'Shoot somebody if necessary,' Leon responded. 'Now listen carefully, because your life, or Kat's life, may depend on this.'

'What the bloody hell is going on here?' Doris stood in the doorway, taking in the scene in front of her.

Leon spun around and saw the small, grey-haired woman, her cheeks flushed with anger.

He turned to look at Kat. 'We appear to have a little old lady standing in our kitchen.'

Tension broken, Kat and Mouse laughed aloud, and a hiccupping Kat introduced her husband to Doris Lester.

Doris stepped into the kitchen and picked up the gun. 'Is it loaded?'

'Not yet,' Leon said. 'I was just about to show these two how to load it and fire it, but now you're here, I'll show all three of you.'

Doris smiled. 'You don't need to show me, but go ahead and teach my granddaughter how to kill people. I'm sure that skill will come in handy one day.'

Leon stood and held a chair out for her. 'Sit, woman.'

She complied, and looked him up and down. 'You're a beautiful man, Kat's husband. You got a father who's looking for a new wife?'

He grinned. 'I do have a father, but he's got a wife, thanks. I'll tell him to put you on a waiting list.'

'You do that. Now, what are you going to tell these two?'

The gun lay in the drawer, and Mouse kept opening it to look at the weapon. She hated it, but she recognised Leon's logic. A burnt-out house, two deaths, Anthony Jackson, a nan on the run from a potential murderer, and two further vulnerable women – the gun was a necessity until the murderer was under lock and key. Leon had made it very clear that it was a deal-breaker; if she refused to consider having it in the bedroom with her, she would have to find someone else's bedroom to hide in.

The biggest surprise of all had been that her nan had handled the gun with ease; she hadn't been lying when she said she needed no instruction, but she wouldn't say why her knowledge was all-encompassing.

Mouse slipped on her nightie and climbed into bed. Knowing Doris Lester was in the next bedroom and not at home in her own house gave Mouse a degree of comfort. She turned out the light, hoping she would sleep without her mind wandering to that alleyway, but it was difficult. Seeing Leon's gun had brought the horror pouring back into her mind, and she knew she had to get over it. It wasn't *the* gun, it was *a* gun, and she could ignore it by putting something on top of it so that she didn't see it whenever she opened the drawer.

She would talk to Kat in the morning, she decided, and they would go to the scene of the murder behind Leon's pharmacy, to see if anything new occurred to her. She needed her memory to open up, the headaches to subside so that she could start functioning properly, to divulge who the hell the taxi driver was. Then she might just need the damn gun in the bedside drawer, she might very easily need it.

13

Kat and Mouse left Doris finishing the deadheading that Kat had started the previous afternoon, and headed down to the village centre. They walked, enjoying the sunshine, and on the way, Kat pointed out various tourist sites, the most notable in Mouse's eyes being the Plague Cottages on Church Street. George Vickers, the hapless tailor who had taken receipt of the damp bolt of cloth from London, had hung it around the fire to dry, releasing the plague infested fleas living within it, the disease that had started with rats.

Eyam's beauty lay in its stone cottages dotted ad hoc throughout the length of the village, cottages that had seemingly been there for ever. It was a typical Derbyshire village; Mouse smiled at the weather vane atop the plague museum, the metal figure of a rat standing in place of a more traditional cockerel.

Mouse stared at the cottages. 'How many died?'

'Two hundred and sixty people over fourteen months, but very courageous people. They quarantined themselves. Others left food and medical supplies for them in the walls surrounding the village, and eventually the plague died out, along with most of the residents of Eyam. But it didn't spread.'

'Such selfless people.' Mouse breathed the words out quietly. 'Everybody knows Eyam is the plague village, but it's only when you stand here looking at the cottages, the graves, the village in its entirety, that you realise the magnitude of it.' She shivered. 'What a wonderful place you live in, Kat.'

'I agree. We waited until a house came up for sale here, and then pounced. It was in a bit of a state when we bought it, but we didn't care. We wanted to preserve it, and keep it safe for all time.'

Kat and Mouse stopped for a moment and took in the beautiful plague cottages, and Kat spoke again. 'You want a bit more information? The children's nursery rhyme Ring o' ring o' roses is from plague times. Ring o' ring o' roses, a pocketful of posies, atishoo, atishoo, we all fall down. Ring of roses refers to the rash a victim develops on the skin, pocket full of posies talks about people carrying nosegays or small bunches of herbs as they tried to ward off the germs, atishoo is the sneezing that was one of the symptoms of plague, and we all fall down means the victim is being overtaken by death.'

Mouse sighed. 'That's so awful. I can't begin to imagine what it must have been like to live here then.'

They continued down into the centre, and Kat grasped Mouse's hand. 'Okay, the pharmacy across the road is ours. The little alleyway down the side is where you and Anthony were taken. You up for this?'

Mouse shivered again. 'I am. It has to be done. I have to know if it will bring anything back.'

They crossed the road, passing along the front of the shop. Kat waved at Neil as they walked by the window, who waved back and immediately picked up his mobile phone.

'Kat's just walked past the shop, Leon. With another woman. Thought I should keep you informed.'

'Thanks, Neil. Can you tell where she's going?'

'Hang on.' He moved across to the screen fed by the CCTV cameras and switched the view to the back door. 'They've gone to the alleyway. Want me to do anything?'

'No, it's fine. They were bound to go there at some point, but I don't want this information going anywhere else. Understand, Neil?'

'Of course.'

'Okay. Thanks for letting me know.'

Neil stared at the screen after disconnecting from his boss, and watched what the two women were doing. The alleyway was free of everything except the wheelie bins, and they walked the length of it, slowly and without speaking. When the dark-haired woman reached the end, she turned around and looked back, and he saw her flinch. Kat went towards her and put her arms around her, holding her tightly. Then they walked back up the alleyway towards the High Street. He switched the screen view back to the shop front door, and followed their progress until they were out of range of the camera.

'Can we go home?' Mouse asked.

'Of course. You remembered nothing new? Don't hold out on me, Mouse, we're not vigilantes.'

'Nothing, I promise you. I still feel I knew that evil bugger. I've met him at some point in my life, I just can't place him yet, but I will. And then watch how well I remember what Leon taught us about using that gun.' Her tone was bitter.

Kat stared at her. 'Come with me.'

They walked a little further up the main road, and then turned off into the churchyard.

'I don't want to go in,' Mouse said. 'I'm too angry.'

'It's because you've been in that bad place, that alleyway. Trust me. This will help. I know you have no faith, but just come and take in the peace.'

She pushed open the door, and led Mouse into the body of the church.

'Pick a seat,' she said.

Mouse walked down the aisle, presuming Kat was following her, and sat down on a pew. Kat was nowhere in sight.

Mouse stared around her and watched the sunlight filtering through the stained-glass windows, creating patterns on the columns and the floor. She waited, still expecting Kat to join her, but she didn't.

It took ten minutes for Mouse to realise a simple fact; there was peace here, whether the belief in God was present or not.

When Kat did eventually arrive to reclaim her friend, Mouse almost felt sorry.

'Now are you ready to go home?' Kat smiled.

'I am, and thank you for this. It's soothed my heart.'

'You're very welcome, and it's always here for you if you feel you need it again.'

Twenty minutes later, they were home, both quiet. Doris was in the armchair, her head to one side, sleeping. They left her and moved to the kitchen.

Kat poured two glasses of water. 'How are you feeling?' she asked Mouse as she passed her drink across to her.

'Not sure. I thought I might sense… something, I don't know what, but I didn't. I went through seeing Anthony's head explode all over again, but I could remember that anyway. It was no big revelation.'

'How do you feel about the funeral?'

'You mean will I be going? I don't think so. I only met him that night. I know we got on well, but it wasn't love at first sight or anything silly like that, and I know I'm still in danger, so I won't be going.'

A knock at the door interrupted their discussion and Kat walked through to the front door. She returned with a parcel.

'Your laptop, I presume,' and she handed it to Mouse.

'Good, now we can really get started.'

'Get started with what?'

'We're going to find out who wants me dead, and we're going to find out why it happened in that alleyway. Now go away, woman, while I connect this to your Internet.'

Kat didn't go away; she watched, fascinated by everything Mouse was doing.

Eventually Mouse sat back, a satisfied smile on her face. 'This is good. It's fast, very responsive – even you could use it.'

Kat's laughter echoed around the kitchen and they heard the voice of Doris as she asked if anybody was making a cup of tea.

'I'll make you one, Nan,' Mouse called, and Kat stood to switch on the kettle.

'Sit down, Kat,' Mouse said, 'you're not here to wait on us. I don't think I'm up to scrubbing floors and cleaning bathrooms yet, but I can make tea.'

Kat hesitated, then sat down. 'Okay, but please don't start scrubbing floors and cleaning bathrooms. I have a cleaner for that sort of stuff.'

Doris joined them in the kitchen, a smile on her face. 'I was just resting my eyes. I wasn't asleep.'

'Nan, you were snoring,' Mouse pointed out.

'Never!'

The two younger women grinned at each other. 'I think you were just a little bit asleep,' Kat said, and Doris nodded.

'Where's my cup of tea?'

'Coming up, Nan,' Mouse said. 'Look at that.' She nodded towards the laptop. 'Mine was burnt in the fire, so I've replaced it.'

Doris moved around the table and sat where her granddaughter had been sitting while setting it up. 'This is nice. Was it expensive?'

Mouse shrugged. 'So so.'

'I'll transfer the money,' Doris said, and pulled the computer towards her. She typed and waited while it loaded whatever it was she had requested. She nodded, and then typed something else.

'Don't, Nan,' Mouse said. 'I can afford it. Keep your money, you've done more than enough for me.'

'Your money won't last forever, and you'll have packed the escort job in now, won't you?'

'What?'

'You seriously thought I didn't know? I just prayed you would stay safe. Seeing you in that hospital bed showed me just how unsafe it was.'

She carried on typing on the computer. 'I don't know how much it was, but I've transferred a thousand. Can I play now?'

'You can. Did you bring yours?'

'Yes, it's upstairs. I need your Wi-Fi password, Kat, please. I couldn't do much last night without it.'

Kat was aware her mouth had dropped open, and Mouse put her arm around her and gave her a hug, pulling her tightly to her. 'Don't look so down, my pet dinosaur. One day you'll learn how to do more than turn it on. Nan got her degree in all things IT related when she was in her late fifties, and she gave me that love of technology. There's precious little we can't handle. I'll teach you, I'm very patient.'

'No!' Kat continued to lean against Mouse. 'I don't want to learn. I've got Leon. My mind just closes down and things break. Like all the wwws. If I find something I want, I never find it again, it disappears. I'm quite happy being a dinosaur, thank you. Besides, when we start up in business together, that can be your specialty.'

Mouse stared. 'Is that what we're going to do?'

'Did I just say that?' Kat shrugged. 'It's a thought though, isn't it?'

'I think it would be good,' Mouse said, slowly and carefully.

There was a moment's pause and Kat spoke again. 'What sort of business? I don't want to be an escort.'

'You haven't made any suggestions about that yet. But apparently I'm dealing with the technical side of it.' Mouse grinned. 'And I promise you that neither you nor Nan will ever have to be an escort.'

Leon arrived before they could discuss anything further, jokingly or otherwise, and he offered to take everyone out for a meal, instead of Kat cooking. Kat was relieved. She wanted time to think and hoped the other two would fill in for her if her mind wandered.

Tessa Marsden faced her team. There was a picture of a burnt-out house attached to the crime board, and she pointed to it.

'Our colleagues in Sheffield have passed this case to us as it is closely linked to our own investigation, so I need to fill you in on the details. Two girls died in the first-floor bedrooms. It seems that the stairs running up the middle of the house, with a bedroom either side at the top, was the core of the fire. This means that someone broke in through the back door, quietly enough to not wake anyone either in the house or the neighbouring houses. This is a professional hit, believe me. He or she knew what they were doing. It seems that the stairs were soaked in petrol, a petrol bomb thrown to the top of the stairs, and then one at the bottom, presumably as our laddo was leaving these two young women to burn.'

Marsden paused and looked around the room. 'This is the important bit at the moment. That house belonged to Bethan Walters, the student who almost died in the back alley in Eyam. The fire-raiser obviously thought she was there, and I think that was the reason for the fire-bomb at the bottom of the stairs. The front room downstairs was Bethan's bedroom. I think he had been there earlier, snooping around. We need to saturate that road, find out if anyone saw anything. It only needed a glance through the bay window downstairs to show him it was a bedroom, so he could then plan accordingly. And keep an open mind. I only said he because it's easier, but it could just as easily have been a woman. Right, I want at least four of you on door-to-door. Dave, you're in charge, take another three with you, and make it thorough. I believe whoever set this fire killed Anthony Jackson and almost killed Bethan Walters. Let's get the bugger off the streets.'

Dave Irwin held a thumb up and turned to select three colleagues. He enjoyed door-to-door work and could always get people talking. It was good to know his boss recognised that.

'And don't spend all day chatting, Dave,' Tessa called as she left the room. 'We need results quickly.'

She pulled her keyboard towards her and brought her screen to life. Then sat and just stared at it. What next?

Why was it so important to kill Bethan Walters? Marsden needed to talk to her again, but maybe at the station, put some pressure on her. Marsden was only guessing, but her guess was that Bethan had to die because the killer had known her, and so presumed she would eventually remember him. Or her.

She pulled up the reports that had already been filed and read them once more. There was nothing new to excite her, to make her think why did we miss that first time around.

She concentrated particularly on the interviews with Bethan Walters but could find nothing that made her stop and think. Was she really unable to remember, or was she holding something back?

Had she really not escorted Anthony Jackson before? Marsden then pulled up the report they had received from the escort agency, where they listed every one of Anthony Jackson's escorts, and Bethan had been the third one.

Marsden made a note of the previous two girls and picked up the phone.

The agency was helpful, once she had said they would be helpful over the phone or they would have to come down to the station and be helpful.

'Caroline Boldock and Gaynor Isaacs,' the disembodied voice said, and then gave their addresses and telephone numbers to a smiling DI.

'Thank you. I'll get back to you if I need further information.'

Tessa quickly typed the information into her computer, aware that she might not remember what had been said, and her illegible handwriting wouldn't help her.

She rang the telephone numbers and made arrangements for the ladies to come down to the station, an hour apart.

Both agreed reluctantly, having became very aware that it wasn't a request, more an instruction.

Kat recognised that Leon was worrying about their welfare; he would be away from home the following night, leaving three helpless females in the house. All three had burst out laughing when he had said it, causing laughter to come from him as well.

'Four years we've been married, and you don't know me yet?' Kat grinned. 'Get on with you, Leon Rowe. I'm as tough as old boots. Stop worrying, we'll be okay, we've got our secret weapon… Nan.' She had taken to calling Doris by the name Mouse used, and she was now Nan to both of them.

'You'll lock all the doors and windows?'

'All of them,' she promised, 'and set the alarm. We'll be absolutely fine.'

14

Caroline Boldock gave her name to the desk sergeant and sat down to wait on possibly the most uncomfortable bench she had ever sat on. She read all the notices posted around the small waiting area and slowly realised just how dangerous it was to be alive in these days of drug dealing, burglary, car vandalism and suchlike.

After twenty minutes of continually checking her watch, she approached the sergeant for the second time.

'Yes, miss,' he said, knowing exactly what she was going to say.

'Have they forgotten me?'

'Oh, I wouldn't think so, miss. DI Marsden will get to you when she can.'

'But I need to be on my way soon.'

The smile disappeared from his face. 'Really? I'm sure DI Marsden will take that into consideration. A note of caution though, Miss…' he checked his pad, 'Boldock, I would recommend you don't voice any complaints to the DI. She's not known for her patience.'

Caroline returned to her seat and said no more.

A further fifteen minutes passed before the door at the back of the reception area opened. Hannah Granger looked around.

'Morning, Miss Boldock. Can you follow me please.'

Caroline followed Hannah down a long corridor until they reached the end room. The walls were mud grey, and the large window on one of the walls was blacked out, letting in no light. A table and three chairs took centre stage.

'Am I in trouble?' Caroline asked, beginning to feel uncomfortable and nervous.

'I'm sure I don't know.' Hannah smiled. 'DI Marsden will be with you shortly.'

Hannah and Tessa stood at the observation window and watched Caroline. She was fiddling with her nails, clearly worried. They waited five minutes, then walked into the room.

'Miss Boldock, Caroline, I'm sorry to keep you waiting. We had a bit of an emergency. I'm DI Tessa Marsden, and this is my colleague, PC Hannah Granger.' She put her file down on the table and reached across to shake Caroline's hand.

Tessa pressed the button on the recording equipment, said the names of those present, and then smiled at her victim.

'Right, Caroline, you're not in any trouble that I am aware of. We want to talk to you about Anthony Jackson.'

'O… kay… Who's Anthony Jackson?'

Tessa and Hannah glanced at each other. 'You haven't heard about the man killed in Eyam?'

'Oh, him! Yes of course I have. I just didn't recognise his name. It's not ten o'clock yet, you know, and I've had to travel from Sheffield to Chesterfield to get here for nine, so excuse me if I'm a bit slow.'

Tessa tried not to let the grin show. This young lady had a bit of a temper.

'So,' Tessa continued, 'we suspect you may know him as Anthony Parkson.'

There was silence for a few seconds, while Caroline digested the information.

'My god,' she said eventually. 'He's Anthony Jackson? The dishiest bloke I've ever had to escort, and he's dead?' Her voice rose marginally higher.

'I'm afraid so,' Tessa said, her eyes on the young woman in front of her, watching for signs of unease, lying, withholding information. She saw nothing except shock.

'Yes. The Newland Escort Agency advised us that you are one of only three girls who provided escort services for Mr Jackson.'

'You're making it sound dirty.' Caroline's tone had changed. 'Don't knock something you know nothing about, DI Marsden. I only provide an escort service, I'm not a prostitute. Some men, and some women, don't have partners they can take along to functions, and that's where we step in. We perform the actions of a partner, for the business side of their lives.'

'You've never slept with any of these men?' Tessa was curious.

'I didn't say that. You're asking about Anthony Parkson… Jackson. I didn't sleep with him. If any of the others die, then please feel free to interview me again.'

'So where did you go?'

'We went to the opening of a gallery, owned by a friend of his. I can't remember the name of his friend, but the gallery is Poseidon, and it's on the main road leading out of Matlock Bath. It actually opened on my thirtieth birthday, so I can even be accurate about the date; 23 of May 2016, if that helps.'

'Thank you,' Marsden responded, making a note on the piece of paper attached to the front of the file. That confirmed the information given to them by the agency. 'And afterwards?'

Caroline took a deep breath, then spoke slowly and calmly. 'He drove me home to Sheffield, and I have no idea what he did after that. It definitely didn't involve me.'

Marsden gathered her papers together and stood. 'Interview terminated,' she said, and switched off the recorder. 'Thank you for coming in, Miss Boldock. If we need to speak to you again, we'll let you know.'

Caroline watched as the policewomen walked out of the room. She stood as the young constable who had been to one side all the time, moved to escort her out of the building.

She wasn't happy. That interview could have been done over the phone, for all the help she had been. She wouldn't have minded a couple of hours in bed with Anthony Jackson, but it simply hadn't happened. He'd been the perfect gentleman.

Even when he'd disappeared for ten minutes to talk to that quite delicious-looking black man, his words had been, *"Susie will keep you company while I just go and have a quick word with Leon."* After his return he hadn't left her at all until he helped her out of his car at the end of the evening.

Gaynor Isaacs told a very similar story; out to a function and when the function had finished he had driven her home. Her evening out was a thank you party he had organised for his employees to show his gratitude for their hard work. She could remember meeting a couple of pharmacy managers, girls who worked behind the counter, and assorted staff from his main warehouse, but there had been nothing memorable about the evening. He stayed at the function about two and a half hours, then took her home.

Tessa thanked Gaynor for her time, apologised for the long trek out from Sheffield, and sent her on her way.

'What did you think?' Tessa and Hannah were taking a break with a cup of coffee and a chocolate digestive.

Hannah thought for a moment. 'I think they were telling the truth. They had no reason to lie. And Jackson obviously didn't hire them to sleep with them, so I guess he must have thought Bethan Walters was pretty special.'

'She is. Stunning to look at when her face isn't covered in bruises, and very articulate. I can imagine any red-blooded man being attracted to her.' Tessa picked up her cup, her face thoughtful.

'It's so puzzling. Why didn't the killer drive them to their destination? He could have killed them both there, and they wouldn't have been found for some time. Instead they're killed in a back alley that runs behind a pharmacy that's not one of Jackson's pharmacies. And yet Rowe is denying knowing him. Says he knows of him, because he's in the same business, but that's all.'

'What business?' Hannah threw the thought into the ring.

'Pharmaceutical. You're thinking…?'

'I'm thinking pharmaceutical in a different way. Having a string of pharmacies is a bloody good cover for non-prescription drugs.'

'Turf war?'

'I don't know.' Hannah looked down at her hands. 'We haven't found any logical reason for his death, so maybe he was killed as a warning to somebody else.'

'Leon Rowe? That's a scary thought. Beth, who is clearly on somebody's hit list, is staying at his home.' She looked at Hannah, thoughts racing through her mind. 'I need you to check every last little thing about Leon Rowe. Everything. If there's anything the slightest bit dodgy, we'll bring him in.'

Hannah nodded, and stood. She picked up her cup and left.

Brian held up the bottle of Glenfiddich, and Leon shook his head. 'No, I'm good thanks. Until this Jackson business is put to bed, I need to stay sober. Have you heard anything from anywhere?'

Brian shook his head. 'Not a thing. It's gone very quiet. Too quiet, if you ask me. For months he's been wanting to talk terms with us, wanting in, and to be honest I was starting to think it made sense. He'd a lot of contacts, and a lot of investment cash. I was almost at the point of thinking you and I needed to talk, to consider our options. This could have been massive for us.'

Leon nodded. 'Exactly my thoughts. So who the hell has taken him out? Who's the third arm? There's nobody else around here until you start getting up towards Newcastle and Freddie Greggs's set-up, and he's getting too old to be expanding. He was making noises about retiring, so I can't think he's behind it. Somebody down south?'

Brian poured himself a small measure of the malt whisky, before answering. 'Could it be somebody in Jackson's organisation?'

'It could, I suppose, but he was adamant he was a one man business. He hadn't even got a partner, a Brian of his own. He was gob-smacked that we work so closely together, he said we could never trust each other fully, not in this business.' Leon looked at Brian. 'I trust you. There's nothing you don't know about me. I have to have complete trust in you.'

'It's always been like that, ever since we were kids. No need to think it will ever stop. God, Leon, we've been together for ever,' he said with a grin. 'It's the main reason I didn't want Jackson coming in with us; our relationship, whether working or social, is special, and he would have changed the dynamics. But I was seriously playing with the idea he could come in on a limited deal, I'd even made some notes to talk it over with you. I've destroyed them, in view of what happened. Didn't want any nosy police turning up doing a search and finding any connection to Anthony Jackson.'

'And Terry? Has he been paid?'

'Well paid. He said the bodies would only surface if somebody took a St Bernard into Ecclesall Woods. Let's hope he's right. I've given him a bit more responsibility as well, that always makes sure they keep their mouths shut.'

'Good. I'll make sure I drop in at George Reynolds' house, tell his wife I'm looking for him because he's not answering his phone, and then give her some cash to keep her going. They've a couple of kids, so I don't want her being without money.'

Leon left the distribution hub feeling marginally better. Brian was always the logical, forward-thinking one; even if he didn't have charisma, or imagination, he was unfailingly reliable, and Leon never had to worry about either the legitimate business or the darker one.

Leon headed towards Sheffield United's ground; Beth had said her home was close by the ground, and he wanted to see the damage for himself. He guessed he would find it easily, and he did.

It was a mess. It was still enclosed within crime scene tape, and he pulled up further along the road. The roof had caved in, but the basic structure of the building was intact, even though it was ingrained with soot. He hoped the two girls had died quickly, they would have been terrified if not. He got out of the car for a short while, and walked around the building. He didn't stay long but drove home, deeply thoughtful. Beth and Nan weren't going anywhere for a while.

15

'I need to get my car back. I'm not happy it being down there, and me a million miles away,' Mouse said. She bit into her scone and sighed. 'These are wonderful, Nan.'

'When are you meeting the insurance people?' Doris asked.

'Tomorrow. Ten o'clock at my very poorly house. Kat's taking me down, because I don't want you in that place. It's got to be dangerous and you're a doddering old woman.'

Doris hit Mouse with the tea towel, and Kat spluttered her tea all over the table.

'Right,' Doris said, a glint in her eye. 'I'll go with you, and I'll drive that thing you call a car back here. You're not well enough to drive it yet, that shoulder is still giving you problems.'

Mouse stood and walked around the table, bent and kissed Doris on the top of her head. 'You're a star,' she said. 'I'd have been fine driving it as long as I didn't have to go around any corners. You won't speed in it, will you?'

Doris laughed. 'Mouse, Minnie's a Mini that was built some time in the stone age. And when do I go faster than national limits?'

'All the time.'

'Okay, maybe a little bit, I'll give you that.'

'Kat, can we follow her home?'

'Of course. Heaven forbid we should have a Lewis Hamilton travelling back from Sheffield.'

Doris smiled and said nothing further on the subject.

The area around Bramall Lane was always busy, thronged with thousands of people on match days, but at half past two in the morning it was devoid of humans, just the occasional cat slinking along in the shadows, or an infrequent dog bark.

The night was warm and he wished he hadn't had to wear black. He had walked for around half a mile, carrying his backpack and prepared to run if he saw any sign of a police car. The moon had helped; it was a mere crescent, emitting very little light. It was almost as if he had planned it that way, but this night was happening because the silly bitch hadn't been in the house when he had razed it.

And now, by calling in a favour, he had found her car just a minute's walk away from her destroyed house. He'd no idea where she was, but eventually he guessed she would need the little red Mini. He could wait.

He'd had to shell out a fair amount of money for the motion-sensor bomb, and the instructions had been explicit. They had to be. It would hardly have fitted in with his long term plans to have blown himself up while trying to destroy Bethan Walters.

He cursed the fact that the Mini was parked underneath a street lamp; Sheffield's street lighting was notoriously bad since they had replaced all the old sodium lamps, and was only efficient if parked directly underneath the light; the Mini was lit up so brightly it glowed. He stepped into a gennel and opened his backpack out of sight of anyone. He took the device out of the bag, held it for a moment and then moved towards the street again. A cat brushed against his jeans and he froze. He gave it a kick and the cat ran.

Taking a deep breath, he moved towards the car, then knelt down as if tying his shoe lace. He slid his hand holding the magnetised bomb under the driver's side of the car, then positioned it directly under the driving seat area.

How to kill in one easy movement.

He stood, dusted his knees, and moved back to the safety of the gennel. He took out the small remote activator, and pressed it twice, watching the green light glow. The man had told him it would remain active for seven days. The bomber hoped he wouldn't have to reactivate it, he needed Bethan Walters dead before her memory re-surfaced.

He walked quickly back to his car, and drove home sticking carefully to speed limits, the remote activator nestled inside an empty cigarette packet.

He was in bed by half past three, his last thoughts before falling asleep were of a Bethan-free future. It briefly occurred to him that meddling Kat Rowe might know where she was, but that was a last resort. He knew the bomb would work, it had to.

The house was an early morning hive of activity; all four occupants had bumped into each other as they tried to get ready and, as they eventually gathered in the kitchen for breakfast, Leon said he would be looking at building an extension on the house if the two ladies were staying with them for any length of time. Luckily his grin told them he was joking. They hoped.

Leon left first, kissing Kat and telling her he was going to see Brian. He would be available all day if she needed him. She kissed him back and said she wouldn't, she was going to wear her clerical collar. That would stop any nastiness on the part of the insurance company, and Mouse would get everything she wanted. She smiled as she said it, but Leon knew his wife.

Doris, Mouse and Kat had a second pot of tea, and then left just before half past nine for their journey into Sheffield.

Doris sat in the back of the car, and Mouse in the passenger side.

'You okay?' Kat asked.

'I will be when I can see some direction after today. And it's getting urgent that I do some shopping. I've very few clothes, Kat. I lost everything inside the house.'

'Get your knickers from Marks and Spencer,' Doris said, absentmindedly, from the back seat. 'They last for ever.' She was busy scrolling on her phone.

'Do I look like a Marks and Spencer gal, Nan?' Mouse said with a laugh.

'You've changed your life.' Doris looked up and over the top of her glasses. 'Are you listening to me, Bethan Walters? It's either Marks and Spencer or a chastity belt. Make your choice.' She returned to her phone to feed the pigs on her virtual farm.

Mouse turned to Kat, her eyes wide. 'If I buy some from Marks, can I shop online at Victoria's Secret? And did you notice she called me Bethan? That means I'm in trouble,' she whispered.

'I'm old, not deaf,' came the voice from the back seat. 'I'll be checking out all parcels that arrive at Kat's house.'

Mouse sank back into her seat. 'I can't win.'

'No, you can't,' it came once more.

Kat laughed aloud. 'You two are amazing. You have a wonderful relationship, but Mouse, you should know this. Your nan will always win, and quite rightly so.'

Mouse sank back into her seat, a smile on her face, hoping Marks and Spencer's didn't just do big girls knickers, and could offer her something with a bit of lace attached. She was getting her car back and in a couple of weeks would be able to escape to different shops...

They pulled up outside the fire-ridden house, and all three sat for a moment and just looked at it. In there, two girls at the beginning of their lives had died, and each person in the car said a small prayer for them. Nobody spoke, they just stared.

Eventually Doris voiced all of their thoughts. 'Can that really be put right?'

'According to the surveyor, it's structurally sound. It will need a new roof and everything knocking down inside it, but it depends what they decide today, I suppose.'

'What do you want, Mouse?' Kat asked.

'I want to re-build it, want to see it looking good again. I'll be selling it, I won't hang on to memories, and I don't want to live here any more, but we'll have to see what they say today.'

A large four-by-four pulled up behind their car, and a man got out clutching a clipboard.

They joined him and he introduced himself as Henry Overend, handing out cards to them all.

Mouse turned to Doris. 'Nan, please don't come in here. It's not safe for you. Wait in the car for us. Go feed your sheep.'

Doris gave a nod of assent. If the truth were to be known, she didn't want to go in. She didn't want to see where those two beautiful young women had died, and she hoped it had been quick. She hoped they had silently slipped away through smoke inhalation, and not had to be burned while they were alive. And she cursed whoever had done this.

Returning to the car, Doris watched as the three people went around the back of the property.

She took out her phone and scrolled through her long list of contacts, stopping at W. She pressed the call button and waited.

'Wendy? You busy for a moment?'

'No, I was going to ring you later. I've missed you. I won last night, but I've saved you your half. Called on number thirteen as well!'

Doris laughed. 'How much? Can I retire to Florida?'

'Sixty pounds each. Wouldn't even get you to the airport. But it's a start. You coming home soon?'

'Not yet. I don't want to leave Mouse. Wendy, I know we said we'd always share even if the other one couldn't make it, but I could be a few weeks yet, so until I get back you keep all the winnings, okay?'

'Nope. It's not as though either of us needs the money, so we'll stick with our arrangement. You would, wouldn't you?'

'I would, so thank you. We'll go out for a meal when I get back, my treat.'

'So how are things? How's Mouse?'

'She's still sore, but getting better every day. She's at her house at the moment, with the insurance chap. I'm waiting in the car. She says I'm too old and doddery to go in.'

Wendy laughed uproariously. 'She's joking, isn't she?'

'I agreed with her. I didn't want to go in. It was a beautiful little house, and now it's just a shell. I'm not sure if they'll recommend demolition or rebuild. It's an end terrace, so it could be knocked down. We'll see when they come out, I suppose. But that's not why I rang. Can you put your taxi head on?'

'I can. You want one?'

'No, I want some info, if you've got it.'

'Go ahead.'

'Does your company have spare black cabs that don't normally get used for jobs, or are a bit dodgy in some respect, perhaps with false plates or something? Or that just sit round the back not working, except if they're needed for specials?'

'Whoosh! You don't want much then. I can state quite categorically that we don't, not to my knowledge, anyway. But ours is the biggest company in Sheffield, so we are very much above board with everything. There are one or two small businesses, though, that are definitely only just legal. Why?'

'Mouse was in a taxi with false plates the night she was attacked, and her feller was killed. You're the only person I know who actually works for a cab firm, so I thought it was worth a try. Thanks anyway. I'll let you know when I'm back home. It should only be a couple of weeks, I hope.'

'Take care, Doris. And I'll text you a list of dodgy companies. See what I can find out.'

'You're a star, Wendy.'

'I know,' she said with a laugh. 'Keep out of trouble, Doris, and if you need anything, just ring. Bye, love.'

Doris held her phone in her hand for a minute, staring out of the car window. She didn't know why she had done that, she presumed the police had everything in hand for the investigation – they just weren't passing anything on.

Three figures came around the corner of the building, spoke for a minute, then Kat and Mouse shook the man's hand. She hoped it meant that they had agreed a way forward that didn't involve demolition.

Doris got out of the car and waited. She needed Mouse's car keys, and they could head off home to discuss the happenings of the morning. She could try to take the horrors of the derelict house, and the ghosts, out of her two girls' minds.

They walked over to her, and Mouse pulled the keys out of her bag.

'It's over there,' she said, and pointed to the side street at right angles to the road on which they were congregated. 'Can you see it?'

Doris nodded. 'I presume it will start?'

'Hope so, but we won't leave you until you bring it to us, and then we'll follow you home. Take care of it, and no speeding,' Mouse said, trying to inject threat into her tone.

'As if,' Doris said with a grin, and crossed the road to walk towards the little car. It was only as she reached the far pavement that she could see the two boys sitting on the Mini's bonnet, enjoying the rays of the sun.

16

'Oy!' Doris yelled, 'Get off that bloody car, you little scrotes!'

Both boys looked around and saw the elderly lady waving her arms at them. They turned to each other and grinned. Joey Cooper and his cousin Will Towers clambered onto the bonnet, waved back at her, and jumped up and down.

Once.

17

The explosion rocked the area, and DI Marsden was on the scene within an hour, once Mouse had explained to the attending police from Sheffield who she was.

The blast had knocked Doris to the ground, and she had shrapnel embedded in her right arm as she had lifted it to protect her face, an automatic reaction that had possibly saved her life. She was still sitting in the ambulance, shocked but with no life-threatening injuries, when Marsden arrived.

Mouse was in the vehicle with her, holding her hand, eyes full of tears.

Doris attempted to console her, to little avail.

'It's my fault, Nan. Somebody wants me dead. You're injured and two more people have died because of me. Two little lads, Nan.'

'Hush, Mouse, sweetheart, none of this is your fault. You're the victim, not the blasted murderer.'

'Beth, Mrs Lester. I'm so sorry, but I just need to find out what you remember.' Marsden climbed up into the back of the ambulance. 'Then they can take you to hospital. I've spoken briefly to Reverend Lowe, but I understand you two were outside your home,' she said to Mouse.

'We were. Nan was going to drive my Mini over to Eyam because my shoulder is still uncomfortable, and we thought it was the safest way of getting it there. Nan had left us to walk to the car, and I heard her shout. We could see her and we could see the Mini. We saw the boys stand on the front of the car and wave at Nan, then they jumped. It was meant for me, wasn't it? Who wants me dead so badly they're prepared to take such a stupid risk as this? I was supposed to sit in that car and it would blow up as soon as I moved.'

'It seems like it,' Marsden conceded. 'It will be some time before we can move what's left of the car, and there are body parts...'

'Oh God.' Mouse sobbed, leaning against her nan's undamaged arm. It was too much. All this death because... because the driver of the taxi thought she had recognised him, but couldn't remember who he was.

She knew she was right. Find the driver, find the man who had killed these little boys as well as her two friends. And Anthony.

She watched as the paramedic pulled the oxygen mask up on to her nan's face, and heard him say, 'Stop talking, Doris. You need to keep this on.'

Mouse smiled weakly. Stop talking. They were asking the impossible.

'Are you going with us, Beth?'

'No, she's not.' Doris once more removed the oxygen mask. 'I want you home with Kat. You're safe there. And don't you move anywhere, not even to Marks and Spencer's, I'm warning you. I don't want to see you, Mouse, until I'm back home with you. Wendy will organise a taxi for me to get me back to Eyam as soon as they discharge me. Are you listening, Mouse?'

'I am.'

'Not good enough. I am and I promise not to leave the house.'

Mouse sighed. 'I am and I promise not to leave the house.'

She kissed Doris, and jumped down from the ambulance. The paramedics closed the back doors, and headed off to the other side of the city; another family member for them to treat.

Mouse walked across to where Kat was talking to DI Marsden. Henry Overend had given his brief statement and been allowed to go, and Tessa Marsden was organising with Kat to go into Chesterfield with Mouse to give their statements.

'No,' she said. 'Sorry, but I've just promised Nan I won't leave the house until she's back there. And even without that promise, this is clearly targeting me so I'm going nowhere outside of our fortress at Eyam. I feel safe there. If you want a statement, you'll have to come to us.'

'Okay, tomorrow morning, I'll be there for ten. I do understand your concerns and we're going to have to look at ways of protecting you, a safe house maybe.'

'I'm in a safe house.' Mouse could hear the challenge in her own voice.

'I meant…'

'I know what you mean, DI Marsden, but I'm going nowhere unless Kat and Leon throw me out. I don't think they'll do that.'

'Of course we won't,' Kat said. 'Can we go now? I don't think we're helping by being here, and it's distressing.'

Marsden nodded. 'Yes and drive carefully. You've both had a shock. I'll see you in the morning. Just an idea, Beth, but have you thought about hypnosis to see if that can revive memories?'

'I haven't, but I'm prepared to try anything. Especially now. Are you thinking what I'm thinking? Find the taxi driver, we find the murderer? And he thinks I know him but haven't remembered his identity yet. You are, aren't you?'

'I am. And we can't force that memory to surface. I'm just concerned he'll finish the job before you remember. Did you know him?'

'I've no idea. There's something in there…' Mouse tapped her head. 'That's like a fleeting feeling, as though I should know who he is, but I really don't. The only thing is, if he is thinking I know him, it means he knows me. But the men I escorted rarely came with their real names, so I wouldn't know him anyway.'

'Get off home, you two. I'll see you in the morning. Think about the hypnosis, Beth, but I'm not going to force it on you. I think your memory will return and we'll know more then.'

'Those two boys,' Kat said. 'Did they live around here?'

'The car was parked outside one of their homes. The other one was visiting. They were cousins.'

The distress was evident on both Kat and Mouse's faces. Innocent lives. All they did was sit on a car; they did nothing to merit such a horrific end to their young lives, lives that had hardly started.

'God bless them both, and their families,' Kat whispered, then pulled a distraught Mouse back to her car. 'Let's get you home. This wasn't your fault, Mouse. It's the fault of the maniac who can't let you go. We have to talk to Leon, see if there's anything else we can do to step up our security until this man is caught.'

Leon was furious. 'You're putting both your lives in danger. And where's Nan? In the bloody hospital because you don't care about anyone's safety.'

'Leon,' Kat said softly, trying to calm him down. 'We do care. It's why we've come to you. We need to know if there's anything else we can do.'

Her words didn't help. He had heard the news of the explosion as he had driven home and although no names had been mentioned, he knew. He didn't ring Kat from the car. He waited.

And then his anger poured out of every pore. He didn't know what he would do without her, and she seemed to have taken the other two women to her heart, putting herself in the firing line alongside Mouse.

'There will be no further disappearances from this house until this murderer is caught. Do I make myself clear?'

'No,' Kat responded. 'Actually, wrong answer, you've made yourself very clear. What I meant was that you can't really issue orders like that. Not to me, and I'm pretty sure not to Doris and Mouse.'

Mouse hoped she wouldn't giggle. The poor man didn't stand a chance against his wife.

He visibly weakened. 'Kat…'

'No, Leon. I watched two young boys blown to pieces this morning, God bless their souls, and if you think I can sit back and take that then you're living on a different planet. You do your job, and I'll do mine.'

'Job?'

Kat looked startled. 'Did I say job? Well… whatever. Now stop trying to lord it over us because it won't work. We're three against one when they've dug the bits of metal out of Doris's arm, and we're not going to sit in this house, scared to death to move because of one man. Now, is there anything else we can do security-wise to make sure we're all as safe as we can be?'

He growled. 'We'll get two bloody big dogs.'

'Tibby won't let them live here. That's not an option. I was thinking in terms of alarms, rather than animals.' She smiled at her husband, he didn't like losing.

Mouse simply sat quietly at the kitchen table and waited for the storm to blow over.

He spoke with less stress in his voice. 'I don't think we need any more alarms but I will check every window and door lock before we go to bed tonight. And if necessary, I can station somebody in our car area, although it is a little full these days, to sit in the car all night and watch the house.'

'What? Is that necessary?'

'Will you behave and stop going out?'

'No.'

'Then it's necessary. Compromise, Kat, compromise.'

Doris arrived home the next day in a taxi to find Mouse with her nose buried in the laptop, notebook by her side filled with scribbles, and Kat laboriously typing up her sermon for the coming Sunday, on her laptop.

She came through the front door and both women looked up, fear temporarily etched on to their faces.

'It's me,' she called out, and both exhaled.

Doris came through into the kitchen waving a heavily bandaged arm. 'Walking wounded coming through.'

Mouse stood and took her nan's handbag from her. 'Come and sit down. Are you supposed to be home? We thought tomorrow at the earliest.'

'I persuaded them. Told them you're a nurse.'

'Nan!'

'Look, they've done their job properly, there's nothing left in it, so it's just a matter of it getting better. Why did I need to take a bed up for an extra night? I didn't. So I rang Wendy, she organised a taxi, and here I am. They did say I needed lots of cups of tea and stuff though…'

'No they didn't,' Mouse grinned, 'but I'll make one.'

Kat stood and kissed Doris. 'We'll both look after you. You want to go into the lounge?'

'Not till I've found out what you two are up to. Mouse, you ordering knickers?'

Mouse laughed. 'No, I'm not. I'm building up a picture of Anthony Jackson, right from him being born. Looking at schools he attended, his reports, his friends, general stuff like that. Somewhere in there is the killer.'

Kat typed a full stop with a flourish. 'I can tell you what I'm doing. I've finished my short and sweet sermon for Sunday. Now I can forget about it and concentrate on important stuff. How can you see school reports and stuff, Mouse?'

The sudden change of subject threw Mouse for a moment. She looked at Kat, keeping her face solemn.

'There are ways.'

'You need help?' Doris threw her offer into the melting pot.

'No, I'm fine on this, Nan, I'm on grammar school reports now. He was very bright, that's for sure. Can you move on to Jackson Pharmaceuticals?'

'I can. Kat, you can do the drinks now you've finished your work, okay? And would you mind bringing my laptop down please, sweetheart? Your legs are younger than mine.'

Kat grinned. God, she loved this feisty old lady. 'I will.' She stood and moved to leave the kitchen. 'Nan, your leg's bandaged.'

'There was a bit in that as well, and apparently it'll stiffen up, so I don't want anybody going on at me about having a limp, it's only until it stops hurting.' She sat down with a thud. 'Now come on, let's get to work.'

Mouse had made a list of people that Jackson had known at school, and who had crossed over as acquaintances into his adult life. It wasn't a long list, and she made sandwiches before beginning her Internet search for details of the six people on the list.

She was surprised to discover that Anthony had been just short of his thirty-first birthday when he was killed; she had presumed him to be older despite his youthful looks because of his seemingly opulent lifestyle.

Michael Damms had been with Anthony Jackson all through his secondary school life. They had clearly been friends, always standing together on school photographs, and even being mentioned together in head teacher notes on Jackson's end of year reports. *Anthony and Michael Damms will go far in their adult lives, probably together.*

Mouse needed to find out if that note had been prophetic, or if university life had set them on different paths. She suspected they had kept in close touch, and delved deeper.

She had already discovered that Jackson had completed his education at Southampton University, and was surprised to see that Michael had headed north, to Durham, effectively splitting the partnership apart.

Jackson had gone on to work in a laboratory, and then to opening up pharmacies in South Yorkshire following an inheritance windfall that had helped him on his way. It seemed he'd had an aunt who had loved him enough to leave him everything she had, except for a £20,000 donation to a donkey sanctuary.

Mouse struggled to find anything about Michael Damms for the first two years after he graduated, but then he arrived on the scene once more, as a pharmacist in one of his friend's shops.

Damms had been married, but Mouse easily tracked down the wedding and divorce dates, five years apart, almost to the day. He hadn't re-married since.

It seemed that he was still employed by Anthony Jackson, deceased, and she wondered who would be taking over the set up. She would have to check on wills; she suspected Michael Damms might feature in it somewhere.

She left him alone once she had the basic information and moved on to Isla Norman.

'Take a break, Mouse,' her nan instructed. 'Just ten minutes, go for a walk around the garden, give your brain and your eyes a rest.'

Mouse smiled. 'I will. You coming with me?'

'We'll all go, have ten minutes in the summer house,' Kat said. 'And you can tell me what you're beavering away at. I wish I could help, but I can't.'

'Leave it to us,' Mouse said. 'And unless something is glaringly obvious, this information we're gathering is for our eyes only. Tessa Marsden gave us nothing this morning, in fact our statements were taken, and she'd gone within a quarter of an hour. What was that about? So whatever we discover is for us. We can talk about what to do with it when we've collated everything.'

They linked arms to head down the garden, both of them supporting Doris, who was being careful with her damaged leg.

They settled around the little table, and Kat lit the citronella candle. 'I've no idea if this actually does keep bugs away, but it looks nice,' she said, looking up at the grey sky. The sun had been missing today, and the bottom end of the garden was dark anyway, with the tree canopy behind the summer house.

'So,' Kat said, 'fill me in on what you're doing, what you've found out. And tell me what I can do. And then tell me why we're doing anything when we have a police force who seem to be working on it anyway.'

Mouse stared at Kat. 'You think they'll find out what I can find out? Or what Nan can find out? The top levels in the force, the IT section, probably could, but ordinary detectives, not an earthly. What I'm doing is kinda... illegal, I think is the right word. I can dig deep, I can hack, and so can Nan. Everything I've found out, the school stuff, isn't freely available, and I promise to wipe everything when we've found out who the little turd was who saw my knickers without my permission in that back alley. This is personal, Kat, and he'll know about it when I have his name.'

'So what have you done to trace him?'

'I've gone back into Anthony's school life, tracked down seven people he kept in touch with after school and university, and now I'm looking at their lives. It won't happen overnight, because I have to be careful, leaving no trace of where I've been, and Nan's looking at Anthony's business in much the same way.'

'Have I met up with the two cleverest people on this planet?'

'Course you have.' Mouse's laughter was infectious. 'Horses for courses, Kat, I couldn't stand up in that church on Sunday and give a sermon. We all have our different talents.'

'Yes, but I can't do anything to help.'

'You saved my life! And you've given Nan and me a home while we recover. You think that's not helping? And you're a listener. That's a massive thing. I can talk things through, knowing you'll have on your sensible head, and you'll point me in the right direction. So don't knock your gifts, Kat. I can't listen, I talk too much and interrupt people constantly.'

'She's quite right about that,' Nan said quietly, a smile on her face. 'Never been any different.'

18

'So has anything jumped out?' Kat asked.

'Not yet. I've done some pretty close checking into the first one on the list, a Michael Damms, who is a long-time friend of Anthony's and a pharmacist in one of his shops. Anthony's funeral is tomorrow, at your church, isn't it? I imagine Damms will be there.' Mouse pushed back her hair, tucking it behind her ears.

'It is tomorrow, but I'm not taking it. It was felt it wouldn't be appropriate. Should we go as mourners? We'll have to tell Leon, I think he was going to show his face, and he'll not be happy if we turn up and he didn't know we were going.'

'Good plan. If we mingle, I'm sure we'll find out who this Damms fellow is, maybe get an up-to-date photo of him. We need a big scrapbook or something, to keep our information in one place.'

Kat smiled. 'I don't think Leon would appreciate a big board in the dining room with pictures of potential murderers stuck up on it. I'm sure I've got something we can use. I've a fair-sized stationery cupboard we can raid.'

They sat in near silence for a few minutes, listening to the gentle sound of the birds and the cascade of the stream, now flowing more strongly after the torrential rain brought on by the storm.

'What if we set this up as an office,' Nan suggested. 'Or even my bedroom? It's big enough. And Leon won't see anything then. What he doesn't see can't upset him, can it?' There was a definite twinkle in her eye.

'You're right. If we're going to be printing off some stuff, we need it away from prying eyes, because he won't approve of us getting involved. What do you need?'

'Couple of small tables. Ordinary chairs will do. It's not as though this is a lifetime thing, we're just trying to find one man who attacked my granddaughter. We can use the top drawer of that massive chest of drawers for putting anything in we don't want on display. Leon could come into the kitchen at any time, and he'd blow a fuse if he thought we were still involved, especially after yesterday. The awful thing is he's in the right. We were in danger, and Mouse particularly.'

Kat stood. 'Right, tea break over. I'll go and find some sort of table. Get you two techno kids set up. And I'll tell Leon later we're going to the funeral so that you can see if anything jogs your memory.'

Doris held up her hand. 'Can we just bear in mind that the killer could be there, and he's looking for Mouse. He might not know where she is at the moment, but he can soon work it out if he sees us.'

'Then we'll not go together. I'll keep away from you two.' Kat's brain was in overdrive trying to work out the logistics.

'It would be better if I didn't go,' Doris said. 'I'm a bit immobile currently, as you know, and to be honest I stand out with all this bandage stuff, so I'll stay home. You two can walk down and back, can't you? Just do it separately, or go down early and wait in the church. It won't seem odd Kat being in there anyway. Can you follow the stream from the bottom of the village, Kat? Maybe that's the way Mouse could get back here, and you walk up the road.'

Kat acknowledged the sense in the plan. 'It's actually quite a pleasant walk, following the side of the stream. Can be a bit muddy in places, but it shouldn't be too bad.'

By three, they had moved everything up to Doris's room, and Kat had ordered a new printer. 'We can't really take Leon's,' she said with a laugh. 'He might think we're up to something. This one will be here tomorrow. Are you okay up here?'

They both held up a thumb, intent on what they were doing.

Isla Norman, the second on Mouse's list, proved to have a husband and two children. She was called Isla Yardley, married to a haulage contractor and living in Stoney Middleton. It seemed she hadn't gone on to university, had started work at the haulage company when she was sixteen and ultimately had tied the knot with the boss's son, Gerry. *Nice one,* Mouse thought. She had remained in Anthony's life through her husband; Gerry and Anthony played in the same cricket team.

Mouse tried hard to find additional information on her, but it seemed the idyllic life she had garnered suited her, and the contact with Anthony once school was over for them was minimal.

She put Isla on a backburner; sometimes the hairs standing up on the nape of her neck meant something, and she knew she would return to this woman, or her husband.

Mouse relaxed in her chair for a moment – *how had Kat managed to find two typists chairs in the house without stepping foot outside the door?* – and let her thoughts roam. She felt she knew the name Peter Swift, but pinning it down to why she knew it wasn't happening.

Peter Swift… Swift… This was somehow connected with her dad, and she couldn't bring it to mind. Had her parents known him? They'd both been dead nearly five years so she could hardly ask them, but she tried to bring her dad's voice into her mind. Peter Swift?

Mouse decided to leave the thought meandering around her head, and moved on to number four. Keith Lancaster. She almost felt she could write him off when she discovered he had emigrated to Australia, but she persevered. Just in case, she told herself, just in case.

He had been very much in Anthony Jackson's life until three years earlier, when he had left his homeland. He had worked for

Anthony in an administrative position, and when she checked his bank statements she saw he had been on a hefty salary, whatever his admin role had been. What had made him leave such a generous employer? She saved copies of the bank statements, ready for printing when the new printer arrived, then came out of the website. She didn't like going into bank's websites, too much hard work.

Mouse knew Keith Lancaster would bear deeper scrutiny; leaving for Australia, on the surface, didn't seem like a sensible plan, so what had made him leave? She would need to check if he had family there, if there had been some pressing personal reason for travelling all those miles, or if he had to leave for some other reason.

He wasn't the murderer, she acknowledged that, but had he had some connection to the taxi driver?

She pushed her pen behind her ear, and took a deep breath.

Typing in Oliver Merchant's name, still puzzling over why Peter Swift linked to her dad, Mouse discovered that Oliver Merchant was no more. He had taken one of Derbyshire's many bends too fast, once too often. She tutted when she saw he had written off a Ferrari in the process of losing his life. She made a note to go check out his headstone after seeing he was buried in Eyam churchyard.

Kat was sitting quietly in the corner of the room, her Bible open and a notepad by her side. She had a Bible Study course coming up, and had decided it was a good time to get in front with the six-week event.

'Peter Swift,' Mouse said and closed her eyes.

'What?' Kat swivelled round to see Mouse's head resting on the back of the chair.

'Peter Swift,' Mouse repeated.

'Footballer, plays for Derby County, I think. Is that what you wanted to know? He still plays for them, if I'm remembering correctly.' Kat frowned, trying to remember if there was anything else she knew about him.

'He was a footballer your dad met at some point, and he really admired him. Don't you remember?' Doris said.

Mouse's face lit up. 'Of course I do. I knew I'd heard the name somewhere, and it was something to do with Dad. He was definitely in Anthony's life in his late twenties, so I'll look him up. Thank you, ladies.'

She recognised there would be quite a lot of information on Peter Swift, so left him till the end. Caroline Phillips was next on her list.

Mouse gasped aloud when the picture of Caroline came through.

19

Caroline Phillips, nee Boldock, born 23 May 1986, Rotherham, South Yorkshire. The picture was of the girl Mouse knew as Caroline Boldock, the same one she had accompanied on a couple of occasions when they had to double up as escorts.

Caroline Phillips? Surely she hadn't married. Mouse had thought they were around the same age; it came as something of a shock to realise she was thirty, not twenty as Mouse had thought, wrongly assuming a shared university life meant a similar age. She followed the routes she had taken to find information on the others on her list, and all became clear. Caroline's father, Clive Boldock, had died when Caroline was only ten years old, and her mother had subsequently re-married. Caroline had changed her name by deed poll to Phillips, her stepfather's name. She had presumably used her original name for her escort life.

Mouse pulled some paper towards her and made notes. She was getting confused; Caroline Boldock seemed to have thrown a bit of a spanner in the works, because it seemed that everyone on the list had actually been in the same class throughout their school life. What linked them now? Knowledge? Of what?

Mouse leaned back and closed her eyes, letting her thoughts wander.

'What are you working through?' Kat's voice interrupted her thinking.

'They're all the same age, all eight of them, including Anthony. Did something happen at school that bound them together?'

'You okay, Mouse?' Doris asked.

'I'm fine. Just needed to stretch. Let me talk through what I've managed to find out, and find out very easily.'

She outlined the seven people on her list, saying she still had one to check, Peter Swift. All seven had gone to school and been in the same class as Anthony Jackson. After leaving school they had lived separate lives, but had kept in touch; all of them, including the deceased Oliver Merchant.

'Something kept them together, something or someone they knew, possibly. None of the names or the photographs mean a thing to me, so I'm not convinced any of them could be the one who attacked me.'

'Should we pass this information on to DI Marsden?' Kat asked.

Mouse grinned. 'No, Kat, we can't do that.'

Kat thought for a moment and then quietly said, 'Oh.'

'Kat, we're on our own with this. I want my time with this man who tried to kill me, before DI Marsden gets what's left of him. And when I go for him, there'll be no bullets involved. Leon may have given us a gun, but we won't need that.'

'So what will you need?' Kat discomfort was showing in her voice.

'A black belt,' Mouse said quietly.

'And we don't need to buy one,' Doris spoke equally quietly, although pride in her granddaughter showed in the way she looked at Mouse.

'You have a black belt?' Kat's surprise showed in the way she raised her eyebrows.

Mouse smiled. 'I do. I've been attending karate lessons ever since I could walk. Mum and Dad wanted me to be able to protect myself. I don't think they ever thought for a minute that it would be from a bullet, but I'm getting the use of my shoulder back, and while I think I would struggle at the moment if any attack came, give me a couple of weeks and I'll be as good as I ever was. Which is bloody good.'

'Mouse Walters, you're an amazing woman,' Kat said. 'Can I learn?'

Mouse laughed aloud. 'Of course you can learn, but you'd never use what you'd learnt. You're too nice, Kat, you'd probably say a prayer for your assailant before you lifted an arm.'

Kat sighed. 'Am I really so obviously useless?'

'No, you're the brains of this outfit. You're the thinker.'

With Leon's arrival, the three women relocated downstairs. Nothing was said about what they had discovered, and they opted for pizza for their evening meal, to save anyone having to cook.

Sitting out on the patio listening to the trickling water and the evening sounds of the village, they felt at peace.

'I'm going to the funeral tomorrow,' Leon casually remarked.

'So are Mouse and I,' Kat just as casually answered.

'What?'

'We're going. Mouse needs to view the mourners, see if she recognises anyone, a stance, a way of walking, anything at all she can pass on to the police. We have to give it a go, Leon, whether you agree or not. There are five people dead now, two of them children. Doris will stay here, she needs to rest. We'll only be away an hour or so, she'll be fine.'

Leon wasn't convinced he liked this attitude coming from his wife. 'I don't think you should go. What if the killer is there, he'll see Beth and know she's with you.' He was steadfastly refusing to call her Mouse.

'No he won't. We won't be together during the service and interment, and afterwards Mouse will come back here using the path at the side of the stream. I'll come home using the main road.'

'I'm not happy.' His eyes flashed at his wife, and she smiled.

'I knew you wouldn't be, but it's my decision, Leon, so forget it. I'll have you there anyway, won't I? You'll be my protector. Stop worrying, it's just an exercise really in trying to see a stranger who could have killed the poor man. Mouse and I know we're not likely to see him, because we don't really think he would be that stupid. He'll know there'll be a police presence, so that makes it safe, I reckon.'

'Let's hope he thinks like that. He's not that bright, he's had three goes at killing Beth, and he must be feeling desperate. Don't you realise he thinks she can identify him.' He looked directly at Mouse. 'Can you?'

'Not yet. And that's the truth, Leon, but what's also the truth is that I think I've seen him before. I thought it when Anthony and I got into that blessed taxi, and I couldn't put my finger on who he was then. But I will remember, one day.'

Leon sighed. 'You three women scare me. Can I trust you to leave this to the police, and not go investigating this yourself?'

They nodded, their faces serious.

He hoped he could believe them.

20

The skies were cloudy, but the weather forecast had showed no rain was imminent. It was warm, and as Kat headed for the church, she was thankful she'd worn her ordinary clothes.

She saw several people as she walked down the main road, and they all asked if she was taking the service. They knew of the part she had played in finding the body, and she had to explain several times why she wasn't officiating, before reaching the sanctuary of the church.

She quickly changed into her clerical garb, and then moved outside, to direct people into the church, keeping her eyes open for strangers. She didn't really expect to suddenly see a man who she could categorise as a murderer, but she felt she had to inspect every male there.

That included her husband. He looked delicious, and well worth inspecting. 'Well, Mr Rowe, you scrub up nicely if you don't mind my saying so.' She reached up and kissed him.'

'Can deacons do that in the church grounds?' he grinned.

'They certainly can,' she responded. 'And I promise we'll go straight home afterwards. I don't want you worrying about us.'

'Too right you will. I'm taking you to the house in the car, before I return to work.'

She watched as he turned his back on her, giving her no time to respond. He moved across to greet someone he knew, and she saw him shake their hand. She was seething. How dare he make her feel belittled.

The church was filling; Anthony Jackson had been a popular figure, it seemed. There were several people from the village, and she greeted them with a hand clasp. They all spoke highly of the deceased, and she thought it was even more peculiar that she hadn't known him.

Mouse arrived and Kat outwardly ignored her. However, she kept a close eye on her as she mingled with the last of the stragglers outside the church, watching her dark hair weaving in and out of the small groups.

The hearse arrived and Kat hurried inside and joined Leon. The mourners rose to their feet, and silence descended as the coffin arrived in the doorway. It was carried in to a classical piece of music that was beautifully uplifting, the notes soaring into the top of the church interior. She couldn't place what it was, and vowed to check the playlist.

There was a brother. His name was Ian, and he spoke of the childhood they had shared, despite the age gap of seven years, and how much he had been devastated when they heard of his death. His friends had been numerous, Ian had reported, and he knew many of them were in the church celebrating his life.

The service ended and everyone filed out to surround the newly dug grave in the churchyard.

Both Mouse and Kat held themselves back, standing on the exterior of the group surrounding the grave. Someone sobbed as the coffin was lowered, and Kat craned her neck to see who it was.

She slid her phone out of her pocket and pretended to do something to it, while surreptitiously taking a photo of the dark-haired woman. She would show it to Mouse later, she thought, along with the half a dozen or so photographs she had managed to take, for comparison with the pictures of Anthony's friends Kat had downloaded from the Internet. The crowd slowly dispersed, and Leon appeared beside her.

'You need to do anything in church?' he asked.

She shook her head.

'Then let's get back to the car. I'll drop you off. Beth's already headed down to the path, and she's okay. Nobody followed her.'

'Thank you. You've been keeping an eye on her?'

'On her more than you,' he acknowledged. 'I know she's the one in danger.'

Kat nodded. 'Then take me home. Let's go make sure Doris is okay.'

With Leon heading back to work, the three women sat around the kitchen table talking about the funeral. Mouse admitted it had been hard; she had enjoyed Anthony's company, he had been refreshing to be with, and she couldn't relate that man to the body that had just been lowered into a hole in the ground.

'And you saw nobody who jogged your memory?' Kat asked. She had deemed it wise not to pose the question until Leon had departed.

'Nobody at all. I didn't imagine there would be so many people though.'

'It's because he was young. The younger the deceased, the large the group of mourners. I knew there would be a good turnout.'

'You didn't see anything to give you cause for concern, Kat?' Mouse asked. 'I noticed you kept opposite me all the time so that between us we had it all covered.'

Kat produced her phone and passed it across to Mouse. 'This girl was clearly upset.'

'It's Caroline Boldock, or Phillips, or whatever she's really called. She's been a friend of Anthony's since school days, and she's one of the group of friends who've kept in touch since they left. I know her through the escort agency. I thought she was a student like me, similar age, but she isn't, she's much older. Thirty or so.'

'Can we speak to her, you reckon?' Kat frowned, considering the negative possibilities to her question. Maybe Caroline Boldock wouldn't want to speak to anyone who wasn't police.

'I can get her phone number,' Mouse said.

Kat's smile was strained. 'Please don't tell me how you're going to do that. I don't want to know. She may have some answers for us though.'

Leon walked into Brian's office, and immediately headed for the coffee pot. Brian was on the phone, and shook his head when Leon mimed pouring him one as well.

Sinking down on to the leather sofa, Leon waited patiently for Brian to finish the call. 'Problems?'

'No, nothing to worry you. Did you go to the funeral?'

'I did. He'd a lot of friends.'

Brian nodded, and bent his head to make a note in his diary. 'So young, you see. Shame he had to die.'

Leon looked at his friend, eyebrows raised. 'You know something?'

'Nothing. Don't really want to know anything either. No, it was just a passing comment. Somebody obviously thought he should die, and I for one think it might not have been a good idea. It'll make the police investigate things they are better off not investigating.'

'There's no word on the streets then?'

'Nothing that's been passed on to me. Maybe Anthony screwed the wrong bird and the boyfriend found out. Perhaps we're looking too deep into this, thinking there might be connections with him wanting in with us, wanting a merger.'

'It's not just about Jackson though. There's been other deaths connected with it. That DI seems clueless. She's clutching at straws. She's interviewed Kat and I twice. All we did was find the body.'

'Forget it, Leon. There's nothing to link us to him. We've no worries.'

But Leon had worries. He had three women at home hell-bent on finding the killer, and to make sure his Kat stayed safe and alive, he couldn't tell anybody.

He finished his coffee and stood. 'That delivery from Rotterdam coming in tonight?'

'That one, and the one from Paris.'

'Paris is early?'

'Yes, quick turnaround by the driver. He'll be heading back again tomorrow.'

'Good. Make sure he gets a bonus. Keep him sweet.'

Tessa Marsden walked up the stairs to her office and threw her bag down on the table. She'd been fooled, and Tessa Marsden didn't take kindly to that.

Sitting at her desk, she counted to ten, then picked up her phone. There was no reply, and she gritted her teeth as she left a voicemail.

'Ms Boldock, please contact DI Tessa Marsden as soon as possible. You have my number.' *And I have yours, madam,* she thought as she disconnected. Only seen Anthony Jackson twice, my arse.

Caroline listened to the voicemail almost as soon as Marsden finished speaking. She had spotted the DI at the funeral, along with others she presumed were police officers from the way they hung back on the periphery of the mourners. She'd also noticed Beth Walters, but she'd kind of expected her to be there, given the circumstances of Anthony's death.

The others sitting around the pub table were subdued: Sarah Hodgson, back in Eyam for the funeral much against her fiancé's wishes, Michael Damms, Isla and Gerry Yardley and Peter Swift, who had already signed at least half a dozen autographs.

'Here's to our missing members,' Damms said, raising his glass. 'To Keith, Oliver and Anthony.'

They all echoed Keith, Oliver and Anthony, then replaced their glasses on the table.

'We're down to six now,' Peter said, staring into his glass of Diet Coke. 'And we're only thirty, thirty-one. That's a bit scary, don't you think?'

'I think it's more than a bit scary that Anthony was murdered,' Sarah said, a frown creasing her forehead.

Gerry Yardley stood. 'What's everybody having?' They gave him their orders, and he headed to the bar.

Isla watched until he was out of earshot. 'Do you think Anthony's murder was anything to do with... you know?'

'With Leon Rowe and Brian King? Nah, that's long forgotten. No, we all knew what Anthony was involved with, despite his clean-cut image,' Michael said, then decided he maybe shouldn't say any more on that subject as he worked for the Jackson empire. 'He probably got on the wrong side of somebody, and paid for it. It's the girl he was with that I feel sorry for. She had never met him before that night, and ended it taking a bullet alongside him.'

'She survived,' said Caroline, spite evident in her voice. She'd asked the agency for any future bookings with Anthony Jackson, explaining that they were old friends from school days, and the agency had confirmed that following their second function Mr Jackson had requested that Caroline not be his escort as it made it awkward for him to act naturally around her.

'I still think we should be on our guard,' Isla whispered as Gerry returned to the table with a tray full of drinks. 'When do you go back home, Sarah?'

'Tomorrow morning. Peter, why didn't you say yes to marrying me when I asked you twenty years ago, then I wouldn't be tied to the south?' she said with a laugh.

'We were only ten, Sarah,' Peter said with a smile. 'I needed to keep my options open.'

'And?' Caroline raised an eyebrow.

'The options are now closed. I have a partner, and as soon as my playing career is over, we'll be married. His name is Robert, but my agent feels it's better if we don't openly admit to being together, not yet. Not good for the image, he says.'

'There's a turn-up for the books.' Michael stood and reached across the table. He extended his hand and Peter shook it. 'Glad to hear it, Peter, and don't forget our invitations to the wedding.'

'My invitations will be heading your way very shortly too,' Sarah said. 'I'd really like it if you could navigate your way to Ross-on-Wye in late September. I realise you won't be able to attend, Peter, because it's a Saturday in the football season, so you're excused, but I really need the support from the rest of you.'

They nodded their agreement and the talk was successfully steered away from Anthony Jackson's murder, although Caroline knew, from the tone of DI Marsden's peremptory voicemail, that she maybe hadn't finished with it yet.

Sarah and Caroline walked back to Sarah's car after she had said her goodbyes to the others, and drove to Caroline's house in Sheffield.

'You know, Caro, I never had you down for a city girl.'

'Needs must, Sarah. It's too expensive to buy within the Peak District, houses in Sheffield are half the price. It was a no brainer, I had to live somewhere, especially as I'm at Sheffield Uni now.'

'Then don't be a stranger. I'm sure Alexander won't mind you coming to stay for a few days.'

'That's his name? You've never mentioned it since you arrived yesterday morning. You call him Alex?'

'No, he prefers Alexander. You'll come?'

'I can't really,' Caroline explained. 'I do an evening job that earns me quite a lot of money. It's putting me through uni anyway. It's taken me years to realise this is what I need, Sarah, to finish my education properly and get a career. I want to go into forensic medicine when I'm through with my degree. But in the meantime I have to earn.'

'What do you do?'

'I work for an escort agency. I had two jobs where I escorted Anthony, and heaven help me, Sarah, I really started to fall for him.'

21

Caroline rang Tessa Marsden a couple of minutes after waving goodbye to Sarah. She was horrified to hear the DI say she had already despatched a police car to arrest her.

'What? But...'

'But nothing, Ms Boldock. If I leave a message for you to ring me, I don't mean sometime the following day. The car will be with you in about fifteen minutes.'

Caroline froze. 'But I'm already on my way to Chesterfield,' she lied.

Tessa smiled. Now she'd got the woman well and truly rattled, she was happy. Maybe they would get proper answers out of her this time.

'Are you sure?'

'Yes. Can't you hear the engine?'

'I hope you're on hands free with your phone,' she said drily. 'I'll recall the squad car. You'll be here by half past ten then, I presume?'

'I will if I can get parked,' Caroline said, and disconnected.

In utter panic, Caroline grabbed her bag and headed out the door. She had twenty-five minutes to get to Chesterfield, park and walk to the police station.

'You're awful,' Hannah said, a grin on her face. 'She'll be a dithering wreck by the time she arrives.'

'Serves her right,' Tessa said. 'She should have told us there was more than two nights out to her relationship with Anthony Jackson. Who knows what else she's holding back...'

Caroline waited in the same interview room as before, but this time it was with trepidation. Marsden had sounded pissed off with her, and she didn't know why.

She looked up as the door opened.

'Caroline, you made it then,' Tessa Marsden said drily.

Caroline didn't answer. She sensed it was a statement rather than a question.

Tessa switched on the machine and logged them in. Hannah's eyes were glued to Caroline, watching her body language. She was scared but that could be because of the threat of arrest levelled at her by the DI.

'Okay, Ms Boldock, shall we start with Anthony Jackson. All that gumph about his name not registering with you, and you only having met him twice was the biggest load of rubbish ever, wasn't it?'

'No…'

'Caroline.' The warning in Marsden's voice was evident.

There was silence and then a tear rolled down Caroline's cheek. 'I've known him for twenty years or so.'

'Thank you. Is there some sensible reason you didn't tell me that last time you were interviewed?'

'I don't know why I didn't tell you. I was scared. Anthony had been murdered and I didn't want to get involved. Working in the escort industry is frightening enough, but when people start getting killed… so I lied and hoped it would all go away.'

'But you went to the funeral…' Marsden prompted.

'I did. I've always had feelings for Anthony. We were at school together, but it never developed beyond friendship. I thought it was the answer to my prayers that first time I was allocated to him for the evening, and we seemed to be fine. Then we had the second date, but still nothing happened. He was polite, we didn't talk much about our school days, and he delivered me back home exactly as I told you.'

'And?'

'And I wanted to see him away from the escort side. I emailed him, asked him if he'd like to meet for a coffee one day, and he kind of fobbed me off with the busy at work excuse, but said if he had a free day he would let me know. I took it as the brush off, but then found out he'd asked not to have me as his escort for future bookings. Which was why Beth Walters was with him that night.' Caroline's head dropped.

'So, talk to us about Mr Jackson.'

Caroline took a deep breath and talked about the group of friends and their celebration of birthdays from the age of fifteen. She explained that Anthony had introduced them all to marijuana at Michael Damms's sixteenth, and after that first night of smoking joints the birthday celebrations had almost run their course. They celebrated hers on the 23rd of May; they had enjoyed Anthony's joints for the second time but then in July they left school, moving on to different sixth forms or colleges to complete their education. Or to start work.

'I was the youngest of us, and the last to get to sixteen,' she explained.

'And where did you go after finishing the term?'

'I went to work in the café in Eyam. My mother's cousin owned it, and she gave me a job. I'd had enough of education, or at least I thought I had. Ten years after I should have started, I'm now at Sheffield University, studying for a degree.'

'Okay, Caroline, now I need names and contact details of all these friends from school. Do you have them? Were they there at the funeral?'

'Most of them were. There were eight of us initially. Two are now dead, Anthony and Oliver Merchant.'

In her peripheral vision, Tessa could see Hannah taking notes of the names.

'How did Oliver Merchant die?'

'He took a bend too fast in a Ferrari, a year or so ago. He's buried in the churchyard too. I took him some flowers before the service yesterday.'

'That leaves six, including you.'

'Keith Lancaster wasn't there. He's been living in Australia for about three years, although before he moved there he was pretty high up in Anthony's business.'

Hannah's pen was flying across the page.

'Was Anthony Jackson selling drugs?' Marsden threw in the question in an almost offhand way.

'Drugs? Of course he sold drugs. He had a pharmaceutical business. You must know that, surely?'

'I didn't mean prescription drugs, Caroline.'

As the penny dropped, Caroline laughed. 'Oh, sorry. No, as far as I am aware, he wasn't a drug dealer in the way that you mean it.'

Tessa stared at her for a minute. Could this thirty-year-old woman really be that naïve? Without statistics to hand, Tessa would hazard a guess that almost every death by bullet was drug related in some way.

'And the other five?'

'There's me, of course, Peter Swift the footballer, Isla Yardley, who was called Isla Norman at school, Michael Damms and Sarah Hodgson, who wasn't there that night.'

'What night?'

Caroline's brain froze. *Shit, shit, shit* echoed around her head.

'That night we first smoked a joint,' she said, aware her voice was off kilter.

'Why not? Why wasn't she there?'

'She'd moved to Ross-on-Wye a month earlier. She'd been to all the others, and she wasn't happy to have moved, but her dad had been promoted so they left Eyam.'

'Did everybody live in Eyam?'

'Yes, I think it's why we were friends really. We all met up in the morning for the bus, and we all came home together at night. We were in the same year as well, so it was natural we'd stick together.'

Caroline could feel sweat on her face. She wanted out of there. She'd almost slipped up saying 'that night', and now she was scared. She wanted to make no mention, accidental or otherwise, of Leon Rowe.

'Michael Damms. What can you tell me of him?'

'He works for Anthony. He's a pharmacist in one of Anthony's shops. He still lives in Eyam, he inherited the house his parents had lived in. Works in Chesterfield, I believe, but don't know which shop.'

'So there are just two left,' Marsden said. 'Isla Yardley and Peter Swift.' She leaned across to look at Hannah's notes, checking her facts.

'Isla is married to Gerry Yardley, the haulage contractor in Stoney Middleton. At school we got on okay, but she left to go to work as well. She started at Yardley's as an office junior, ended up marrying the boss's son, who is now, of course, the boss.'

It briefly occurred to Hannah that Caroline must be pretty damn scared of Marsden to let all this information pour out of her.

'And Peter Swift?'

'When Peter left school that summer, he joined Stoke, went to their academy. Haven't you heard of him?'

'Yes, I've heard of Peter Swift, the Stoke striker, but it doesn't automatically follow it's your Peter Swift.'

'Well, it is. He was at the funeral, and joined us at the pub later, but he was kept busy signing autographs and posing for selfies.'

'So, who was at the pub?'

'Myself, Sarah Hodgson, Michael Damms, Isla and Gerry Yardley, and Peter Swift. We stayed a couple of hours, talked wedding invitations, toasted absent friends and then as far as I know, split up. I took Sarah back to my home in Sheffield, and she left for Ross-on-Wye just after ten this morning.'

Marsden stared at her for a few seconds without speaking. She guessed Caroline was being garrulous for a reason; to hide something she didn't want to talk about. She stood. 'DI Marsden and PC Granger are leaving the room. Interview terminated at 11.48.'

She paused at the door. 'PC Irwin will escort you out, Caroline, but we'll probably need to speak to you again. Please leave telephone numbers of everybody on this list with the constable.'

Caroline sat in her car and frantically worked her way down the list, telling Sarah, Michael, and Isla that they needed to prepare for a phone call from a DI Marsden. She left voicemails for Peter and Keith.

She hoped she'd done enough to cover her slip up and that DI Marsden hadn't read anything sinister into it. Whatever happened, she wasn't going to be the one to mention Leon Rowe's name. She may not have recognised him when Anthony went to speak to him on their first "date", but she certainly had known his name for nearly fifteen years.

The sight of him at the funeral had been enough to make her legs go weak, and it wasn't his jaw-dropping stature and good looks that had turned her to mush. It was the memory of what he had done to his victim that night.

No killer had ever been found, no gun had ever surfaced, and yet seven people had witnessed events from that night. Seven people who had met up fifteen days later for Caroline's sixteenth birthday, and had made a solemn pledge to never speak of what they knew.

Sarah knew nothing and for that Caroline was grateful. Under police pressure she would have folded.

Caroline leaned her head back on the headrest and closed her eyes. Her friends were really not going to appreciate being dragged into Anthony's murder investigation; she simply hoped none of it would prove to be justified.

She opened her eyes, leaned forward and turned the ignition. The sooner she got home the sooner she could curl up in a ball and escape the world. The memory of that night had been buried once, she could bury it again. Buried, just like Anthony Jackson.

22

'Can I trust you two ladies not to get up to any mischief this morning?' Kat asked, smiling at Doris and Mouse across the kitchen table.

'Of course,' they answered in unison, then smiled at each other.

'Is it a full day meeting?' Doris asked.

'No, I should be home for around one. It's only in Castleton.'

'I'll make sure lunch is ready for when you get home,' Doris promised.

'Thank you. I can't see how this will help in any way, but how about a run out to Anthony's home this afternoon. It might give us more of a feel for the man, and the police will have gone. Think about it, we'll decide later.'

Mouse nodded. 'Good idea, then we'll have a chat about what we've found out so far. Consolidate everything. And I've got somebody I want to ring but he'll probably be in lectures. He's a supplier for some of the students and I thought it might be worth a chat. He probably won't tell me anything, but he's asked me to go out for a drink with him a couple of times...'

Kat grinned as she stood. 'Go, Mouse. Just don't agree to anything till this killer's out of the way. Oh, and Nan, we've a Tesco delivery coming today. Between ten and twelve, I think. If you can't sort it, I'll put it away when I get back.'

They heard her car pull away, and Mouse went upstairs to the chest of drawers, pulling out the print outs she had done.

Doris had cleared the kitchen table, and Mouse spread everything on it.

'It seems really strange that these eight people have stayed in touch. They were friends in school, and going back into their email accounts, they're all still friends now. Something is holding them together and I don't think it's school. Most people leave school and go on to live separate lives because they make new friends in whatever field they move to. This was a group of eight teenagers who probably liked a drink, and that really isn't enough to bind them together for life. And now two of them are dead.'

Doris pulled some of the paperwork towards her. 'There's a lot of information here, Kat. I hope you covered your tracks well.'

'That really doesn't bother me, Nan. Somebody tried to kill me and they tried three times. Legalities are the least of my worries. I'll be quite happy to pass all of this on to the police if I come up with the answer.'

'So,' Doris mused, 'we have Anthony Jackson and Oliver Merchant dead. Was there anything suspicious about Merchant's death?'

'I'm not sure. I've read the newspaper accounts from the time, and the inquest was an open verdict. His family and friends all seemed to say he was an exceptional driver, took good care of his Ferrari, and he knew the road very well, travelling it twice a day for work. He worked in Sheffield, but still lived in Eyam. There was no reason for him to leave the road and hit that brick wall.'

'You're thinking two people murdered out of these eight? That puts the others at risk, surely.'

Mouse nodded. 'It does, and I think we need to talk this through with Kat. Something happened when these kids were sixteen or so, that bound them together, even as adults. I'm going for a walk down to the church, have a look at Oliver Merchant's gravestone, try to clear my head.'

'Then take my car. Think you'll be okay driving?'

Mouse moved her arm and smiled. 'It's much easier, gets a little better every day. But I can walk if you're going to worry.'

'I'll worry more if you walk,' the old lady responded. She handed the car keys to her granddaughter. 'Maybe we should think about a new car for you.'

'Soon, Nan, soon. I don't feel ready yet. Those two little boys…'

Doris nodded. 'We can share mine while we're here. Don't worry about it.' She cursed herself for being thoughtless.

Mouse collected her bag and headed for the door. 'I won't be long and I have my phone if you need me. Rest, Nan, please. And if things are hurting, take the damn painkillers!'

'I don't need them. Now go.'

Mouse parked on the road outside the church and walked through the large wooden doors. She chose the same seat she had used before, and sat for a while, enjoying the peace and allowing her thoughts to roam. She knew she was on the right tracks with thinking they were linked by something; how hard could it be to work out what it was? Would Caroline talk to her? Even if she did, she knew she wouldn't talk about something that was so big it had tied together eight people, with none of them breaking the chain.

Mouse didn't say a prayer, she didn't really know how, but she did walk to the front and light four candles, two for Jo and Millie, and two for the boys killed by the explosion in her car.

She walked out into sunshine that hadn't been there when she went in, and blinked. With her eyesight adjusted once more to light, she walked around the churchyard. Crossing to Anthony's grave, she stood quietly and looked at the wreaths that covered the mound. There were many; she took out her phone and photographed each one.

Her task finished, Mouse left Anthony's grave and searched for Oliver Merchant's. It wasn't difficult to spot. The large stone marking his last resting place gleamed white in the sunshine. A family of wealth, she decided.

She took two photographs of it, and slipped her phone back in her bag, before returning to the car. Her phone wasn't ready to head home to Kat's house just yet; it pealed out as she was fastening her seat belt.

'Nan?'

'Mouse, are you still at the churchyard?'

'I am. Just about to head home.'

'Then can you go back in and see if there's a grave or a plaque for a Craig Adams. He used to live in Eyam, but I've not found out if he was cremated or buried. I'll explain more when you and Kat are both here, or I'll be doing everything twice.'

'I'd decided to wait till Kat was home, I've got loads of photos to print off so by the time I'm finished she should be with us. I'll see what I can find and then I'm heading home as well. Love you.'

She locked the car and walked back into the graveyard. It took her a quarter of an hour, but she found the small dark grey headstone, buried in long grass. It looked neglected, and she cleared as much of the overgrown grass and weeds as she could. It seemed Craig Adams had been twenty-two when he died, and once more she took out her phone to take the photograph. The date of his death hit her with a thud to her brain. The 8th of May 2002.

Kat's car was parked out front when Mouse arrived. Mouse picked up her bag, her mind reeling with the discovery in the churchyard.

'I'm back,' she called as she went through the front door. There was silence, so she headed for the kitchen. Nothing.

She glanced down the garden in the direction of the summerhouse then headed towards Doris and Kat, holding her phone.

Kat frowned at her, just as Mouse had known she would. 'You've been out.'

'I have indeed. Taking pictures of this beautiful place.'

'You haven't. Nan says you've been to the churchyard.'

'And the church,' she retorted. 'I sat for quite some time, then lit four candles. *Then* I went to the churchyard.' She emphasised the second "then" to confirm she had done what she said she was doing.

Kat shook her head. 'Three attempts on your life, and still you take risks. Wait for me next time, will you?'

Mouse sat. 'Lunch looks lovely. Are we eating all of the Tesco delivery?'

'No,' Doris said, 'but I think Kat feels we need feeding up. I've never seen so much food. We have to start paying our way, Mouse.'

'No you don't,' Kat interrupted. 'Leon foots the bill, and he just pays it, so don't worry about it. He'll not even notice the difference.'

She picked up a sandwich. 'Eat. We have work to do apparently.'

It took Mouse an hour to print off three copies of every photograph she had taken. She left Kat and her nan to put away the huge amounts of food and wine, clear up after the delicious lunch, and settle themselves at the kitchen table with glasses of wine.

Mouse joined them, clutching three plastic envelopes containing photographs.

'Right, these are the pictures I took this morning. I photographed every wreath, every spray on Anthony's grave, then went to find Oliver Merchant's, which was spectacularly large, followed by Craig Adams's. I had to do some weeding around that one. Nan, you want to talk through Craig Adams first?'

'I do. I knew the birthdates of the kids, so took 2001 to 2003 as my points of reference, and trawled through newspaper accounts and... well, you don't need to know all the details of my research. Suffice to say the only unsolved murder in this area was of an Eyam young man, killed in Bakewell. This set of kids went to school in Bakewell. I don't think for one minute they had anything to do with the murder. I think they saw it. And I think fear has been the over-riding thing with all of them because they know the person or persons who did it.'

Kat and Mouse digested the information and Kat nodded. 'You're right. It makes sense, doesn't it. But we have to tell the police.'

'Soon,' Mouse said. 'Not yet. We can't be confessing to things that could potentially put us in prison, so our stories have to be along the lines of we came across something accidentally.'

'But all of these people are in danger,' Kat protested. 'It seems whoever did it is taking them out one by one. He or she has clearly found out they witnessed it, and if we don't tell the police, they're unprotected.'

'Let's get our stories right. Let's go through these photos, and I mean scrutinise everything carefully because there may be something in them that will ring bells with us. Now, what about Leon? Will he walk in on us if we utilise this table?'

'He's away overnight,' Kat said. 'Let's get going with this, because I'm feeling a real sense of urgency in it.'

Mouse handed out the files, and the three women began their epic bout of scrutinising every picture, making notes rather than interrupting the others; it would be easier to discuss when they all reached the end.

It was as Kat reached the spray of flowers sent by Sarah Hodgson that she remembered the photos she had on her phone from the funeral.

'I have some pictures,' she said, and Mouse looked up.

'Of?'

'Of people I believed were these friends. There's no guarantees I got the right ones, because those pictures we saw that you downloaded were from when they were younger. You want to see them?'

'I'll go and print them for us. You two carry on here, I'll only be a few minutes.'

She ran upstairs, and Doris topped up the wine glasses. 'We're going to need this,' she said.

23

Two hours later, they were ready talk. They had moved on to coffee, recognising that maybe the wine might fudge their thoughts a little.

'So, first thoughts. Nan?'

Doris turned to Kat. 'The main thing to strike me was that the flowers from his friends of old all mentioned the past. Without exception. And to me that means they think Anthony died because of what they shared. So why is nobody talking? They must be scared. Or do they think that Anthony is somehow involved deeply in a criminal life and asked for it? That he had done something that merited being punished that they haven't done?'

'I couldn't agree more with that. Let's look at Caroline's wreath. *RIP Anthony. A life ended much too early. You didn't deserve this, we stuck together. We would have worked. All my love, Caroline. Xxx.* To me, this is saying the group stuck together. The second we is personal, she means her and Anthony. Was there something between them?' Kat queried.

'I can partly answer that,' Mouse said. 'Caroline was Anthony's escort a couple of times. If she came on to him a bit heavy, he would back off. I wouldn't mind betting she used their long-term friendship to try to snare him properly. He must have asked for a different escort, because the agency tend to use the same ones if the client says they're happy with the arrangements. Enter me. And that night he said he wanted to use me as his escort as a permanent thing, circumventing the agency and just ringing me to book me. That is most unusual. That tells me he was wanting to be well away from Caroline.'

Doris nodded. 'So what do you think to Peter Swift's card?

Kat pulled the picture towards her. '*We kept the faith, Anthony, we kept the faith. RIP, mate, till we meet again.* If you didn't know, or even didn't guess, at the circumstances, you would gloss over these words assuming they were personal between sender and recipient. I wonder if DI Marsden is mulling over these cards just as we are.'

Mouse laughed. 'She might be, if she knows about the connection between all of these people and Anthony. Bet she's found out the legal way though.'

'I can vaguely remember this Craig Adams murder happening,' Kat said. 'They found him in the river Wye, but he didn't drown. He was shot. We couldn't go near the river for ages, they had it cordoned off. But that's as much as I remember.'

Mouse smiled at her. 'That's what the Internet's for, Kat; you no longer have to remember things. It's all on there for the taking. Let's have a quick look at these pictures you took at the funeral, make sure we all know what they look like now.'

It seemed Kat had picked out the right people, and once they'd agreed on that, the pictures were stuck into the book they had set aside for information collated that was accurate.

Doris said she would take charge of their murder book, and did they think DI Marsden would give her a job because she was quite enjoying doing this research.

'Nan, you're in your sixties, I think it's a bit late to be looking at a new career.' Mouse laughed. 'I think we need to look more into Craig Adams, find out his background and why somebody would want to kill him. I know it's not definite he's the link, but the date of his death and the date of that birthday where they all met up suggest they're connected.'

Kat stood. 'I'll make a pot of tea. We got any buns?'

'Butterfly buns in the blue box,' Doris said. 'Made them this morning.'

Kat blew her a kiss. 'Doris, when Mouse finds her new home and leaves us, will you stay on here please?'

'With pleasure. Having that hunk of a Leon pottering around the house is a bit of a bonus.'

Kat grinned. That was exactly how she felt.

Isla headed downstairs after reading to the children, trying to put her tongue and brain back into English after reading Dr Seuss yet again. The children loved the books, but after reading them many many times, they became a little tedious.

Reuben, at nine, was old enough to appreciate Harry Potter, and she couldn't wait for Nancy to reach eight, when Isla felt she would be ready to tackle the villainous Malfoy. One more year…

She headed for the kitchen, glad that Gerry's trip to Southampton had merited a night out. The whole bed to herself, utter luxury. She loaded the dishwasher, tidied away the children's paints – the pictures they had created were nothing short of wonderful, if you liked Picassoesque paintings – and bagged up the garbage to take out to the wheelie bin. She looked around the kitchen, checking there was nothing else to go in the black bag before tying the drawstring, then placed it outside the back door. The bin would be emptied just after seven, so it had to go by the roadside before she went to bed.

She watched the last half hour of a documentary about Chester Zoo animals, and decided to have an early night.

The garbage bag was heavy and she threw it in the already full black wheelie bin, pressing down hard on the lid to try to flatten the contents. The darkness engulfed her, and she glanced up at the stars, so many in evidence on such a clear night.

It took considerable effort to get the bin to the pavement; it meant crossing the yard that lorries continually ploughed up then flattened, and the terrain was anything but smooth. She reached the road, stood the bin by the wall that marked the boundary of their property, making sure it didn't block the pavement, then turned to go back inside.

She saw nothing, she felt nothing. The bullet exploded into her brain and she dropped to the floor.

The shadowy figure, dressed in black, followed the wall around, and headed across the spare land, hugging the stone wall as closely as he could.

PC Ray Charlton had called to the pub for just one pint after driving home from work. He lived with his wife and son, but he was considering suggesting a house move, and he thought things through better with a pint in his hand.

He was considering selling up and moving nearer to Chesterfield; he couldn't see himself changing stations, he enjoyed working under Marsden even if she did knock him a bit for his timekeeping, but his timekeeping depended a lot on traffic. If he didn't have that lengthy journey, he would be there on time. Perhaps.

He had a lot to consider. The house in Stoney Middleton had been his parents and his grandparents, and they'd done a lot to it following his mum and dad dying within a year of each other. They would get a tidy sum; not enough to buy a helicopter to make travelling to work easier, but definitely enough to not need a mortgage for a property in Chesterfield. The biggest issues were it would make his wife's commute to the library for work about ten minutes longer, and Ben would have to change schools. That wouldn't be easy for him as he approached GCSE time. Ray definitely needed thinking time.

He'd been tied to a computer all day, following links to the people who had left wreaths, reviewing the video of the funeral that showed all the mourners, and his eyes ached. He was ready for bed. He downed the last of his pint and stood, his thoughts still no clearer.

'Quiet tonight, Margaret,' he said to the landlady. 'You on your own?'

'Yes, I've enjoyed it,' she smiled. 'The darts team are playing at Bakewell, and I think all the customers must have gone to support them. You any closer to finding out who killed Anthony?'

'Getting there,' he said. 'Getting there. You knew him?'

'A little bit. He was in the Bradwell cricket team, along with Sam, the husband who was on bar duty tonight until he decided he couldn't miss the darts tournament,' she said with a wry grin. 'There are three of our regulars in that cricket team.'

'Good bloke, was he? Jackson, I mean, not your missing Sam.'

'Very pleasant. Never caused any trouble, bought rounds without expecting anything back. He once threw somebody out for me who'd had a bit too much, and Sam was out... again.'

'We're following every lead,' Ray said. 'There's half a chance we'll turn up here to talk to you and Sam.'

He placed his pint pot on the bar, and said goodnight.

The pub door closed behind him, and he stood for a moment looking up and down the road, the main one running through the village. It was eerily quiet. He stepped to the pavement edge and saw the clothing on the floor, half in the haulage yard and half on the pavement.

He knew it wasn't just clothing; he knew there was a body inside the dress. He reached it in seconds. The blood and brain matter was scattered far and wide, and he didn't need to check for a pulse.

He took out his phone and spoke to control.

Margaret could see the flashing blue lights reflecting in the pub windows, and she went to the door to look outside. Her hand went to her mouth as she saw the number of cars, the road block that had been set up, and the body lying on the ground. Isla Yardley. She recognised the blue and white spotted fabric of her dress that she had worn earlier in the day when they had bumped into each other in the Co-op.

She saw Ray looking towards her as she stood framed in the doorway, and he waved. He headed across the road.

'You'd better contact the darts team, tell them not to come back to the pub. The road's going to be closed for a while.'

'It's Isla, isn't it?' Margaret whispered. 'That's the dress she had on earlier. We met in the shop then went for a coffee. Is she...?'

'She is. I'm sorry, Margaret. Did you hear anything?'

'No, but you were in the pub anyway. Did you?'

He shook his head.

'She's been shot?'

'Yes. We've got somebody in watching the children, but they say their dad is on an overnighter. They're not sure where.'

'Southampton. She mentioned it earlier. Said she was looking forward to an evening on her own. Gerry doesn't do many runs these days, but they've two drivers on holiday, so he took this one. If you want to bring the children here, I can look after them until Gerry gets back. We've spare beds the grandchildren use and the kids know me. They'll be very welcome, poor little mites. They must be scared, and it's going to be a few hours before Gerry gets back.'

'Thank you,' he said. 'I'll tell DI Marsden, when she... oh, she's just arrived. I'll let you know what she says.'

Within an hour, the children were sleeping at the pub, both too tired to take in what was happening, and both wanting their mum.

The CCTV from Yardley's Haulage had been downloaded and would be checked back at the station, along with CCTV from the pub.

Gerry Yardley had switched off his phone when he went to bed, and saw the missed calls when he woke at five, ready to start the long journey home after he'd had a hefty breakfast in the truck stop.

He didn't get his breakfast, set off immediately and arrived back in Stoney Middleton mid-morning. He couldn't get near the yard, so left the lorry on the main road with hazards flashing. He hoped no speeding drivers would smash into it.

He gave his name at the crime scene tape, and the PC ushered him under it, and pointed out DI Marsden, who had settled for three hours of sleep in order to be back at the scene when Gerry Yardley arrived.

His wife's body had been removed to the morgue, and a fingertip search of the yard was taking place, along with the field outside the yard, bordered by the stone wall.

Marsden accompanied Gerry inside his home, separated from the yard by a high fence. 'I'm so sorry for your loss, Mr Yardley,' were her opening words. 'Your children are safe with Margaret, at the pub. We took them there last night.'

He nodded, the bleakness in his eyes heartbreaking to see. 'Thank you. Why? Why would anybody want to hurt Isla? She hadn't a nasty bone in her body.'

'There hadn't been anything unusual over the last few weeks then? Nothing to cause you worry? Your business doesn't have problems?'

'Nothing, as far as I'm aware. The only unusual thing has been Anthony Jackson's funeral. We were there for that. But apart from them being old school friends, that was it. In fact, I knew him just as well as Isla, because we were in the same cricket team. I've known him for about five or six years. And that's it. Our lives just go on, we don't do anything different, rarely venture any further than Bakewell, we like… liked… the country life. We've never been abroad, don't really have holidays, the business doesn't allow it. So why did she deserve to die?'

Marsden let him talk, sensing this was a man who didn't let his feelings show, and the talking was the result of hours of silent driving from Southampton, knowing what he had to face when he arrived home.

He frowned. 'Was she putting the bin out?'

'We think so. We've had to turn the bin lorry around, couldn't let him by, and we're going to go through yours before it's emptied anyway. Just in case.'

'Can I see the children?'

'Of course. I have no more questions for now, but we will find this man.'

'You think it's the same man who killed Anthony?'

'Yes, I do, but we have no proof, not yet. We'll know more after the autopsy. We will need you to formally identify your wife. The landlady at the pub recognised her dress because they had been for a coffee together, and Isla had been wearing it then.'

He nodded slowly. 'This is a nightmare.' He stood abruptly. 'I'm going to get my kids.'

Marsden watched him walk across the road, and saw Margaret enfold him into her arms. The children squeezed around her and he gathered them tightly to him. He could say nothing to them, not yet; he didn't know what to say.

With Leon back home, Kat had put everything away in the top drawer that held quite a lot of paperwork and photographs.

He had offered to take them all out for a meal, and Kat booked a table for half past six, so that Doris wouldn't become overtired.

The first item on the local news was the murder of Isla Yardley, wife of the managing director of Yardley's Haulage Ltd.

Kat's eyes were huge as she turned and looked at Mouse. 'Oh my god! Now we have to tell Marsden what we've worked out, these other people need to be protected.'

Mouse held a finger to her lips. 'Sssh,' she whispered. 'Leon's coming downstairs. He'll panic that we may be in danger.' She picked up the remote control and switched off the television.

Doris came downstairs five minutes later, and they set off for the restaurant, Kat and Mouse unusually quiet in the back, and Doris in the front, casting admiring glances at the impressive man by her side.

24

Marsden faced the room, and everybody stopped talking. 'Good morning, everybody. This investigation has stepped up another level. Isla Yardley was shot and killed outside her home yesterday, and the list Caroline Boldock gave us is now down to five remaining people. I have spoken with Sydney police and asked them to contact Keith Lancaster and give him protection. We now need to secure the other four, Michael Damms, Caroline Boldock, Peter Swift and Sarah Hodgson. Sarah Hodgson is already in a safe house somewhere in Herefordshire, and is being interviewed by police there. Michael Damms has stated that he does not require babysitters, he can handle himself, and we have yet to contact Caroline Boldock. She doesn't appear to be at home. Penny, can you contact the agency please, and find out if she had an escort job last night.'

Penny held up a thumb in acknowledgement.

'Ray, thank you for everything you did at the crime scene yesterday, exemplary work. Can you have a look at Oliver Merchant's death for me. I know he crashed on a bend, but interviews suggest he was a safe and careful driver who valued the Ferrari too much to risk damaging it. Did something happen to cause him to lose control? I don't know how we'll ever prove it, but I'm thinking maybe somebody stepping out into the road causing him to swerve. We know the car hit the stone wall and overturned. Why did it swerve so much that it hit the wall? Anything at all, Ray, find me anything at all.'

'Yes, boss.' This made a change to punishment duties for being late for work.

'I'm going to organise a patrol car to go past Michael Damms's house at odd times during the day, take note of car registrations near his place, that sort of thing, but if he doesn't want to move to a safe house, I can't force him. It's a priority to find Caroline Boldock, and trust me, that young lady will be going to a safe house. And that leads us to Peter Swift. I need somebody to go to Stoke County Football Club and…' Seven hands shot into the air.

She looked around the room, grinned and said, 'Right, I'll go then, in the absence of any volunteers.' There was a groan that reverberated all around, and she closed her notebook. 'Let's get on with it, I want information on absolutely everything.'

Ray Irwin moved across to his computer, and clicked on the email that had come in at some point during the briefing. He read it and looked up. 'Boss, some information just come in. The bullet removed from Isla Yardley came from the same gun as the bullets removed from Anthony Jackson and Bethan Walters. But there's something else. The gun was used in another crime, back in 2002. Somebody called Craig Adams was killed and dumped in the Wye.'

'Was there an arrest?' Just for a moment, Tessa Marsden thought it could be case over.

'One minute,' Ray said, and keyed in the name. 'No, boss, nobody ever arrested, cold case.'

'Brilliant. So we're adding bodies from everywhere in this bloody case. Okay, Hannah, take a look at this Craig Adams case, will you. We'll discuss it this afternoon. Penny – you tracked our Caroline down yet?'

'No, she wasn't working last night. She could be anywhere, boss.'

'Right, I'll leave her a voicemail. That'll get her in pretty damn quick.' Tessa allowed herself a small smile as she remembered the panic in Caroline's voice when she had told her she was about to be arrested.

'I'm off to Stoke. Who's coming with me? First to the door gets it.'

There was a mad scramble but one of the new PCs assigned to the murder investigation, and sitting at the desk nearest to the door, won by a mile.

'Smart move, Claire,' Tessa said with a grin. 'Let's go talk to footballers. You like football?'

'Sheffield Wednesday season ticket holder, ma'am,' Claire said proudly, and the room groaned.

'Shouldn't be allowed,' someone shouted from the back of the room, and it was followed by a different voice, shouting, 'Yeah! Up the Owls!'

The two women left the room to moans and groans. 'And don't call me ma'am, Claire. Boss will do.'

'Okay, ma'am,' Claire said.

Tessa sighed. It was going to be a long day…

Peter Swift wasn't there. He hadn't turned up for training, he hadn't responded to telephone calls to his mobile phone and upper management at his club were deeply concerned.

Tessa spent a quarter of an hour explaining the situation, and she could see panic begin to infiltrate the meeting. It seemed that footballers valued their jobs, and didn't go missing without due reason.

'I'll need details of his address and landline please. I only have a mobile number for him.'

She was handed a slip of paper with everything she needed on it, and Marsden and Claire left, promising to ring the club if they should track Peter down, especially if he were ill. The club doctor could then be despatched to medicate the footballer safely.

It only took twenty minutes to arrive at the large detached home of the type favoured by footballers the world over; surrounded by high walls and an electronic gate, the house seemed impregnable.

Claire pressed the speaker button on the gate and a male voice answered. She explained who they were, flashed her warrant card at the camera, and the gates widened to allow them passage.

The front door opened as they climbed out.

'DI Marsden,' Tessa said, holding out her hand. 'And you are?'

'Robert Newstead.' He shook her hand, and motioned for them to go in.

The entrance hall was huge, immaculately decorated in creams and golds, and had several doors leading off it, as well as a magnificent staircase leading to the first level.

He led them to a lounge, where he had obviously been reading the newspaper as they had arrived.

'I'm sorry to disturb you, but we're looking for Peter Swift.'

'He's at the club. You know he's a footballer? Plays for Stoke County?'

'Yes we do. He's not there. We were hoping to catch him here. He's not contacted the club to say he's not fit for training, or anything.'

'What?' Robert stood. 'But he left around half past eight this morning. I'm expecting him back sometime in the next hour.'

'Can I ask your relationship to Mr Swift please?' Tessa asked.

'As long as you keep it to yourself, you can. I'm his partner. We've been together nearly three years, but Peter's agent doesn't want him to go public on it until he's finished playing. Creates bad vibes on the terraces apparently, and the chants will be pretty nasty it seems. We will marry when he leaves football behind, but until then…'

'So can you think where Peter will have gone? Has he ever done this before?'

'Oh my god, no. He's been with Stoke since he joined the academy at sixteen, he lives for that club.' Robert took out his phone and listened intently. 'Straight to voice mail.'

Tessa stood, followed by Claire. 'Thank you, Mr Newstead. When you hear from him, he must contact me.' She handed him a business card. 'He is in considerable danger, and I need to make sure he's safe.'

'What if he's not safe now?' His frowning face told of his worry.

'He isn't safe, Robert. I must speak to him as a matter of urgency.'

Tessa rang the club and explained that Peter had set off for training that morning, and she wanted to know immediately if he should happen to turn up there.

'You think he's already in trouble, boss?' Claire said quietly.

'I do, Claire. We'll head back to the station and see if anyone has come up with anything new.'

They were two minutes away from the station when Marsden's phone rang out. She listened intently for a few seconds, then told Claire to pull over.

She continued to listen and then said, 'Which hospital?'

A further minute passed and then she thanked whoever she had spoken to, before disconnecting.

'Okay, Claire, Northern General as quick as you can. Peter Swift has turned up, he's been taken there by air ambulance. It seems a hiker found him at the bottom of a steep drop, trapped in his car. He couldn't get out, his leg's broken but he's alive. He was conscious when they airlifted him away, so let's try to get there quickly, before they put him under for any operations he might need.'

'You're all heart, boss,' Claire said with a grin. 'Hold tight.'

Peter was a little drowsy; he had needed some industrial-strength painkillers.

'I'd been there hours,' he explained. 'I thought I would die there. My phone was in my bag on the back seat and I couldn't reach it. I kept sounding the horn, and in the end I think that's what brought that feller to me. His dog kept licking my face.'

'You lost control?'

'You tend to lose control when you've got a laser beam blinding you. I had no vision, DI Marsden. The car carried on in a straight line, and I was on a bend. I went over the top. I don't remember coming to a halt, so I think it must have knocked me out, the fall, but I came around eventually and that's when I started hitting the horn.'

'I've notified your club, and your partner, so they should be with you very shortly. However, you will be under guard while you're in here. Somebody is trying to kill you, Peter, and I need to know who it is. I think you know. He's already killed Oliver Merchant, Anthony Jackson and Isla Yardley.'

'Oliver? But Oliver died in a...' His voice faded away.

'You've realised it's a copy of your accident, have you? Losing control for no reason. I'll bet my job on it being a laser beam that caused him to overturn that car. He didn't survive, Peter.'

'Did you say Isla?'

'I did. She took a bullet, just like Mr Jackson. One of you has to start talking, I know you're all hiding something.'

Peter pressed the bell and a nurse arrived at his bedside within what seemed like a split second. 'I'm in too much pain for this, nurse,' he said. 'I need to be on my own.'

In no time at all, Tessa and Claire found themselves outside his room. They spoke to the PC who had been allocated the first shift of guard duty, and headed back to the car.

'He's not going to tell you anything, is he?' Claire said.

'Then we'll find it out ourselves,' Tessa responded.

25

'This is a lovely house,' Kat said, as the three of them stood peering through the wrought iron gates sealing the property off from the rest of the world. 'I know we can't get in, but I don't think that matters. We've seen where the late Anthony lived, and it kind of sets him in my mind now.'

'You sure you don't want to have a look around?' Mouse asked. 'I can go back home and find out how to neutralise the gates and turn off the house alarm.'

Kat grinned. 'No, you're okay, thanks, Mouse. I can live without getting inside. I don't think it will tell us anything new anyway, the police will have gone through it carefully and taken anything away that could possibly help. No, it's enough to fix this in my mind. We seem to have turned into private detectives, haven't we?' Kat added with a laugh.

'Yes,' Mouse and Doris chorused.

'Private detectives working from a bedroom.' Doris smiled. 'I think we're wasting our time here. Kat's right, this house can tell us nothing, other than Anthony Jackson was a very rich man, and to be honest, do we need to know anything else about him?'

All three turned away from the gates and headed back to Kat's car.

'I've been thinking,' Mouse said. The other two groaned. 'No, listen to me. Whoever that taxi driver was, he knew this area pretty well. He calculated exactly how to make us end up on the floor as he took the bends in the village – and they were right-angled bends for maximum effect – so he either lives here or he knows somebody very well who lives here. I need you to think carefully at this point, Kat.'

'Can I think carefully when I get home? I'm driving.'

In a fluid movement, Mouse reached forward and hit the volume button on the radio. 'Shhh,' she said. 'They just mentioned Peter Swift.'

Kat indicated and pulled to the side of the road. They listened without speaking, only turning to share looks of horror as the item ended.

'That's another one of the group. Anthony, Oliver, Isla and Peter.'

'Peter survived, thank the Lord,' Kat said.

'Only by...'

'The grace of God?' Kat said, smiling at Mouse.

'No, I was going to say the skin of his teeth if he went over any one of Derbyshire's bloody stone walls. Bet his car's a mess as well as him.'

They drove the rest of the way in silence, although Mouse's thoughts were on Australia. As were Kat's. As were Doris's.

They sat around the table, each of them staring into the mug of tea in front of them.

'Keith Lancaster,' Mouse said. 'The one in all of this who is out of the loop. We need to know why he headed off down under when he had such a good job with Anthony. But more than that, we need to know if he's been back recently. Or is here now.'

Mouse's phone pealed out and she looked at the screen with a frown. 'Overend? Who do I know called Overend?' She was about to reject the call when her face cleared. 'Oh,' she said, 'Mr Overend, good to hear from you.'

There was a pause while she listened to the caller, then she said a series of yeses, before thanking him and disconnecting.

'Insurance,' she said with a smile. 'The builders are moving into the house on Monday, and it should take about four weeks.'

'Brilliant,' Doris said. 'Will you put it on the market straight away?'

'I will. So now that's in progress, we can maybe look around for another one for me.'

'Don't rush into anything,' Kat warned. 'You're safe here, you and Nan.'

Mouse nodded. 'I won't. I'm looking for something a bit more substantial, rather than a home I can share with other students, so I'll take my time, I promise.'

They continued to sip at their tea, until once again Mouse broke the silence. 'I'm going to ring him, this Keith Lancaster. If he answers, I'll make something up about investigating the murders; I just need him fixed in Australia at the moment, to rule him out of being the actual murderer. If he's not there, then I'll start digging to track if he's over here.'

'You can do that?'

'As long as I tread carefully. Very carefully. You can find everything out really. Want the codes to launch a nuclear missile?'

Kat smiled, hoping Mouse wasn't serious.

It seemed that Keith Lancaster didn't want to answer his phone; Mouse waited until she knew it would be daytime in Sydney, but there was no response. She tried three times but there was nothing. The landline and the mobile number seemed to be mocking her, telling her Lancaster's life was nothing to do with her.

She had no way of knowing if he was simply on vacation in Australia, so she decided to take the route of checking passenger lists for incoming flights. Again there was nothing. He hadn't entered the UK, not under his own name. She hoped he wasn't dead already.

Mouse walked down to the summerhouse carrying the file Doris had prepared with everything she had been able to find out about Craig Adams, and her laptop.

He was only twenty-two when he died. What on earth had he done so early on in his life to upset somebody so much they had shot him, she mused, her tongue sticking out between her teeth as she dropped deeply into her thoughts.

He lived in Bakewell with his mother Sally, father not on the scene. There was an address, but it was the house he had lived at in 2002, so it was doubtful that Sally Adams would still be there.

Mouse opened her laptop, and a minute later was checking the electoral role. Sally Adams was still at the same address. Mouse would talk to Kat, persuade her to drive them there, but felt it would be better to leave Nan at home; she would be safe with Leon.

She pulled the photograph of his headstone towards her and studied it. It told her nothing really, but she just felt a sense of... something as she looked at it. Okay, so he had probably become involved with the wrong people, but did he have to die? And something would have died in Sally Adams with her son's death. He hadn't had any siblings at the time of his murder, and Mouse doubted any would have followed.

With the file put tidily back in place – Doris's words of *keep it in the right order* rang out clearly in Mouse's mind – she sat back in the chair and closed her eyes for a moment.

Kat appeared in the doorway carrying two cups of coffee.

'Where's Nan?'

'I've just taken her a coffee. She's up in her bedroom. She looked a bit tired, but she's on her computer so I didn't ask what she was doing. I probably wouldn't have understood,' she added with a grin.

'Then shall we nip to Bakewell? I was going to suggest going Saturday and leaving Leon to keep an eye on Nan, but if she's working in her room we could go now.'

'What for?'

'To see a lady called Sally Adams, Craig Adams's mother. I'm positive that whatever binds these eight people together, it's connected with Craig Adams's death, and maybe if we can talk to his mother she'll be able to help, especially if we push the idea of her finally finding out who killed him.'

'Finish your coffee and we'll tell Nan, then go. He died fifteen years ago, it's a bit of a stretch to think his mother will still be there.'

'According to the electoral roll, she's still there,' Mouse confirmed. 'I checked just a minute ago.'

Kat looked at her under lowered lids. 'I should know better by now than to query it, shouldn't I?'

Bakewell was busy, as always. It's beauty, especially by the river, drew many visitors every day, and Mouse decided Kat was blessed to only live six miles away from such an awesome place.

'I love it here, it's got everything,' Mouse said. 'Loads of shops that aren't phone shops, craft shops, the riverside, the ducks, amazing place.'

'Then maybe this is where you need to be looking for a house to buy. It's a cracking place, and the Monday market is superb. Busy little town every day though, not just market day. Have you given any thought to what you want to do?'

'Not yet, something will happen that will tell me what to do next.' Mouse nodded, as if agreeing with herself.

Kat pulled up outside a small, stone-built terraced house; the bright yellow curtains both upstairs and downstairs gave it an air of being a much-loved house. She glanced at Mouse. 'This is the address. What do we say?'

'I think we tell the truth. We're investigating Craig Adams's death, and we're looking for his mother. We'll see what she says after that. We can't let on we know she still lives here.'

They got out of the car, and Kat checked her clerical collar was on straight. She led the way up the path and knocked on the door.

There was no answer, and so Mouse knocked again.

They saw movement of a yellow curtain, and waited patiently. Eventually the door was opened and a woman of around sixty spoke through the gap afforded by the chain being on.

'Yes?'

Kat hesitated. 'I'm sorry to trouble you, but we're looking for a lady who lived here at one time, a Mrs Sally Adams.'

'Why?'

'We're investigating the death of her son, Craig Adams.' Kat held her breath.

The door closed and they heard the sound of the chain being removed. This time the door opened fully.

'Are you police? You're wearing a dog collar.'

Kat smiled. 'No we're not police. My name is Katerina, Kat for short, and I'm the deacon at Eyam church. This is my friend Beth.' Kat removed her ID badge from around her neck and showed it to the lady.

She examined it briefly, then handed it back. 'I'm Sally Adams,' she said. 'You'd better come in.'

'Can I offer you a drink?' Sally had led them through to the kitchen, and indicated that they were to sit at the table. The oven was on, and it seemed she was baking. 'I'm sorry to bring you in here but I'm baking for a cake sale, and these are nearly ready to come out.'

'No problem,' Kat said. 'And I'm sure we could manage to drink a cup of tea,' she added with a smile.

Sally flicked the kettle switch, and joined them at the table. 'What do you mean when you say you're investigating Craig's murder? You're not the police.'

'No, we're kind of private investigators,' Mouse said.

'Okay. I'm asking because I had the police here yesterday hashing everything up again. A DI Marsden. She was nice, but I'm not convinced they'll solve it any more than they solved it the first time they had a go. I lost my only son, and nobody's paid for it.'

'Not yet,' Mouse said with confidence. 'I went to his grave, pulled up a few weeds, gave it a bit of a tidy up, and told him we'd sort it out. And we will. Starting with a chat with you. We don't want to know where he was on that last day, at least not from you, because he was an adult and I imagine you wouldn't know.'

Sally paused. 'No, you're right, of course. I didn't know. He came home at lunchtime, which was a bit unusual, and that was the last time I saw him alive.'

'What was he like, your Craig?' Kat asked gently.

'Primarily, he was kind. He would help the neighbours, go shopping for them, mow their lawns, that sort of thing, and I always felt I'd brought him up right, even if I did have to do it on my own. His father died just after he was born, an accident at work. He was doing some overtime because we were saving for a holiday, and he was on his own in the factory when some steel pipes rolled. He was crushed, died immediately so they told me.'

'I'm so sorry,' Kat said.

'Thank you. It's why Craig is buried in Eyam churchyard; his father is there, because he came from Eyam. When I die I will go in the same plot as Craig. His father's plot is owned by his family. They insisted he be buried there, and I didn't have the gumption or the strength to argue.'

'And you've never married anyone else?'

Mouse would have applauded Kat if she could have; she had a fantastic way of empathising, and Sally Adams was responding.

'No, never loved anyone else. Craig was enough for me. We had a lovely time until he reached sixteen or so. Then he seemed to change. Being a little bit naïve, I certainly didn't initially recognise his behaviour as being connected with drugs, but it seems it was. His post-mortem revealed cocaine and marijuana. I knew it would, and it did occur to me at the time that maybe it wouldn't be investigated as thoroughly as it might have been if drugs hadn't been present.'

Sally Adams stood as the kettle clicked off and made cups of tea. She handed out the drinks and re-joined Kat and Mouse at the table.

'This was what I did that last day with Craig,' she said, looking down at the cup she was cradling in her hands. 'I made us a sandwich and a drink and we talked.'

A timer pinged, and she jumped up, took out the tray of scones and switched off the oven. Once again she sat down.

'Was it a nice talk? One to remember?' Mouse asked, trying to imitate Kat's gentleness.

Sally picked up her cup and took a small sip before responding. 'No, it wasn't a nice talk. It was the point I realised the hope I held that he would stop with the drugs was never going to happen. He asked if I could give him two thousand pounds.'

Kat and Mouse remained silent, understanding that something important had just been said.

'He knew I had it, of course, I was paid compensation after my husband's death, which I received. We bought this house out of it, and the rest sat in the bank. Most of it is still there. I asked Craig what he needed the money for, and he said he owed it to somebody. I didn't argue, he was my son and he needed help. I went to the bank and withdrew the money. I pushed it with him to try to find out who he owed it to, and he told me he would tell me once it was paid. He stormed out of the house before we'd finished talking about it. I never saw him again.'

'What did the police say about this?'

'They don't know. Nobody's ever asked me. They knew he lived at home with me, but nobody ever said when was the last time you saw him. I suppose that's because I said but I only saw him this lunchtime, when they came to tell me they'd found his body, late that night. In my statement it says we had lunch together, but nothing about the conversation.'

'And you still don't know who he wanted the money for?' Kat reached across and touched Sally's hand. The woman had gone through hell; and still was, fifteen years later.

'I've an idea. I asked a couple of his friends the next day – they called round to say how sorry they were – but two days later they'd disappeared. One is in prison for murder, and I've never heard anything of the other since that one and only visit.'

'Would you be prepared to give us their names? I realise we probably won't be able to track them down, but it gives us the whole picture. And I promise you, Mrs Adams, we'll give this our best shot. You've been honest with us and you didn't need to be,' Kat said, and pushed her empty cup to one side.

'Of course I will. The one in prison is Don Truman, used to live in Bakewell but arson seems to have been his speciality and he burnt a shed down on an allotment not realising there were two teenage girls in it, smoking joints. They didn't get out. His best friend, and the one who has disappeared, is called Mark James.'

'And do the police know of their connection to Craig?' Mouse was beginning to think the police had done very little to find Craig's killer.

'Not from me. They may have found out from other sources, but nobody asked me, and I was shocked, mainly not in this world for a long time after I lost Craig, so I didn't really tell them anything. I didn't say much yesterday, but they did tell me Craig's death had cropped up in another investigation. It's brought it all back and I spent last night with it churning through my mind. Thank you for coming. I think I needed to talk.'

Kat passed her a card. 'You ever want to talk again, and not just about this, about anything, you give me a ring. Beth and I are accidental private investigators, we don't have a licence to do the job, but Beth is the girl who was shot when Anthony Jackson was killed in Eyam. What we're looking for is information that will lead us to her attacker, and Craig's murder was thrown up by our following another lead.'

Sally nodded. 'Then thank you. I hope you solve it all, it will be everything I have ever wanted.'

Kat and Mouse stood. 'Thank you, Mrs Adams…'

'It's Sally,' she said, and followed them to the door. 'If I remember anything else about that conversation, I promise I'll ring you. And Kat, give my regards to your mum. I've known her many years. We were in junior school together, although went to different secondary schools.'

'I will,' Kat said with a smile, and headed back to the car.

26

Doris was asleep when they returned home. Mouse quietly collected her laptop and headed back down to the kitchen.

'Nan's sleeping,' she said. 'I think taking that shrapnel out of her was a bit more debilitating than she let on.'

'Mouse, how old is she?' Kat asked.

'Okay, she's sixty-seven, but...'

'Exactly. She's sixty-seven. My mum is fifty-seven, and she nods off in the afternoon. I think it's more because they can, rather than because they need to. So let her sleep all she wants, she's earned it.'

'It scares me that she's getting older,' Mouse said thoughtfully. 'I'm not sure how I'd manage without her. She's not just my nan, she's my mentor, my... everything.'

'I can tell.'

Mouse switched on the laptop and sat at the kitchen table.

'You doing anything I don't need to know about?' Kat asked, not wanting an answer.

'I'm looking up getting a licence to be a private detective. I think this is why I'm with you. Your negotiating skills and my technical skills give us the perfect working relationship, and I think this is more than a possibility for us.'

'I wasn't looking for a job,' Kat smiled. 'I've got one.'

'You haven't, you don't get paid for it. That's not a job, that's a calling. It's different, and you can still do that while you're setting up our business. I'll finish my degree, because Business Studies will come in damn handy and will motivate me to get it, and we can advertise complete confidentiality. We need to be licenced, I think, so I'm doing the research, getting the forms and stuff… what do you think?'

'Talk to me when you have details. Have you really thought this through? And what do you think Leon would say?'

'Kat Rowe, be your own woman. Leon will love you no matter what. Tell him it's better than being an astronaut, your second choice of career,' she said with a grin. 'I'm serious, Kat, I think we're really close to finding out who the hell shot me, and I won't kill him because to be a PI you have to have an impeccable record. So you're saving me from prison by agreeing to this really.'

Kat walked over to the window. 'We would need premises, a shop of some sort…'

'Already thought about it. I need to find somewhere to live. I'm quite happy for that to be around here, but supposing I buy a shop with a flat above it. When the business starts to make money I can rent the shop to the business, but until then it's peppercorn.'

'And Nan? What do you think she'll say?'

Mouse was quiet.

'She'll say it's crazy, we know nothing, and it's dangerous,' Kat said. 'And she'll be right, but bloody hell, it's exciting.'

'You'll do it?'

Kat walked back from the window, her hand held out. She shook Mouse's hand. 'Of course, partner. We need full details though, and I won't lose Leon through this. If it looks as though I might, I will have to pull out.'

Mouse's smile lit up her face. 'You were the first one to suggest this, you know, right here, in this room. My memory serves me well.'

'Mouse, if there's one thing I've learnt about you, it's not your phenomenal memory that's going to be a major help in our business, it's the black belt.'

Neither of them noticed Doris leaning against the door jamb. They did, however, hear her.

'It's a brilliant idea,' she said. 'I won't need a job with DI Marsden, I can have one with you. I know I don't have a black belt, mine's only brown, but I'll be back to full fighting fitness when my leg and arm are working properly again.'

Kat laughed. 'Hi, Nan, you heard all of that?'

'Enough.'

Kat and Mouse exchanged a glance. 'You think it's feasible?' Kat asked. 'It's not just some airy-fairy thing Mouse thought up?'

'I think it's logical, clever, tailor-made for you two, and I'll be your receptionist, won't I? I don't want paying, just want to be involved, to keep an eye on you. I can do lots of the research stuff from the office, while you two are out and about.'

'You sure? You're sixty-seven, and retired. Why would you want a new career at your age? You should be settling down.' Mouse put her arm around Doris's shoulder.

'I want a new career because I'm sixty-seven, retired and bored. These last couple of weeks have brought me back to life. Now do you want my brown belt skills or not?'

'Is she serious,' Kat asked. 'She has a brown belt?'

'Oh, she's serious alright,' Mouse said. 'The only reason she doesn't have a black belt is because she won't do the grade.'

'I feel inadequate,' Kat moaned.

'You are,' Doris said with a smile, 'but Mouse and I will soon sort you out. We'll get you into a class with five-year-olds aiming for their white belt, you'll be fine.'

Kat shivered. 'No thanks. I'll stick to prayer as my skill. The only thing I will say is that you have no financial stake in this, Nan, because if it doesn't work, I don't want you losing anything. This will be a fifty-fifty business for Mouse and me, equal partners. And if you insist on not being paid, all car expenses will be covered by us. Understood?'

Doris nodded as she thought that over. 'Okay, understood.'

After much discussion, Doris agreed that as she was a retired old lady, albeit one with a brown belt in karate, she would take on the task of finding out the pros and cons of her two girls making what they were doing more official, and booking them on to any courses that might be going. She would sort out the licensing, and begin to look for premises that would incorporate a flat upstairs.

In return, Kat and Mouse had to go step up a notch and find a murderer.

Easy.

27

Peter Swift was surprised to see the lady vicar, but actually quite pleased.

'Hello,' he said with a smile. 'They let you in then?'

Kat returned the smile. 'They did indeed. He checked my ID, and here I am. I just thought I would see if there's anything you need, and if you're a practising Christian I can offer you communion.'

'I received communion last Sunday,' he said. 'So, thank you, no. I take it with my partner every week, so I'll wait until we're back in our own church, even if he has to carry me.'

Kat nodded. 'Anyway, my name's Katerina, Kat for short, and here's my card. If you need to talk, or need anything, I'm available on that number.' She handed her card to him and he placed it on his locker.

'You've broken your leg?'

He touched the cast. 'I certainly have, so prayers would be appreciated. I would hate this to end my career prematurely, but I am nearly thirty-one...'

She pretended to be unknowing. 'Ending your career at thirty-one? I don't understand.'

'I'm a footballer, Kat. And the fracture's pretty bad. I had a car accident, although the police think it maybe wasn't so accidental, this tumble down a mountain side. I was blinded by a laser beam.'

'Oh, no! How awful. Who would want to do that?'

'Somebody who wants me dead, presumably. Hence the policeman sitting outside my door.'

'And you don't know anyone who wants you dead?'

'Maybe the Arsenal goalkeeper, I scored last week. I've never known a goalie want to kill somebody before though,' he joked.

'So nobody from your past, maybe?' Kat knew she had to tread carefully.

'Not that I can think of.' His eyes stopped smiling.

She changed her tone. 'Then let's hope they find whoever did this awful thing. Is it just your leg that's injured?'

'I took a blow to the head that knocked me out for a while. In fact, I think that's the reason I'm still in here; they've sorted the leg, just need to keep an eye on my head. Kat, will you ask your congregation to pray for me? Which is your church?'

'St Lawrence, in Eyam. And of course I will. We pray for all the patients I visit in any of the hospitals.'

'So I'm not the only one?' Suddenly she knew she needed to leave.

'No, I'm moving down the corridor now.' She stood. 'Take care, Peter. Stoke needs you.'

She moved towards the door and he picked up her card.

'Kat,' he said, reading her name, 'you knew I played for Stoke?'

'Not until you said you'd scored against Arsenal. I'm an Arsenal supporter,' she lied.

'And your surname is Rowe? Are you married?'

'I am. Don't forget, if you need anything, call that number,' and she slipped out of the door, said goodbye to the officer and left the hospital.

Peter Swift followed her figure as she quickly left the room; he was deep in thought. He picked up his phone and rang Michael Damms.

'Michael? Can you talk?'

'I can. You okay, pal?'

'No. It seems it was attempted murder. Somebody shone a bloody laser beam into my eyes, blinded me. I was lucky to survive. The thing is, that DI thinks Oliver died the same way. There was nothing on the road the night he died, and she thinks the same thing happened to him.'

'Stop panicking. Caroline and Sarah are in safe houses, and I've got police cars running round here like there's no tomorrow. I told them I was staying put. You and Isla have got the entire police force on high alert, I think.'

'For God's sake, don't get blasé about it, Michael. Go to a safe house, tell that DI Marsden that you've changed your mind. We may have to start talking before that murdering bastard Leon Rowe kills any more of us.'

'We can't tell anybody. We'll always be looking over our shoulders for the rest of our lives if we do that. Do you think Leon Rowe in prison is any less dangerous than Leon Rowe in his bloody chemist shops? If we talk, Peter, we'll all be dead within a year.'

'As opposed to six months, you mean? Can't you see he's working through all of us? He started with Oliver, it now appears, then Anthony, Isla, me – that's four of us targeted already, and three are dead.'

'You can't say anything without agreement from Caroline and Keith. And me. We promised.'

Peter groaned. 'I know, but we never expected this. I'll bite my tongue for the moment, but there's something we've not talked about. Who told him? And why? Somebody's talked, Michael, and there were only seven of us that knew, because Sarah had already left by then. So who broke our promise?'

'That had occurred to me,' Michael conceded. 'And the only one I'm sure didn't talk is me. But somehow he's found out, and somehow he knows all our names. For fifteen years or so we've been safe, and now…'

'And now we're not. If we tell the police, where does that leave us? Criminal charges because we didn't say anything at the time? Or possibly now, 'cos we've not said anything even though our friends are dying.'

'I imagine there would be charges of some sort but a good solicitor would sort it. But it's not about that, Peter, it's about a promise we made. We seem to be okay for the moment, people are in safe houses, you're in hospital and presumably guarded, and I have… my own security.' Michael held up a thumb to Jack Mitchell; he had called Jack in as protection, after being forced to explain why he couldn't go into work at the present time.

'Okay, we'll wait,' Peter said, 'but if anyone else is injured or killed, I'm straight on the phone to this DI, whether we made a promise or not.'

'Speaking of being injured, how are you?' Michael finally got around to the enforced part of the conversation.

'I'm fine. On enough painkillers to floor a baby kangaroo, but getting there. Speak to you soon, stay safe, Michael.'

'You too, pal,' Michael said, and disconnected.

Shit, Peter thought, as he cleared the call, *I didn't mention this bloody vicar woman's surname.*

Kat walked quickly through the hospital, aware that there had been a change in Peter Swift's attitude. She didn't know why, and she hadn't wanted him alerting the policeman outside the door, so she thanked God for the bit of information that she'd managed to glean from him and left. The pale green painted corridors seemed to stretch forever, and she breathed a sigh of relief as she exited the automatic doors of the Huntsman building. She took out her phone and rang Mouse.

'Mouse, can you hear me?'

'Roger.'

'Who's Roger? Anyway, I've just spoken to Peter Swift. He was blinded by a laser beam, which could very easily be what caused Oliver Merchant's death. Luckily Peter has survived.'

'Roger.'

'Mouse, for Heaven's sake, I'm not on a two-way radio.'

'You coming home?' Kat heard the laughter in Mouse's voice.

'Roger.'

She grinned as she climbed into her car, hoping that Mouse had managed to track down Caroline Boldock who seemed to have vanished.

Much to Kat's surprise, Mouse had managed to track down Caroline, in a not very useful sort of way.

It seemed that Caroline wasn't allowed to answer her phone, so she had slipped it into her pocket, gone to the toilet and texted Mouse.

Mouse handed her phone to Kat, and Kat clicked on the message.

Hi Beth. Sorry can't speak. In a police safe house. Three people dead and they scared it will happen to me. Will contact when they let me out.

Kat laughed. 'Short and sweet. She doesn't sound too bothered, does she?'

'I don't know her all that well, but she is a little bit scatter-brained. Clever though. I would have thought she would have recognised it's a serious situation. Depends how much the police have told her, I suppose. And Peter Swift? How did you get on with him?'

'Fine, until I asked him if he'd upset anybody in his past. Then he shut down, so I got out as fast as I could. I left my card with him, and came back here. Where's Nan?'

'Working upstairs. Leon called in to collect his suit, said he's off to London, might be home, might not, and he'll ring you later. He asked where you were, so I said you'd some church business to see to.'

'Maybe an early night then. I don't feel too well, got a sore throat and that's not good when I've a sermon to deliver tomorrow. I'm going to nip down to the village to Neil, get him to tell me what I need. Do you want anything bringing back?'

Mouse shook her head. 'No, I'm fine thanks. Drive carefully.'

Kat picked up the car keys she'd only just put on the table, grumbling to herself that she should have called in to the village on the way back, instead of having to go out again. She met Doris at the bottom of the stairs and gave her a kiss.

'You okay? I'm nipping down to the pharmacy if you need anything.'

'No, nothing I can think of. Can we all have a talk when you get back?' She waved a file at Kat. 'I've got loads of information we need to go through if you're both serious about this.'

Kat laughed. 'Oh, we're serious about it. Can't promise to talk, got a rotten sore throat, but just give me half an hour to go get something for it, and I'll be with you.'

'Open your mouth.' Neil pressed Kat's tongue down with the depressor. 'Ouch, that looks sore. How long have you been like this?'

'About three days. It's not getting any better though, and I'm giving the sermon tomorrow.'

'You need an antibiotic. And it'll be at least two days before you can see a doctor.' He looked at her, a troubled expression on his face. 'I'm going to give you a course of antibiotics. Throat sweets aren't going to have any healing effect on it, although they might soothe it a little to get you through your church service tomorrow. The first dose needs to be a double one, to kick-start the course, then it's two tablets every six hours. Drink plenty of fluids, and I don't mean wine, Katerina Rowe,' he said smiling. 'You'll soon start to feel better. Wait here.'

He disappeared into the back of the shop and returned with a bag with the medication, along with some throat sweets. 'Don't go mad with the throat sweets, they're strong but they're good.'

She thanked him and left the shop. She paused with her key in her hand, ready to unlock the car, and stared across the road at the empty shop that had been vacant for months, ever since the craft shop had closed its doors for the last time. The sign outside said it was for sale or to let, shop and flat. Enquiries were to be directed to an estate agent, and she took out her phone and photographed the hoarding.

Driving away, Kat didn't notice Neil pick up his phone.

'Morning, boss. I've just had Kat in, and I've given her some antibiotics. She's a hell of a sore throat.'

There was a pause.

'No, she was alone.'

Neil put down the receiver and stared out of the window. He hated spying on Kat, she always seemed such a lovely person, and yet Leon insisted on knowing her every move. The hold that Leon had on him meant that he had to comply, but it didn't sit easy with him. He glanced at his watch. Five minutes to go and he could head off home until Monday morning.

Unless the boss needed him, of course.

Kat swallowed the four tablets, grimacing as she did so. They felt like horse tablets going down her throat, it was so sore. She also took a couple of paracetamol, hoping they might deaden the pain a little.

Doris and Mouse had papers spread all over the table, and Doris had produced a complicated spreadsheet that had Kat's eyes wide open.

'Wow,' she said, 'couldn't you sleep?'

Doris laughed. 'It's easy peasy when you know how. And you will know how. I was going to book you on a course for IT, but then I changed my mind. You're going to need a certain amount of knowledge, Kat, and all it will take is for you not to be scared of it. So what I've decided is that I am going to write a course, and I'll work with you. However, it will be at set times, and you will be there, no excuses, until you've passed and received my certificate. Understood?'

If Kat's throat hadn't been so sore, she would have gulped. 'Yes,' she acknowledged.

'It will only be basic IT, nothing too complicated, and we'll have lessons twice a week, two hours each time, then it's not overfacing you. And you can work through the booklet under your own steam, but I will be there with you to answer any questions. You won't become a hacker, I promise, but you'll be able to do more than type your sermons.'

'Be afraid, be very afraid,' Mouse whispered, and Kat saw the grin on her friend's face.

'I am,' she responded.

'Okay,' Doris continued. 'That's out of the way. There are courses you will both need to take. The Institute of Professional Investigators runs an IPI Level 3 Professional Investigators Course, so you're both booked on to it. It's an online course, extremely comprehensive, and will give you everything you need to begin your new careers. Kat, it's time to tell Leon.'

Kat nodded. 'I know. He'll be a little surprised to say the least. But we haven't sorted any finances out yet, surely there's a cost to these courses?'

'There's no cost to your IT course, silly girl, and I've paid for the other one. When the business is making money, you can pay me back.'

'Nan, how much have you paid out?' Mouse raised her eyebrows.

'I'll send you my bill.'

Mouse smiled and blew her a kiss.

'We may have to sort some finances out sooner than we think,' Kat said, and opened the photographs on her phone. She passed it first to Mouse.

'It's a shop in the village, been empty for months so I don't know how good it is inside. You can't tell, because the windows have been whitewashed. However, as you can see from the noticeboard, it has a flat upstairs. Would it be worth a look?'

Mouse looked, passed the phone to Doris, and grinned.

'It'll be bloody perfect, Katerina Rowe. And if it's scruffy inside, we'll send Nan in with a bucket and mop. She'll soon put it to rights. First thing Monday morning, I'll give this estate agent a ring, arrange for a viewing, and we can take it from there. I don't imagine it'll be spectacular inside, but we can sort it.'

'I'll buy a new bucket and mop,' Doris said, and handed the phone back to Kat.

28

Leon sat in his car on the M25 and knew he wouldn't be going home that night. He had managed to change the meeting time from two to four o'clock, but the stationary traffic made him think that even that was being optimistic, and he should have said five.

He never enjoyed being away from Kat, although since the arrival of Beth and Doris he felt a little easier knowing she wasn't alone with only a cat for company. He dialled her phone and she answered quickly. Her voice was sultry, quirky.

'Hi, babes. What's wrong with your voice?'

'Sore throat. I've been to see Neil, and he's given me some antibiotics. I'll be okay in a couple of days. My two nurses are looking after me.'

'I thought the idea was that you were looking after them.'

'Role reversal.' She laughed.

'You're sure you're okay? I'm not going to get back tonight, I'm stuck on this blessed M25, not moving. I've had to change the time of what I expected to be a short meeting, but now it's not starting until five, so I'll book in to the Hilton as usual. Ring me if you need me though, won't you?'

She could hear the concern in his voice.

'I'll be fine, honestly. I'll have an early night, with a hot toddy. I'm more concerned that I might not have a voice for tomorrow – I'm taking the service.'

'Okay,' he said. 'I'll not ring you again tonight, I don't want to risk waking you. I'll give you a call tomorrow morning before you go to church. I love you, Kat, so take care. And do what the nurses say.'

'I will, I promise. Love you too, Leon. Speak tomorrow.'

She disconnected, and turned her attention back to the paperwork on the table.

'So is that it? One course and we've cracked it?'

Doris smiled. 'Not quite. There's a foundation course to complete first, before you go on to the level 3 one, so there's plenty to keep you occupied. I've applied for licences for both of you, but if I find I need one as well, I'll apply for one at that point. I don't want to intrude, but we have no idea how busy you're going to be, and we don't want to turn work away for the sake of not having enough operatives. I accept my limitations, before you two say anything about my age, but there's nothing wrong with my brain, I drive, and when I haven't got bits of shrapnel in me, I walk. And what's even more important, I have a lifetime of knowledge. You two have the same, but your two lifetimes don't even add up to my one. All I'm saying is don't dismiss my value.'

Mouse and Kat looked at each other and burst out laughing.

'As if we'd dare,' Mouse said.

'You've got the position, whatever it is,' Kat said, 'and write your own job description.'

Doris handed out paperwork, explaining what each piece was, and slowly it dawned on Kat and Mouse that it wasn't simply a case of sitting in an office and waiting for someone to walk through the door asking them to follow an errant husband they suspected of playing away. There was a lot more to it than that.

They read through everything, then handed it all back to Doris to put in the file.

'You can start the IT course in two weeks, Kat,' Doris said, without looking up. She missed the fear that flashed across Kat's face.

'Oh, jolly good,' Kat said faintly.

Doris looked over the top of her glasses. 'Katerina Rowe, are you being sarcastic?'

'No,' she said, 'it's my voice that's gone a bit wobbly.'

Tessa Marsden sat at her desk, once again viewing the CCTV from outside Steel, focusing on the taxi driver's face, but could still tell nothing from it. She took it back to watch again, but this time she caught the action of the bouncer as he called for the taxi for the couple, Beth Walters by his side, Anthony Jackson to the other side of her.

She pulled the statements on to her screen, and found the man's words where he had said very little, just that he had called one of their dedicated taxis from around the corner to take Mr Jackson and his partner to Eyam.

Dedicated taxis. She understood that the Sheffield nightclubs had taxis on standby, but why had this particular taxi, driven by a murderer, turned up at exactly the right moment to get Jackson and Walters?

Who did that bouncer contact? Was he following instructions? She looked at the bouncer's name – Billy Hart – and decided there was maybe something to be followed here.

'Dave, Claire, go and bring Billy Hart in, will you?'

Dave Irwin looked up from his screen. 'Sure, boss. Who?'

'Exactly,' she said, leaning on her office door jamb. 'Somebody insignificant, who may actually know something significant he's neglected to tell us. Bring him in, put him in that scruffy interview room and leave him. Then come and find me. He's the bouncer who called the taxi with the murderer in it. Let's see what we can shake out of him.'

Tessa and Hannah stood looking into the interview room watching Billy Hart squirm uncomfortably on the plywood chair. It seemed he had been in bed when Dave and Claire arrived, and he had been extremely vitriolic towards them, so Claire had handcuffed him, before putting him in the back of the car.

He was quiet now, handcuffs removed making it easier for him to chew his nails.

'Let's go and have a cup of tea, Hannah,' Tessa said. 'Then we'll come and talk to Mr Hart, see if we can't get him to remember how he got that particular taxi to arrive at the Steel entrance that night.'

Hannah smiled. 'Okay, boss. Think he'll want one?'

'Probably. He's not getting one though. I think he didn't tell us everything he could have done, so no drinks until he does.'

They high fived, and walked to the canteen.

Half an hour later, they were preparing to go in the interview room. Hart looked even more uncomfortable.

They opened the door, and Hannah switched on the recording equipment. Marsden listed everyone present and the time, then they sat, facing the burly man.

'Mr Hart, you were on duty at Steel the night of the murder of Anthony Jackson and the attempted murder of Bethan Walters. Is that correct?'

Hart nodded.

'Speak for the benefit of the tape please, Mr Hart.'

'Yes.'

'Please take us through what happened from them coming out of the nightclub. Leave nothing out, Mr Hart.'

'Do I need a solicitor?'

'Do you? Have you done something wrong?' Marsden stared at him, her eyes like flint.

'No, nowt,' he muttered.

'Then answer our questions and you can go home.'

He grunted.

'Let's start with what time they left Steel.'

'I think it was around midnight. It must have been just before because midnight I swapped for the inside job.'

'Inside job?'

'Yeah. We have one security in the foyer, just stands in a corner and observes, two outside checking bags, checking ID cards, stopping them if they're already high on either drugs or drinks, that sort of thing, and one security round the corner at the taxi rank making sure everything's okay there. We swap positions at certain times, and it was my turn to stand in the foyer at midnight.'

'Did you know Anthony Jackson?'

Hart hesitated. 'Yeah.'

'How?'

'He's been to the club before. He brought a load of his friends that night, but he left before any of the others did.'

'So now we get to your part in this.' Tessa gave a small smile. 'Quite a large part as it turns out, considering that the driver of the taxi murdered Mr Jackson.'

'I've given my statement once,' he responded, anger showing in his face.

'Mr Hart, would you rather we left this until tomorrow, give you time to think about what really happened?' Marsden smiled again.

'Yeah,' Billy said, and stood up.

'Very well. PC Irwin, will you take Mr Hart down to the cells please?'

Dave Irwin moved away from the wall that had been supporting his not inconsiderable frame, and headed towards Hart.

'Whoa!' Hart said, panic showing in his eyes. 'I need to go home.'

'Not till you've given an amended statement, Mr Hart. This time with truth in it.'

He sat down, and Dave Irwin retreated back to his original position.

'We're carrying on?'

Billy Hart nodded.

'Okay. Who came out first?'

'I've already told you this. Her, the bird. I didn't know she was with Jackson until he joined her. I jumped to it then.'

'Why? You scared of him?'

'No. I'd been told…'

'Been told what?'

'I'd been told if he wanted a taxi to use a different band on the walkie talkie to order it.' His face blanched as if he couldn't believe he was saying the words telling of the action that had condemned Anthony Jackson to death.

'And if you'd been inside? How would that have worked?'

'I was told to follow him outside and make sure I was the one ordering a taxi, because I was the only one with the band number. And I was told I couldn't go off duty until Anthony Jackson had left that club.'

'You didn't query any of this?'

He shrugged. 'Nah, things like this happen regular like, because we get quite a few celebrities in the club and they usually have taxis organised. It's not the first time I've had to call on a different band. Didn't think anything of it.'

'So here's the killer question, Mr Hart. Who told you?'

'I have no idea. It was a text.'

She held out her hand. 'Phone please.'

He reached into his jacket pocket and took out an iPhone; a diagonal crack bisected the screen.

'Is the text still on it?'

He shrugged again.

Tessa went into settings and made a note of the phone number. She handed it to Hannah. 'Get this to the tech boys please, PC Granger, and tell them I want a log of both calls made and received, plus texts. Unless you've remembered, Mr Hart?'

'Didn't think about it, it was just a number, but that's not new either. Celebs have their own security, just assumed it was from somebody on Jackson's payroll.'

'We'll give you a receipt for this.' She put the phone in an evidence bag and handed it to Hannah, who left the room. 'You can have it back in a couple of days, if we don't need it for the court case.'

'Eh? What court case?'

'This is a murder investigation, Mr Hart. Concentrate please, we've a lot to get through.'

Billy rubbed his sleeve along his forehead, the fabric absorbing the sweat.

'So, Ms Walters came out first. How long was it before Mr Jackson joined her?'

'Not long. I'd just finished admiring her boobs, to be honest, when he appeared, so maybe thirty seconds to a minute. I asked him if he needed a cab and he said he did. I called on the bandwidth I'd been given, and somebody said *okay*. Before you ask, I didn't recognise the voice. I walked down the steps with them, the black cab came round the corner within seconds of me making that call, and he helped her in. Nice legs. Then he got in, I shut the door, and they went.'

'Okay, big question coming up, Mr Hart. Did you recognise either the driver or the vehicle?'

'No to the driver, but I can't say I looked at him, 'cos she'd got a nice arse as well as cracking long legs. But the cab... Give me a minute.'

He closed his eyes, and Tessa said nothing. He appeared to be cooperating, which was more than she could have expected at the start. Hannah came back into the room, and nodded at Tessa's eyebrows raised in query. Tessa spoke for the tape, indicating Hannah's return, and still Billy's eyes were closed.

'I know what it was,' he said slowly and opened both eyes. It was only then that Tessa realised one was blue and one was green.

'Sorry about that, DI Marsden, I had to walk through it in my mind till I got to the bit I needed. On the door that I opened, there was a really deep scratch, about a foot long. It looked too deep for a key to have done it, more like a screwdriver. Nearside back door, it was.'

'You're sure?'

He nodded. 'I am. Sorry, didn't think about it before.'

'Okay, Billy,' Tessa said. 'Thank you for your cooperation. I'm going to leave you with PC Granger and PC Irwin, and once you've signed your statement, you can go. Don't go on holiday without letting us know, will you. And if you remember anything else, contact me immediately. That gorgeous girl you ogled almost died that night, and Anthony Jackson had his head blown off. Consider that, will you.'

She logged herself out of the room and switched off the recording.

'Ray, I need a list of all taxi firms within a forty mile radius of Eyam. I want a team putting together to visit them, and I expect every black cab to be checked for a scratch on the nearside back door.'

'Yes, boss. It paid off bringing Billy Hart in?'

'It did. He went into a sort of trance, and when he woke up he told us about the scratch,' she said with a smile. 'Do you know he's got odd eyes? One blue and one green. Quite striking really.'

'I've never felt the need to stare into Billy Hart's eyes. He once stopped me going into Steel, said I was drunk.'

'And were you?'

'Yeah, but…'

'But nothing.' Tessa laughed. 'The man was doing his job. We're having his phone checked. I don't expect it to be of any use, because I think the phone the text was sent from will prove to be a throwaway one. We've still to check it but I'm not holding my breath. I think this scratch could be the clue we've been looking for. And I also think this cab is kept specifically for when somebody needs a vehicle that blends into the background and nobody takes any notice of it. I'm positive it's not used as an ordinary cab, picking up customers. But it's got to be garaged somewhere, and where better than with a fleet of black cabs. Let's go find the damn thing.'

29

Brian looked up, fear etched on his face, as the office door slammed opened and crashed into the wall behind it. The last time someone had entered his office in that manner, they'd been holding a gun. It had taken some persuasive talk to make the young lad put it down, but when he had laid it on the desk he had burst into tears. The lad's dad had been found dead, and he had been told Brian King was behind it. That young man now worked for the company.

This time the entrant was Terry Vincent, trying manfully to balance a huge box, and failing miserably at stopping the door from crashing inwards.

'Sorry, Brian,' he panted, 'but there's news, and I didn't want to leave this in the motor.'

'What news, and what's in the bloody box? It's not even eight o'clock yet, for Christ's sake, and you're already bringing me trouble.' He was covering his fear with words.

Terry opened one of the box flaps, and took out a bag of white powder.

'Shit, Terry, not in this bloody office,' Brian groaned. 'Take it downstairs and get Ginger to book it in and secure it. Where's it from?'

'Jackson's place. Without him there, it's falling apart. He ran it on his own, and now there's nobody taking charge, so my contact said. I turned up and bought this for £500. Bargain, I reckon.' Terry's Yorkshire accent grew stronger as he shared his news and good fortune with his colleague.

'News? You said there's news. What about?'

'Oh, yeah. Some fuckin' jogger found that grave we buried George and Paddy in. I tell you, Bri, it's allus a bloody jogger or a dog walker that finds bodies. Anyway, the police have blocked roads off, and they're digging 'em up as we speak.'

Brian had turned a shade of grey that didn't suit him at all.

'You said they'd never re-surface,' he finally managed to say.

'I know.'

'Tell me there's nothing on them that could lead anybody to here.'

'Nah, we'll be fine.'

'Terry, we'd better be fine. I don't doubt Leon's heard about this by now—'

The door crashed open for the second time, and Leon Rowe strode in.

'What the fuck!' he roared. 'Have you heard? It's all over the local news.'

Brian nodded. 'Two minutes ago.'

Leon turned to face Terry. 'If that bloody DI turns up asking questions of me again, I'll sell you down the river, Terry. Now get out of my sight.'

Terry picked up the huge box of drugs, and edged out of the door. Brian stared at Leon; he'd never seen him so angry. He was normally cool and calculating even under extreme pressure, but this was something else.

'For fuck's sake, Brian, I could do without this. I've enough on my plate at home without this little issue. The police are going to turn up here, or at the shop, because they'll track down who they worked for.'

'Leon, go home. Leave this with me. As far as the police are concerned, we're a respectable business. They can look at what they want, check what books they need to see, they'll find nothing. We can even say Paddy and George worked for us, officially on the books, and I can show proof of that. It's the other books that tell the full story. The police'll not see them. I'll tell them they just upped and left as far as we were concerned. Now go, and stay away. Stick to the shop, I'll manage here, and when they've been and gone I'll let you know. Trust me, everything is in order.'

'George's wife knew he worked here. She thinks he's run off with somebody else. She'll tell them he worked for Rowe's Pharmaceuticals.'

'That's fine. He did. What he did outside of work is nothing to do with us, and he clearly got in with some bad people. Maybe it's worth a suggestion that we were investigating them ourselves because we suspected them of removing stock. Go home so that I can calm down. At the moment it's obvious we're stressed, and I don't want them to see me like that.'

Leon stared at him, then nodded. 'I'll head back to the shop. Let me know after they've gone, and what Marsden's plans are next. I just know it'll be her who starts connecting dots on this.'

He held out his hand, and Brian clasped it. 'Thanks, Brian, I don't know what I'd do without you. Make sure we're clean, and she'll have to go away.'

Kat inserted the key into the lock. The door swung open easily and the old-fashioned bell above the door pinged. She hurried to the back of the shop and entered the code given to them by the estate agent.

'So far so good,' she said with a laugh, her voice throaty. It felt marginally better, and she blessed Neil for letting her have the tablets without a prescription. 'That could have been embarrassing if I'd got the code wrong.'

Doris and Mouse were already walking around, inspecting the amenities in the shop which were proving to be a little sparse.

'We'll need to get everything out and start from scratch,' Mouse said. 'You okay with a paintbrush, Kat?'

'I paint a lovely Picasso.' Kat laughed. 'For walls I tend to get a decorator in. I think we just get shopfitters, if it proves to be what we want. We'll need this front area for Nan, so that's going to need a swish new reception desk, and then the whole of the back area can have a stud wall erected, splitting it into two offices for Mouse and me. We'll get a couple of good desks – first impressions count and we need to impress clients. Maybe get two decent ones from the antique quarter. By then, of course, and according to Nan, I'll be able to do more than switch on my laptop.'

'You mean you'll be able to switch it off as well?' Mouse grinned. 'Kat, I think this is perfect.' She opened a small door and wrinkled her nose. 'It needs a new toilet and handbasin in here.'

The light in the shop space was tinged to a luminous grey quality by the whitewash that had been painted all over the front window courtesy of the previous incumbents.

Kat walked across and rubbed a little bit of it to give a clear six inch square of glass. 'We'll be able to wave at Leon and Neil,' she said. 'The pharmacy is straight across from here.'

'Headache tablets and throat sweets on tap then. This really is perfect. We'll have to take down the hoarding covering those two back windows, or we'll have no natural light in our offices, but we can make them secure. Security in here will be a priority, we could potentially have some files that could do damage in the wrong hands.'

'Nan? You haven't spoken.'

'I'm still trying to decide what colour chair I want.'

'You think this meets our needs?'

'Totally. It's much larger than I expected, and I think you'll both be surprised by how much space you get even splitting that back area into two. However, the real crunch is that flat upstairs. If that's no good for Mouse, then the shop is irrelevant. And I also think that although the property is up for sale or let, we should try for an initial six-month rental, followed by an option to purchase outright after that rental period. I think there'll be no problem getting business – I've already got the advertising schedule worked out – but after six months we'll know whether or not it's right for you two.'

'My god, she's a wise old bird, this nan of mine,' Mouse said, and kissed the much smaller woman on her head. 'Shall we go and look at the flat then?'

They exited the shop, locking it behind them, and then unlocked a red door at the side. They climbed the stairs and all three paused at the top.

'Wow.' Mouse spun around. 'This is fab.'

It was a huge room, an open-plan kitchen diner and lounge, with three doors leading off the main room.

The bathroom had been newly refurbished and, apart from a layer of dust, was immaculate. Both bedrooms were doubles and both had built-in wardrobes. They were of similar size, and the smile on Mouse's faced increased exponentially.

'I would have wanted this place even without the shop,' she said. 'Whoever lived here looked after it.'

'Hello?' A man's voice floated up from the bottom of the stairs.

'We're up here, Mr Smythe,' Kat called.

The estate agent joined them. 'Sorry I couldn't be with you earlier, but I'm free now. What do you think?'

'This is beautiful. Apart from a flick around with a duster, it's been well looked after.'

'That's because nobody has lived in it.' Carl Smythe smiled. 'When the previous owners gave up the tenancy, the flat was refurbished with a view to selling it as part of the whole property. The shop was left alone because there's no point refurbishing that as, for example, a bakery, if whoever buys it wants it for a fish and chip shop. So we concentrated on the flat. It's newly rewired and plumbed, new bathroom suite, the wardrobes are new – there was nothing in the bedrooms before. This large living area was initially a very tiny kitchen with a sizeable living/dining area, but we knocked down a wall and made it open plan.'

Mouse was even more impressed. 'I love it.'

'You've been in the shop?'

'Yes, we've already built walls in there.' Doris laughed. 'The whole thing is perfect. How would the owners feel about an initial six months' rental with an option to purchase after six months?'

'The owner is my father. I'll talk to him, but I know he's keen to sell as soon as possible. He doesn't want to die and leave issues for my brother and me that need to be dealt with. He's a bit old fashioned.'

'Okay, leave it,' Doris said. 'We'll work with the initial purchase plan, and get back to you by tomorrow, after we've discussed everything fully.'

'Then I'll leave you for now. Can you drop the keys at the office please. Take as long as you need, and don't forget to set the alarm as you go out.' He smiled at the three women and left them to walk around.

They returned to the shop and Doris took out a notepad. 'We need a list,' she said. 'I like lists.'

Kat looked through the square cleaned section of the window and saw that Leon's car was still at the pharmacy.

'Okay,' she said. 'It's time I spoke to Leon. I'll be back in half an hour or so, possibly divorced, but I'll be back. Then we'll return the keys and go for a coffee and a talk in the tea rooms. That sound good?'

They nodded, and she walked across the road to the pharmacy.

'What?' Leon felt angry that Kat's plans had reached the point of getting premises without his knowing anything about them. He was trying desperately to keep that anger hidden.

'We're a good team. We've done a lot of tracking with Mouse's attacker, and we have the capabilities. I believe this is what I've been looking for, and I also believe this is why I was meant to meet Mouse. And Nan. It won't take anything from my church work; I've made that very clear to both of them. As you know, God has always come first with me, and always will.'

'And what about the baby we've talked about? Where will that fit into your plans?'

'It will. I need a couple more years of you, and then we'll have our baby. I can become a silent partner, doing deskbound work when I get too big to move, and we'll manage. Doing this as a job,

Leon, doesn't mean I don't love you, you know. You're my world, but my world needs a little bit of readjustment right now, and I know this is it.'

'Come on then.' He picked up his coat. 'Let's go and have a look at this shop. I know a bit more about this subject than you do, and I have contacts for you for fittings. But it needs to be right in the first place. If it's too small, you can't make it bigger. Shops are what they are, in the main.'

He led her out of the back door of the pharmacy, and she couldn't help glancing back to where she had first seen Mouse.

Leon held the door open for Kat to enter before him. He smiled as he glanced up and saw the old-fashioned bell that tinkled as he had pushed open the door.

'Don't lose that,' he said. 'It's lovely. Ours is electronic across the road, soulless.'

He glanced around, taking everything in. 'It's big enough,' he finally conceded.

'We thought splitting this back area into two with a sound-proofed stud wall which would give us an office each for Kat and Mouse,' Doris explained. 'We don't expect cases to be about solving murders – this has been a steep learning curve finding out who killed Anthony and attacked Mouse – it will be more about following random husbands for evidence of adultery, chasing down missing persons, that sort of thing. Our list for our advertising campaign is quite comprehensive, and all above board.'

'Can we just take a step back there.' Leon smiled at the older woman. 'Finding out who killed Anthony and attacked Mouse?'

Doris shrugged. 'We're sure they've killed before, and we're even more convinced Anthony knew who had killed a young man who died some years ago. We'll soon have the answer. Then we go to DI Marsden with what we know, what we think we know, and what is indisputable. She can take it from there. All the recent murders are linked of course; they were all teenagers together, friends, and they've stayed friends. We found all this out, Leon.'

Leon felt as if he was having a day when his world was crumbling around him. Two bodies with a direct link to him, a wife heading off on an already agreed path that he knew nothing about, and now three women, all living with him, telling him they were within an inch of sending him to prison for life.

He said very little as they showed him around the flat, and he headed back to his own office sanctuary, leaving them to return the keys to Carl Smythe. Leon had given Doris the name of his shopfitters to add to her list, and as he sat back down at his desk, he poured a large glass of whisky. He needed it.

30

Tessa Marsden was having a bad day. The discovery of not one but two bodies in the extremely shallow grave in Ecclesall Woods had led to Sheffield police contacting her when one of the victims proved to have an Eyam address and the other lived in Bakewell.

George Reynolds' wife had seemed quite blasé about the fact that her husband's body had been found, and had presumed it was something to do with his job. And then, quite suddenly, she had begun to sob. It seemed she had thought he had left her for another woman but he had been too scared to tell her to her face.

'Mr Rowe stopped by to ask if I'd heard from him, and when I said no, he left me some money to help pay the rent and stuff.'

The figure of £10,000 had been somewhat surprising to Tessa, a little bit over the top for a missing employee, and from the Reynolds' house she had headed to Rowe Pharmaceuticals.

Brian King had been less than forthcoming; he confirmed George Reynolds had worked for the company, in the distribution department, but one day neither him nor Patrick 'Paddy' Halloran had turned up. No explanation, nothing. King said that Mr Rowe had been to see Mrs Reynolds, wanting to know if she had heard from George. He had been a valuable member of the team; not so much Paddy Halloran who could be a troublemaker.

When Marsden mentioned the payment of £10,000, Brian King had smiled.

'It would be out of his own pocket, DI Marsden. It certainly didn't go through the company books. But that's what Leon's like. The Reynolds had children, and that would have been the reason behind the money.'

'So do you know where Mr Lowe is?'

'When I spoke to him earlier, he was at the shop in Eyam. He'd been in Bakewell and Baslow earlier, but he generally finishes in Eyam. As you know, he lives in the village.'

She thanked him and left, then turned around and went back.

He was on the phone, and disconnected when he saw her framed in the doorway again. 'You forgot something?'

'Just one last question. Who would want to kill these two men? Any idea?'

'None whatsoever. I can understand a little bit that Paddy would maybe upset someone enough, but George... he was an alright bloke. Good home life, good work life. Intelligent, loyal – no, I've no idea.'

'And Craig Adams?'

'Who? That's two questions.'

'Craig Adams is a cold case we're investigating, but it's linked to everything that's happening in the Eyam and Bakewell areas. He was shot and thrown into the Wye in 2002. Do you know anything about that?'

'I can't even remember it happening. I would have been... twenty-one, twenty-two or so, and probably out having a good time every night at that age.'

'Craig Adams was the same age and in the same class at school as you and Leon Rowe. You still don't remember him?'

'That Craig Adams? Shit. I didn't know anything about it!'

Tessa nodded, and left his office. He wiped the sweat from his face, and picked up the phone.

Kat, Mouse and Doris ordered afternoon tea for three, and then stared in wonderment at the assortment of food that appeared before them.

'We'll not need to cook tonight,' Doris said with a laugh. 'There's enough here to feed a small army.'

'Tuck in,' Mouse said. 'My treat, no argument. I've had good news in that I need to go inspect the house as soon as possible;

they've finished three days earlier than they thought. Once I sign it off, I can get it on the market.'

They munched their way through the sandwiches without speaking much; it's hard to speak with a mouthful of chicken and grape sandwich, followed by cheese and egg, followed by Yorkshire ham. They slowed down a little with the jellies and strawberries, and really struggled with the scones and the truly exceptional cakes.

'If we don't fall asleep when we get home,' Kat said, 'I want to look at the Craig Adams file again. I'm convinced there's an answer somewhere in there for us, and now that I've got Leon's blessing, although a little half-hearted, it seems as though a weight has lifted and I can take on the world. I knew he wouldn't be ecstatic, but he actually took it quite well.'

They didn't fall asleep; Mouse and Doris went on their computers, and Kat utilised Doris's bed to spread out all the paperwork from the file on Craig Adams. Kat looked through the initial reports in the newspapers, when identification hadn't been completed, to the heartbreaking photograph of Sally outside her front door, tears on her cheeks, to newspaper reports showing the funeral of the young Derbyshire lad. There was a queue of mourners, and Kat stood to go to her own room to fetch a magnifying glass.

Settling back down, Kat studied every face in the long line, and gasped as she recognised two of them.

Mouse looked up. 'You okay?'

'I'm not sure. Just come here a minute.' She handed the magnifier to Mouse and pointed at the picture.

Mouse leaned forward. 'Shit.'

'Don't use that word, Mouse,' Doris said.

'Come here, Nan,' Mouse said. 'Look at this.'

Again the magnifier was employed, although Doris made no sound. She simply looked up at the other two, and said, 'It's Leon. A much younger Leon, but I imagine there weren't many black people around here back then. Did you recognise anybody else in the line, Kat?'

'Leon, and the man who runs his Sheffield operation, the distribution centre. Brian King. I don't think I would have recognised him from this picture, but because he's stood at Leon's side, I know it's him. What does this mean?'

'I'm not sure. If he knew Craig Adams, and he clearly did or he wouldn't be at his funeral, maybe he has information he doesn't realise he has. You have to pick your moment, but you have to ask him.'

'I know. I suppose I just don't like this suddenly being close to home.'

Kat sat in silence for a couple of minutes, then took out her phone. She scrolled through until she found the number that had only been in there for a few days, and rang Sally Adams.

Sally answered almost immediately. 'Hi, Kat.'

'Sally, just bear with me on this, and I'm sorry if this is upsetting you all over again.'

'It isn't. I've heard nothing further from the police, so I'm not daring to believe they'll solve this. You might though.'

'Why?' Kat could feel Mouse's and Doris's eyes on her.

'Because of who you are.'

'But I'm only a deacon.'

'I didn't mean that. It's who you're married to.'

'Leon? That's strange, because that's what I was ringing about. Was Craig friends with Leon and Brian King? I've seen the photograph in the newspaper of the funeral, and the long line of people who attended. Leon and Brian were there.'

'Of course they were there. I've got to go.' And she disconnected.

Kat stared at her phone, bewilderment on her face.

'You okay?' Mouse asked.

'Not sure. What am I missing here?'

She recapped her conversation with Sally to Doris and Mouse, feeling more troubled once she'd repeated it.

'Where did you meet Leon, Kat?' Doris was gentle in her questioning.

'At a church barbeque. He came with a friend, we were together all evening and the friend went home in a taxi. We sat in Leon's car for hours, just talking. I'd never met anybody like him. I think I was in love when I finally went home. We've never been apart since.'

'And did you know how he made his money? He's obviously very well off.'

'Yes, he has numerous shops scattered around Derbyshire, Nottinghamshire, that sort of area, all pharmacies. He runs the shops, or so I understand, attends assorted meetings with drug companies, and Brian King, who has been a lifelong friend, is his Distribution Manager at their place down Sheffield's East End. I've never been involved with his business. Maybe if I hadn't been so committed to my church life, I might have taken more of an interest, but we work well the way it is.'

Doris looked down at her hands. 'Stop me if this gets too much, Kat. There is a reason Sally Adams put that phone down on you. I think Craig Adams *did* tell his mother who the two thousand pounds was for, and I think it was either Leon or this Brian King.'

Kat couldn't speak.

'Then why didn't she say anything before?' Mouse asked, belligerence evident in her tone. 'Why didn't she tell the police when Craig's body was found?'

'Fear,' Doris said. 'I imagine she was all too aware of what they were capable of. Her son was dead. It's my guess that instead of paying the two thousand to Leon, he bought more drugs. Drug dealers don't do second chances, and this was probably Craig's second chance because he was a friend of theirs. They'd all been at school together. I don't know how we prove this, or even if Kat wants to prove it, but I'm pretty sure this is the right scenario.'

Kat felt breathless. She couldn't take in what she was hearing, yet somewhere in the back of her mind was the feeling that Doris was right. Leon a murderer? Did he still deal in drugs? She knew without any shadow of a doubt that he hadn't been involved in Mouse's attack and Anthony's death, so why would anybody think he was guilty of Craig's murder?

Tears filled her eyes, and she turned to the two women. 'He couldn't have been involved with Anthony's death. He was with me at the restaurant, then with me all night after we'd got back from the restaurant.'

'When people are murdered and it's pre-planned,' Mouse said gently, 'they can easily have paid someone to do it. They're just as guilty as whoever pulls the trigger or uses the knife. We need to know if Leon still supplies drugs, and we need to get into Rowe Pharmaceuticals' accounts, although I doubt they'll show anything. If he is dealing, there'll be a second set of books that aren't on any computer. They'll be handwritten. Kat, are you okay?'

'Of course I'm not bloody okay. The Leon I know isn't capable of this.'

'Then we need to prove he isn't. If he's as innocent as you believe, we'll find a way of proving it. Tell us about Brian King.' Mouse, like her nan, was treating Kat very gently, all too aware of the distress inside her.

'Brian is a lovely man. He has ginger hair, and the temperament that goes with it. He's completely loyal to Leon. They grew up together, right through infant school and on to the end of school days. Now Brian is Leon's most senior employee. He knows as much about the business as Leon – in fact probably more.'

'Can we visit the distribution centre? Preferably when Leon isn't there.'

'I suppose so. I can say I'm showing you around. Doris, you stay home please. There are lots of metal steps, and I don't want you falling; I know your leg isn't right yet. According to marital laws, I suppose half the business is mine, so Brian can hardly object to me looking at my half of it. We won't tell him we're going, we'll just turn up.'

'You'll be careful?'

Kat smiled. 'We will, Nan, I promise. I also want to see Sally again. That was so strange, the way she cut the call short. There's something she's not told us – or the police.'

'You're keeping an open mind on Leon?' Mouse was clearly worrying about her friend.

'Kind of. I can't believe he would kill anybody. And I'm a hundred per cent sure he's not involved with drugs, it's a respectable business operation he runs. I'm certain I would have sensed something.'

Mouse nodded. 'Maybe. Shall we go see Sally after we've been into Sheffield tomorrow? I can call and inspect the house, sign it off if it's done, then we can go and see this Brian King. On the way home we'll have a few minutes with Sally. Sound like a plan?'

'A plan indeed. Let me check the calendar in the kitchen first though, see if Leon's put anything on it. If he has fixed meetings, he puts them on that so I know what he's doing, it's only the unexpected meetings that aren't on there.'

Kat headed downstairs and checked Leon's itinerary; she saw he was heading to Derby first, then Chesterfield, so it was probably an early start. He came through the front door as she reached the bottom of the stairs.

He leaned forward to kiss her. 'Last night was superb,' he whispered. 'I'm available for a repeat tonight, if it's on offer.'

'You're insatiable, Leon Rowe,' she whispered back. 'It might be though.'

She tried to smile, but the discussion of earlier with Mouse and Doris was lodged very securely in her mind.

He kissed her again, and they headed upstairs. 'I'm having a shower. We eating out or in?'

'Don't think any of your ladies are eating at all. We had afternoon tea at the tea shop, we might never eat again. Can we decide in a bit? It may just be you I'm feeding.'

He paused on the landing. 'Have you made a decision about the shop?'

'Yes, we're having it. I'm contacting your shopfitters tomorrow, to set the ball rolling. It will only be a bit of a chat, we're some time away from getting them to do any work, but I need to give them a head's up.'

'You need money?'

'No thanks, we're okay.' The thought came unbidden. *I don't know where your money has come from any more.*

He nodded. 'If you need any sort of help, just ask. I'm not here tomorrow, by the way, but back tomorrow night.'

'I know. I just checked.'

He disappeared into their bedroom, and Kat continued along the landing to Doris's room.

'Leon's home,' Kat announced.

'You're okay?' Mouse asked.

Kat shook her head. 'No, I don't know what to believe any more, or if I can still trust him. I just feel sick thinking about it, but it's not something I can ignore. I have to know, don't I?'

31

The road where Mouse's Mini had exploded had been repaired, marking with fresh black tarmac the site where the two boys had died; an eternal memorial that had driven their parents into leaving the area. Mouse could see the repair from the bedroom window, and she felt sick.

Kat moved to stand by her, and put her arm around Mouse's waist. 'I'm here for you.' Mouse nodded.

They drove to the distribution centre, Kat wondering if she was doing the right thing. She could explain the impromptu visit to Leon by saying she had been telling Mouse about the spread of the business, and decided to take her to see what she had talked about. But how would they explain it to Brian King?

Kat parked the car outside the fenced compound, aware that lorries were in and out all day long, and set the handbrake. Mouse climbed out of the car and waited for Kat to join her on the pavement.

Kat nodded towards a lone figure standing near the gate. 'It's almost as if he's expecting us,' she said. 'That's Brian King.'

Brian's back was to them, so he would be unaware of their presence. His head was angled slightly to the left, watching the progress of an articulated vehicle as it traversed the crowded yard.

Mouse stared, her face losing all colour. 'Kat, can we go?'

Kat glanced at her friend and, without speaking, pressed her key fob. They climbed back into the car, and Kat started the engine. She reversed into a small side road, and drove back the way they had taken to get there.

Kat pulled up by the side of the road and switched off the engine. 'What's wrong?'

Mouse was trembling. 'He's the taxi driver. And what's more I escorted him to a do, some time ago now. That's why he seemed so familiar in the taxi. My brain just wouldn't accept that the man I'd escorted that night, who appeared to be wealthy, charming and quiet, could be a taxi driver. And it's obvious why he wants me dead. He knows I'll join the dots eventually.'

Kat grasped Mouse's hand. 'What do we do now? This is my husband's business, he's heavily involved with Brian… Shall we go home? We need to tell Doris and we need to listen to her advice.'

'Or do we go straight to DI Marsden?' Mouse said. She leaned forward and cried. Kat pulled her towards her and held her close.

The tears slowed and Mouse tried to apologise.

'Don't worry,' Kat said. 'You've had a shock, on top of seeing where the two lads died. But we have to talk to somebody. I simply don't know what to think about Leon. Do you still feel up to seeing Sally on the way home?'

'Yes. Once we set up our business, we won't be able to pick and choose what we do, who we see, so let's start as we mean to go on. I'm going to have to tell Marsden, but maybe tomorrow. This gives you tonight to either talk to Leon, or ignore it and let the law deal with him.'

They drove back to Bakewell in almost complete silence, although Kat kept reaching across to Mouse and squeezing her hand. She looked grey, distraught.

'We'll talk to Nan when we get in. She'll calm both of us down.' Kat blinked away her own tears as she spoke.

Mouse nodded, not sure she wanted to say anything yet.

They reached Sally's house, and this time it was opened within seconds of them knocking on the door.

'I was going to ring you later, Kat. Come in.' She led them through to the kitchen. 'Are you both okay?'

She peered closely at both of them. 'You've been crying. What's wrong?'

'We're good,' Kat said. 'Just had a bit of a shock, that's all. We'll recover, especially if there's a cuppa on the go.'

Sally smiled. 'Always, in this house.'

'So what did you need to ring me about?'

'Firstly to apologise for putting the phone down on you. I'm not normally rude, either on the phone or face-to-face, but I'd just had some news. I'll talk about that when I've made this drink.'

Nursing mugs of tea, they sat around the kitchen table and looked at each other. 'Did you want to see me about anything in particular?' Sally asked.

'No, not really. It was more to try to jog your memory for anything else, something you may have forgotten, or even just a theory you had. The last thing we want to do is upset you. You lost your son, that's enough for anybody to handle.' Kat spoke soothingly, not wanting to alienate Sally any further.

'I've got something to tell you. Just wait here a minute.'

They heard her footsteps as she went upstairs, and then her voice, speaking softly to someone.

A minute later, she was back downstairs, and pouring out a fourth mug of tea.

'I've somebody upstairs I want you to meet. He's agreed to see you, but he's a scared man. Bear that in mind.'

Kat and Mouse looked at each other, then nodded. This time the footsteps they heard were heavier, and a short stocky man with a tanned complexion walked into the kitchen. His hair was cut very short, and he had the deepest blue eyes Kat had ever seen. He looked to be about forty, although neither Kat nor Mouse would have put money on it.

'Kat, Beth, this is Mark James. Remember I told you Craig had two close friends. Don Truman is in prison, and Mark James disappeared just after Craig died.'

Mark dropped his head. So far he hadn't spoken a word.

'Last week,' Sally continued, 'Mark's mum passed away. Mark is only here until the funeral, then he's going back to Spain where it appears he's been all this time.'

'Thursday,' Mark said. 'I daren't stay any longer. I slept here last night, lying low. I don't want anybody knowing I'm back. I'll not be obvious at the funeral, I can't be.'

'I don't understand,' Mouse said,. 'You're saying you can't be at your own mum's funeral. Why not?'

'I would be killed,' he said simply. 'I arrived yesterday and booked into a Premier Inn, nice and anonymous. I contacted Sally, not expecting her to still be living here, and she told me to take no chances. She said to come here, she had a spare room, so here I am.'

'But you've been away fifteen years… surely whatever you did will be forgotten by now.'

'What I did? I did nothing. I was Craig's friend, that's all. And Craig was with me and Don when they came for their money. Now Don's serving a double life sentence, he'll never get out, and I ran before they could kill me.'

Mouse frowned. 'Let's take a step back, here. Are you saying Don shouldn't be serving a life sentence?'

'Definitely not. Whoever put those two lasses in that shed and set fire to it, using Don's petrol can from his garage with his fingerprints on it, was an out and out bastard. I know Don didn't do it. He was with me, getting drunk. By the next morning he was arrested and I was on a plane. I knew who had set him up, and I knew I was next. This is my first time back since and I can't let anybody know I'm here. Sally vouched for you two. I hope she's right.'

Kat nodded. 'Your story's jumping about a bit though. Start at the beginning will you, Mark?'

'Sorry.' He sighed. 'My head's all over the place. Don and I were with Craig that afternoon, and he was saying his mum had given him the money to pay off his debt, the one he had with Leon Rowe.'

Kat sucked in her breath, and felt her heart begin a rapid beat. 'Go on,' she whispered.

'Craig was a blethering idiot, because sometime between him leaving his mum's house with the two thousand pounds, he bought some more weed. By the time he met up with Rowe, he hadn't got all the two thousand quid, he'd managed to shrink it to eighteen hundred. They came for him that night, Rowe and that Brian King, and took him. They knew we'd seen them take him, so later on they went to Don's garage, got his can with his lawnmower petrol in it, filled two lasses up with drugs and put 'em in a shed, then set fire to it. The can was left near the shed.'

He paused for breath. 'They arrested Don next morning, and I legged it. I knew nobody would believe that he'd been with me, and while I was being his alibi, Rowe and King would have come for me. I've been in Spain ever since.'

Sally's eyes never left Kat's face all the time Mark was speaking. He picked up his cup and drank.

'Your mum is Valerie James?'

He nodded and put down his cup. 'She is. You know her?'

'I'm doing her funeral on Thursday. I saw your sister last Friday when I did the funeral visit. If you come to the church early on Thursday, you can stay in the vestry throughout the service. Wait there until everybody has gone, then you can leave in safety.'

Kat could see his eyes glistening with tears he hadn't dare shed before. 'I have to go now, Mark, but unless you're dead set on living in Spain, I don't think it will be too long before you're back in England.'

'I can't drive, Mouse, not even this short journey.' Kat opened the driver's door and got out of the car. Mouse opened her own door, then walked around to take the seat Kat had vacated, wondering if she ought to confess to never having driven an automatic vehicle before.

'You just want to sit for a bit?' Mouse asked.

Kat nodded, not ready to speak.

Mouse waited, knowing eventually the brutality of her predicament would hit Kat, and she would recognise what she was about to lose.

'Tomorrow,' Kat murmured softly, 'tomorrow we will take all our findings to DI Marsden. Tonight I will say goodbye to Leon. I can't live any longer with all this knowledge inside me, and do nothing about it. When we start our business properly, Mouse, we must never take on any case that is personal to any one of us. It hurts so damn much.' She began to cry.

Mouse held her close until the torrent of tears had ended, and then started the car. 'Shall we go home?'

'Yes. I think so. It's time for me to grow up. To face facts.'

Mouse pressed gently on the accelerator and marvelled at the smooth way the car took itself through the gears. Her little old Mini had never felt like that.

Mouse parked carefully in the forecourt, aware that the car that was already there was strange to them, and it would presumably need to move out at some point.

They walked around the back and through the kitchen door, to find Doris enjoying a cup of tea with a woman of around forty, hair slightly greying but with beautiful deep brown eyes, eyes that swivelled towards them as they walked through the door.

Kat held out her hand. 'I'm sorry, I can't remember your name, but you're George Reynolds' wife, aren't you? I met you at one of the Christmas parties, if I remember correctly.'

The woman nodded, and stood to shake her hand. 'Yes, I'm Lorna. I came to speak with your husband, but he's not here. Mrs Lester made me a cup of tea, because I cried on the doorstep.'

'I'm here. Can I help you? I've no idea what time Leon will be home.'

'I don't know. It's George, you see. They found his body buried in the woods, in the same grave as Paddy Halloran. It's not right.'

'What do you mean?'

'My George wouldn't have anything to do with Paddy Halloran. He detested him. Thought he was lazy, and didn't like they way he spoke about Mr Rowe. I just wondered if Mr Rowe knew anything about it, and I know the police are wondering why Mr Rowe gave me all that money. So, you see, I may not be the brightest button in the button tin, but I'm not daft. Something stinks.'

'Leon gave you money? When?'

'A few days ago. Maybe eight or nine. You see, I presumed he'd run off with somebody else, my George, because he didn't come home. When Mr Rowe turned up, he gave me an envelope. There was ten thousand pounds in it, Mrs Rowe. Why? What did he know? I want to ask him that. I want to ask him why my George is dead, and if he knows who killed him. He gave me that money long before George's body was found.'

Kat leaned with both hands on the kitchen table. 'I can't answer you,' she whispered, 'because I don't know the answer. What do the police think?'

'Huh. It's like speaking to donkeys. Or they think I'm one. I get the impression they think Halloran killed George, but Halloran showed evidence of torture. Burnt feet, two fingers chopped off, that sort of thing, and although they didn't say it out loud, I'm sure somebody else made Halloran speak, perhaps to tell them what he'd done with George. Your husband liked George, they got on really well, and he would have been mad that George was dead, he was in charge of the Chesterfield side of the distribution pipeline, or so he told me.'

'Distributing what?' Kat looked puzzled, although she was tipping over the abyss as she understood more and more of what Leon had never told her.

'Drugs. Cocaine in particular. He never touched it himself; George liked to be in control, and taking drugs, you're out of control. But he'd worked hard for Mr Rowe to build up that area.'

'And you've told this to the police?'

'Not really. I wanted to see Mr Rowe first, to let him know that ten thousand quid won't buy my silence if he had anything to do with George's death.'

Doris couldn't take her eyes off Kat. She knew this must be killing her inside, tearing her apart.

'Lorna, by tomorrow this nightmare will be resolved, one way or another,' Doris said. 'Can I ask you to keep quiet until the police want your statement? That will happen, I promise you. But Kat needs to deal with her husband first. Let me take you out to your car. For your safety, I don't want Leon to know you're here. Do you understand?'

Lorna blinked, and stood. Doris grasped her hand, took her out of the kitchen door and around the side of the house, then watched as the younger woman climbed into her car. 'Trust us, Lorna, this will all be sorted by tomorrow.'

'It had better be, Mrs Lester, it had better be.'

Kat was ringing Marsden as Doris re-entered the house, and she heard 9am confirmed. Doris couldn't help but think what a brave woman Katerina Rowe was proving to be.

32

Leon arrived home to a quiet household. He waited in the hallway, and then called Kat's name.

She came through from the lounge and looked at him. 'Leon.'

He moved towards her and kissed her on the cheek. 'Hi, sweetheart. I'm just going up to have a shower. We eating in or out?'

'I'll come up and talk to you,' she said, desperately trying to inject an iota of enthusiasm into her voice.

'You okay?' He looked into her eyes. She clearly wasn't fooling him.

'We'll talk in the bedroom.'

Leon stepped back, and ushered Kat in front of him. She turned around immediately they entered the room. 'Shut the door please, Leon.'

He obliged, and pushed it closed. 'What's wrong? You have a problem?'

'I do. My problem is that Craig Adams, along with one or two others that I know about, is dead. He died on the 8th of May 2002. It's a cold case as far as the police are concerned, but it's a cold case that has been reopened since Anthony Jackson's death. Anthony Jackson witnessed that murder, as did Oliver Merchant, Peter Swift, Isla Yardley and three more of their friends who were in their circle. Tell me, Leon, do you have plans to kill the other three? Or do you think four deaths will make them keep their mouths shut?'

'But I was with you the night Jackson was killed! And I'm sure your little friend downstairs will confirm it couldn't have been me driving that taxi, I'm sure she would have noticed if the driver were black.'

'We know who was driving the taxi, Leon. The person who was with you on the night you killed Craig Adams.'

Leon sat on the bed with a thud. 'What? Brian? He was the taxi driver?'

Kat laughed. 'So I don't need to ask any further questions, do I. Was that a confession, Leon? You'll need it for tomorrow, we've asked DI Marsden to be here for nine in the morning. I should imagine she's at the point of picking you up anyway, because everything we've found out has been easy to follow. The crunch piece of information she doesn't have as yet is that Mouse can identify Brian King as Anthony's killer, and her own attempted murderer. You have tonight to sort things out with the legitimate side of your business, but that's all. And just for the record, Leon, I know all about the other side.'

Leon's beautiful black face was slowly turning grey. Brian had brought all this down on their heads? Why? What the fuck was going on? His long-time friend had said nothing. Brian had been working behind his back, but to what end? To get rid of him? To take over the business fully?

Leon's head was whirling with Kat's body-blow, and he suddenly remembered the last proper meeting he'd had with Brian, ostensibly called to discuss Anthony Jackson's potential investment in their business. At that meeting, Brian had mentioned it becoming a three-way split, with him becoming a partner, as opposed to an employee.

He had come away from that meeting saying no to both Brian and Jackson. Was this the result of that decision? Was he being set up to take the fall for everything? But what had Kat said? Beth recognised Brian? That accounted for all the attempts on Beth's life; it was pure luck Leon had never mentioned to Brian she was staying with him and Kat.

Leon stood and moved towards Kat, who shrank away from him. 'Kat…'

'Keep away from me, Leon. And don't think you can escape this, we have files and files of proof. When Michael Damms, Caroline Boldock and Keith Lancaster start talking, you're going away for life, and in your case it will mean life. You're scum, Leon Rowe, absolute scum. How many have you killed with your drugs? And how many have you ordered to be killed? What about George Reynolds? His wife was here earlier, telling me about the ten thousand you gave her. Hush money, was it? I've wasted four years of my life on you, and it ends tonight.'

'Don't push me, Kat,' he threatened, and punched her. Unable to keep her balance, she stumbled across the room and crashed her head into the dressing table. Her scream reverberated around the house.

Darkness descended and Kat gave in. She slumped to the floor, unaware of the blood gushing down her face.

Leon stared at her, anger overcoming everything. He moved towards her slumped form, knowing that it was him or her; if he were to escape a prison sentence that was unending, she had to die.

The bedroom door burst open and Mouse stood in the doorway, the gun held in shaking fingers.

'Move!' she commanded. 'Get away from her.'

'And if I don't?' His tone was mocking. He'd seen the reaction of this young woman to the gun, and knew she wouldn't be able to hit him at three paces, never mind the length of the bedroom.

'If you don't, I'll shoot and make sure your fingerprints are on the gun.'

He laughed. 'You think you're good enough to place a bullet in my brain, in exactly the right place for it to look like suicide? You really think that, you silly cow? No, Beth, you kill me and you'll go to prison for most of your adult years.'

Mouse felt a hand come around her arm and take the gun out of her trembling hands.

'Mouse might not be able to place a bullet accurately, Leon Rowe, but I certainly can.' Doris took a step into the room, levering Mouse out of the way with her hip. 'Now, how do you want to do this? I don't want to kill you, but I will if I have to.

Step well away from Kat, get to the other side of the room. Mouse needs to attend to your wife.'

'No. Now what are you going to do?'

Doris raised the gun slightly and fired. His left hand exploded and he screamed. 'You want anything else rearranging?' she asked.

He staggered to the other side of the room, cradling his hand in the elbow of his right arm. Mouse moved towards Kat, who was opening her eyes.

'Stay where you are, Kat,' Mouse whispered. 'I need to get clean cloths and water, you're going to be fine.'

'Leon? Where is he?'

'He's at the other side of the room. He's only got one hand, but he's under control. I'll be ringing DI Marsden in a bit, we can't wait till tomorrow now. He's injured you, so Nan had to injure him. He was going for you again, Kat.'

'Is Kat okay?' Doris asked.

'She will be. I'll get her downstairs and see to her when we've decided what we're doing with the pathetic little man cowering in the corner.'

Kat used the side of the bed to haul herself to her feet. She stared at Leon, who was wrapping a towel around his hand in an attempt to staunch the flow of blood.

'Get out, Leon,' Kat said calmly. 'Get out of my life, and make it for ever. Tomorrow we will be handing everything over to DI Marsden, so I'll tell her you disappeared during the night. If you can't drive, get a taxi. And don't ever come anywhere near me or any of my friends or family again. You have this one chance to escape justice, Leon, I suggest you take it. I hope Marsden tracks you down, I really do, because that's the right thing to happen, but I can't hand you to her on a plate.'

'Kat, are you sure about this?' Doris looked concerned.

'I'm sure. Go now, Leon.'

Doris stepped aside, and the three women watched as he walked out of the room. Nobody moved until they heard the front door bang, followed by the sound of a car engine starting.

'Good job I shattered his left hand and not his right, isn't it?' Doris said. 'He clearly thinks it's okay to drive with just one hand. I should have shattered his kneecap, I suppose.'

Mouse helped Kat to stand, and all three of them went downstairs. The blood from Kat's head had stopped dripping down her face, and Mouse cleaned the wound, then dressed it. She handed over a couple of painkillers, then made Kat sit in the lounge, her feet raised on the recliner, and rest.

'I'll make you a cup of tea now Mouse has put you back together,' Doris said, 'and then we'll talk. We might have dealt with the murdering scumbag who fooled us all, but there's another murdering scumbag out there. Will Leon go to Brian King, do you think?'

'I doubt it. I saw the shock on his face when I said Mouse had identified Brian as the taxi driver. He'd no idea. I imagine he's doing lots of thinking about Brian. He's used to total loyalty, not the disloyalty after over thirty years of friendship. He's probably ringing somebody right now to make arrangements to have Brian sorted once and for all.'

'You think?' Mouse raised her eyebrows.

'Yes, I do. I've learnt a lot of things about my husband today, and nothing would surprise me.'

'So do you think we should ring Marsden now?'

Kat sighed. 'I don't know. My Christian beliefs say of course we should try to prevent any more deaths, but I'm not just a deacon, I'm also a human being, and I can't help but feel that both Brian and Leon deserve everything that's coming to them. Am I wrong? When I think of Sally Adams and Lorna Reynolds…'

The cup of tea, with just a tot of brandy in it, calmed frazzled nerves, and forced them to think logically.

It occurred to them that the crime that could cause them serious issues was the firing of the gun, and removing most of Leon's left hand. Fortunately the blood splatter had been confined to the bed; he had helped them massively by landing in that direction, so Mouse went upstairs and stripped the bedding. She checked around and saw one tiny spot on the bedhead. Scrubbing removed it from sight and she hoped it would also defeat any technical wizardry by the police. He had saved the blood from going everywhere by clutching his arm to him, and then wrapping it in a towel which he had taken with him.

The bullet was embedded in the skirting board, in the joint where it met the floor. Mouse prised it out, washed yet more blood away and dropped the bullet into her bowl of water.

The blood from Kat's head was a different matter, and there was a small pool on the wooden floor. It was easier than removing it from a carpet would have been, but still took some time and with no guarantee it wouldn't be traced if the police found it necessary to check.

Mouse made the bed ready for Kat, but guessed there would be no sleep.

'All done,' Mouse announced a minute later, the washing machine confirming it. 'I can't see any more blood but I'd like you two to have a look, in case I've missed any. However, let's not forget he hit you and you bled considerably, Kat. They've no reason to suspect the blood is Leon's unless they actually catch him. You have fresh bedding on, so even if they find Leon and he tells this strange story of a mad pensioner shooting him, we can simply deny it. We'll just say look for Brian King, he probably shot him. Or one of the others he's managed to upset in his crooked lifetime. There's bound to be many who would like to see Leon dead. Now, of course, we need to get rid of the gun.'

'Already done. Did you find the bullet?' Doris asked.

'What?'

'I said it's already done. Don't ask me anything else until this is over, then I'll tell you where it is. I just need to add the bullet to it.'

Mouse handed over the tiny object. She knew it would be well hidden.

'So now what?' Kat said. 'We ring Marsden?'

'Let's give Leon a couple more hours, because ideally I'd like him to get far away. Is his passport still here, Kat?'

She shook her head. 'No, he leaves it in his car. He frequently nips over to Holland and France, so keeps it with him. Why did I never see it, this link to drugs? He was always going to Holland, and he knows Paris better than Bakewell.'

'Then let's hope he realises it's all up for him, and legs it to Holland again. That actually will be the quickest way of getting away, Holland on the overnight ferry from Hull. Security's nowhere near as strict on the boats as it is on planes.'

Doris looked at her two girls as they discussed hoping the thug that was Leon Rowe had escaped, and she knew they were protecting her. 'Listen, you two, if this does go pear-shaped and I don't get away with shooting Leon, I don't want any heroics from either of you. You go ahead with your plans, make me proud, and I'll do my time. I've not killed anybody, so it won't be for too long, but hopefully he'll disappear, never to be heard from again. And Kat, my love, I'm so sorry this has happened. I know you loved him and I can't begin to imagine how you're feeling, but we're both here to help you through it.'

Doris made them a sandwich, forced them to eat it, and then Mouse rang DI Marsden. Mouse listened to the phone ringing out and was on the verge of putting the receiver down when Marsden answered.

'DI Marsden.'

'Hi, it's Beth Walters. Are you busy?'

'Sort of. I was just on my way out of the office to get a statement from somebody before I head out to yours in the morning.'

'Are you too busy to come out here tonight? I think you should. There have been developments.'

'With Leon Rowe?'

'Definitely with Leon Rowe.'

'I'll be there by eight.'

Tessa disconnected the call, picked up her bag once more and went to find Hannah.

Hannah Granger was sitting patiently in the driving seat, waiting for her boss to join her.

'Sorry, Hannah, if anybody's expecting you home early, can you ring them and warn them you'll be late. After we've seen Caroline Boldock, we're heading to Eyam, to Leon Rowe's house.'

'We're right about him, aren't we? He's behind all of this.' Hannah frowned. 'I can't help but feel sorry for Kat Rowe though. I don't think she's any idea.'

'Maybe she didn't have, but I get the feeling that's changed. I think tonight is the time we'll get the answers we need. They're pretty savvy, Kat Rowe and Beth Walters, and I think whatever we haven't managed to tie together yet, will be bundled up in a nice little package tonight.'

33

Caroline Boldock was the first of the seven to break. Incarceration in the safe house had emphasised the need to tell the truth; her life couldn't be lived in fear of Leon Rowe turning up with a shotgun.

Tessa and Hannah listened to her story, a simple one of teenagers celebrating a sixteenth birthday, until evil had arrived in the form of Leon Rowe and Brian King. She confirmed it was definitely them – you couldn't miss Leon Rowe, even from the back. On that warm May night, he had worn a T-shirt, and they had all recognised him. They had known Brian King's voice, and he was never more than a couple of feet away from Leon anyway.

Caroline repeated the words still etched into her brain, the words Craig Adams had said as he pleaded for his life while being dragged along the riverside walk. And then she confirmed the sound of the shot and the splash.

It felt cathartic to Caroline to finally speak of that night with someone other than the seven people who had witnessed it. Tessa organised her conveyance to the station for the next morning, to give her formal statement, and then sorted the instructions to get Michael Damms and Peter Swift brought in to give their statements, and for them to be told that Caroline had already divulged their part in the cover-up. Keith Lancaster in Australia could wait. And sweat.

Tessa left the safe house with a smile on her face. Now to arrest Leon Rowe and Brian King. She contacted the station to request a backup car meet her at the Eyam house, and they headed there, hopes high it was coming to an end.

Hannah could see how angry Tessa was, and chose to keep quiet through the tirade. It seemed that the three ladies had watched Leon Rowe go, and hadn't told anyone.

'But I asked you to come tonight instead of tomorrow,' Mouse said, deliberately putting a puzzled expression on her face.

'You didn't exactly stress the urgency,' Tessa replied.

'There was no urgency, Leon had already walked out, and to be perfectly honest, DI Marsden, we were more concerned with sorting out the damage to Kat's head.'

'Do you need an ambulance, Mrs Rowe?'

Kat gave a weak smile. 'No, I'll be fine. Head wounds always bleed heavily, but the cut is relatively minor. I've just got a bit of a headache, that's all. Beth and Nan sorted it, cleaned up the blood, changed the bedding – I think that's why Leon vanished so quickly. He saw all the blood.'

'You two were in the room when he hit Mrs Rowe?'

'No,' Mouse replied for both her and Doris. 'I heard Kat scream. He was standing over her, and I told him to leave her alone, I needed to see to her. He went while we were looking after Kat.'

Tessa looked at the paperwork laid out on the coffee table, the files, the scribbled notes, and recognised that they probably knew as much as she did.

'How did you get this information?' Tessa asked.

'Just by chatting to people. They'll do so to us quite openly, but talking to police is another matter.' Mouse spoke calmly.

'No clever computer work then?'

Kat laughed. 'I can barely switch one on.'

'I didn't mean you, Mrs Rowe. I meant Miss Walters.'

'Beth and I are very competent with technology,' Doris said, acid in her tone. 'What exactly are you suggesting, DI Marsden? Do you want these files or not? The whole situation as we have tracked it, is notated here. The only thing that is missing is what has happened tonight. Beth's memory was finally triggered by a visit to the Rowe distribution centre where she saw Brian King, so you now have your witness identification you have hassled her for; just take everything we have discovered. If something doesn't match up with yours, then ours will be the correct one.' Doris limped out of the room and went to the kitchen. *Jumped up little...* she turned to find Hannah following her.

'Shall we make a pot of tea?' Hannah smiled. 'Take no notice of the boss, she's not slept properly for weeks, and just when she could see the end, that damn man disappears. Come on, let me help you. I think we all need to calm down.'

Doris looked at her, then filled the kettle. 'We didn't realise he'd gone for quite some time, you know. We were busy cleaning the blood off Kat, and sticking her back together, then changing the bed, washing the floor, getting the blood-stained sheets in the washer. It all took time. It was only when we realised he wasn't downstairs that we thought to check for his car. It's gone, let's hope for good.'

'I've just had a message to say Brian King's been picked up, so Leon's obviously not gone there for sanctuary. Heaven only knows how Mrs Rowe will deal with the fallout from this. She's going to need a lot of help.'

'We're here for her. She knows that.'

Hannah carried the tray of drinks through to the lounge, where she handed them out to everyone. Marsden was looking through the files.

'You spoke to Peter Swift?'

Kat nodded, then winced. The movement hurt her. 'I did. I didn't lie to get in, told him my name, gave him my card, and just chatted with him. Offered to give communion, but he declined, saying he would wait to go to church with his partner. Nice man. Then I left. I really went to see if I could get him to say anything accidentally, but as you can see from the notes, he clammed up, so I came away.'

'Am I okay to take all these files with me?'

'Of course,' Doris said. 'That's what they're there for. We've got duplicates of everything anyway. As you would expect.'

Marsden gathered everything, then dumped it all back down before picking up her mug of tea. 'I don't want to fall out with you three, and thank you for all of this. But you put yourselves in danger, and that's not good. If Leon does get in touch, I need to know immediately.'

'Of course,' Kat said. 'But this is the plague village, DI Marsden, and trust me, he'll avoid it like the plague. I know him, he'll not risk coming back here.'

Marsden allocated four of her people to go through the files she had brought with her from Eyam, and she headed down to the interview room where Brian King, accompanied by his solicitor Olivia Jordan, was impatiently waiting.

Marsden didn't care; she was tired, and she guessed he had no intentions of saying anything. Thank God for Caroline Boldock and her bravery in finally speaking out, and thank God that Beth Walters had recognised Brian as the taxi driver. And she had said it was purely from the angle his head was at when he was tracking a lorry in the yard. On such small actions, whole cases are resolved, she mused.

She stood at the window alongside Hannah, looking into the room. 'Okay,' she said, 'I'll take the lead. If you think I'm missing anything, jump in.'

Hannah laughed. 'As if. I've sat in on dozens of interviews with you and not noticed you've missed anything so far.'

'There's always a first time, Hannah, and this one's a slippery customer. Look who he's got for a solicitor.'

They moved towards the door, and Tessa stopped for a second to survey the occupants. Within a couple of minutes, the recorder was activated and she began.

'Mr King, I need to take you back fifteen years or so. Can you tell me where you were on the evening of the 8th of May 2002?'

'No.'

'Okay, is that a "no you won't tell me", or a "no you can't remember"?'

'I can't remember. As you said, it's fifteen years ago. And I don't keep a diary.'

'Then let me remind you. You walked along the riverside path in Bakewell around nine in the evening, with Leon Rowe and a young man called Craig Adams.'

'Did I? Who's Craig Adams?'

'A young man who was in the same class at school as you and Mr Rowe. You actually knew him quite well. Well enough to kill him, it seems.'

Olivia Jordan held up her pen, and looked about to speak.

'Okay, Ms Jordan, we're not in a court of law, not yet anyway. I'm just after the truth, which, by the way, we have in the form of statements from witnesses to the events of that night.'

'Witnesses?' Brian King said.

Olivia reached across and touched his knee, warning him to be careful what he said.

'There were seven witnesses. Three are now dead, and one seriously injured. Three are still alive, and they have all given statements telling the same story.' She crossed her fingers at the lie; they still only had Caroline's statement, but Peter and Michael were coming in later. They would be interviewed and statements taken, which she guessed would match Caroline's. The Australian statement would be a bonus.

'No comment.'

'That's a surprise. Let me jog your memory a little bit more. In the afternoon of that day, Craig Adams had tried to pay two thousand pounds to Rowe, which he owed for drugs. He was short of the full payment. We have two witnesses to that as well, so don't waste your breath denying it. You returned at night and took Craig. The same witnesses saw this. Are you with me so far?'

'No comment.'

'Okay. Fortunately we don't need your comments. You manhandled Craig Adams along that riverside walk, not knowing that initially your voices were recognised, and then the two of you were visually recognised. I have the exact words Craig used as he pleaded for his life, but it was to no avail, was it, Brian? You took him to the deepest stretch of the river and you shot him. Oh, don't bother asking, the shot was heard, along with the splash as he went into the water.'

'No comment.'

'Okay, let's move on to later that night, to a crime that was solved pretty quickly. It was a case of arson, and right outside the shed that was burnt down was a petrol can with fingerprints on it. Those fingerprints belonged to Donald Truman, currently serving two life sentences for the murder of two girls who were inside that shed. We still have that petrol can, and there are massive improvements in testing these days. It's already with forensics, and if either you or Rowe even breathed near that petrol can, we'll know. We believe you gave those girls drugs in that shed, and then set up Don Truman, one of the witnesses to the abduction of Craig Adams, for the murders. That petrol can, according to a witness who fled from this country because he also knew about the abduction, was in Don's garage. He used it to store petrol for his lawnmower. What did you do to keep Don quiet? Threaten his family? His little sister? You don't need to answer that. We have somebody interviewing Don Truman right now, and once we reassure him that your whole operation, and you, is about to be closed down permanently, he'll tell us everything.'

'No comment.'

'Okay. Let's move on to more recent deaths. Let's talk about Anthony Jackson. Let me tell you what I believe. I think Jackson wanted to join your outfit as a partner.'

'I'm not a partner in any outfit.'

Tessa could sense the undercurrent in his voice. There was anger there.

'Really? You're not a partner in Rowe Pharmaceuticals? Or even Rowe Drug Empire?' She smiled.

'No.'

'You're not happy about that, are you, Brian? So did it make you even more unhappy when Jackson came around wanting part of the action, and you were still a lowly employee.'

'Hardly lowly.'

'Nevertheless, an employee.'

Tessa consulted her notes, and King shuffled uncomfortably on his chair. She ignored him.

She took out a photograph, and pushed it across to him. 'Recognise him?' She took out a second picture. 'Or her?'

King didn't flinch at the gruesome sight of a faceless Anthony Jackson. 'No face,' he said. 'How am I supposed to recognise him? And I don't know who the slag is.'

'She said you called her slag when she got out of the taxi you were driving. That was thirty seconds before you shot her.'

'I shot nobody.'

'We'll find out when we find the gun. Your apartment is being torn apart as we speak, so I'm hopeful that the gun and the laser will surface by the end of today.'

'Laser?'

Marsden knew she had him. Somewhere in his home was that laser. Maybe they wouldn't find the gun; he would be stupid to leave that where it was easy to find, but the laser was there, the one to blind Peter Swift and likely Oliver Merchant, she'd stake money on it. She stood. 'DI Marsden leaving the room. I'll send coffee in. You could be here for a long time.'

'Dave?'

'Yes, boss.'

'Have you found anything? Tell me it's gun-shaped.'

'No gun, but he sure keeps lots of paperwork here. I think it relates to drug shipments, but not sure they're connected with Rowe.'

'Have you found a laser?'

'I haven't personally, but let me get back to you. I'll go check with the others.'

Dave Irwin disconnected, and headed upstairs. 'Listen up folks, we're specifically looking for a laser – oh, and the boss says anything gun-shaped.'

'Just bagging a laser now, Dave,' he heard from another room.

Irwin moved across to the second bedroom, and was handed an evidence bag. Inside it was what, at first sight, seemed to be a torch. It was unnerving to think that this small item had probably killed one man and seriously injured a second.

He took a photograph then sent it to Marsden. His text was brief and to the point. **Found in second bedroom.**

Marsden headed back down to the interview room, clutching a newly printed photograph of the one Dave Irwin had sent.

Olivia Jordan and King were finishing their coffees, Jordan making notes at the same time.

'Sorry to keep you waiting.' Marsden pressed the recorder and logged herself back into the room, then sat down. 'Okay, Brian. As I said, we have a team of officers in your home, and I'd like you to tell me what this is.' She pushed the picture across the table.

He looked at it for a moment, then turned to his solicitor. She too briefly scanned the print, then spoke directly to Marsden. 'I'd like to speak with my client away from this room, alone please.'

34

Brian King was charged with the murders of Anthony Jackson, Isla Yardley and Oliver Merchant the following day. It was understood that other charges would follow.

They had statements from Caroline Boldock, Keith Lancaster, Michael Damms and Peter Swift, all telling the same story of witnessing the murder of Craig Adams aurally, and seeing Brian King and Leon Rowe dragging the young man along the riverside path.

King categorically denied shooting Adams, he said Rowe was responsible for that. Leon Rowe was the one Craig had upset, by withholding some of the debt.

He confirmed that Jackson had told him of the identities of the seven people who had witnessed the killing; Jackson had hoped by giving this information to King, and thereby to Rowe, that it would give him an in to their business. Instead, King had kept the long-time secret to himself, and had set about removing the problem, one death at a time. Leon Rowe would have been the final execution, leaving King with everything.

Tessa Marsden felt drained. It had been a long traumatising case. She had to admit to herself that Kat Rowe and Beth Walters had pulled out all the stops, although Marsden was convinced that some of the information they had gleaned had come about through the technical wizardry of a certain elderly lady and her granddaughter.

It seemed that Leon Rowe had disappeared. He hadn't gone abroad, not in his own name anyway, and there had been no sightings of him despite lots of publicity in the media. He was currently the most wanted man in the UK, and there had been reported sightings, but nothing that produced anything to make them think the sighting was genuinely Rowe.

One day, Leon Rowe, Marsden thought, *one day, and you'll be behind bars for the rest of your natural.*

Terry Vincent waited until midnight, then headed to the compound. He negotiated his way around two Corsas, a Land Rover and a Mondeo, reaching the taxi at the back of the lot without damaging any part of himself. He carried a petrol can in each hand.

The alcohol from the seven pints he had consumed earlier was causing his legs to work independently of the rest of him, but he climbed into the taxi and started it with the key kept in the ignition so the vehicle was always ready to go.

He did a three point turn in sixteen moves, and finally reached the compound gates. He climbed out, opened them and drove the taxi out on the road, before returning to lock up.

This was what Brian would want. Terry walked back to the idling black cab, and climbed into the back first. He felt around the seats and looked on the floor, in case any wallets or phones had been left, but the only thing he found was a house key. He climbed back out and into the driving seat, after throwing the key over the gate and inside the compound. He didn't think anybody would be reporting it as lost property.

He drove the cab to a patch of land where other cars tended to end up in flames, and hoped he would be able to walk home without his legs giving way altogether.

Sprinkling the petrol around took no time at all, and he saw no one. He threw in the match and there was a huge whoosh. He staggered, then ran. Brian would be pleased with him, that would get rid of any evidence there might be in the vehicle. Another job well done. And hopefully another hefty bonus come payday.

Epilogue

Two months later

Kat and Mouse stood holding a pair of scissors between them, the points resting on the bright royal-blue ribbon that trailed across the double shop door and both windows. The paintwork gleamed in the bright late summer sunlight and the name of *Connection* sparkled, the blue of the name contrasting vividly with the white background.

Kat, Mouse and Doris had sent out three hundred invitations to the opening, and Kat was convinced everyone had arrived, complete with a plus one. She hoped there was enough wine and cheese to go around.

Mouse grinned at Kat and whispered, 'Go on then.'

Kat half turned to face the people gathered around, many of them spilling on to the road, and smiled.

'Welcome to our grand opening, everybody. Thank you all for coming, and please come in and grab something to eat and drink. I now declare our new shop, our new investigative agency, *Connection*, well and truly open.'

Kat and Mouse cut the ribbon, and everyone cheered. They walked through the door holding hands, followed by a beaming Doris.

For the next hour, it was bedlam, but slowly the crowd dispersed. Doris had made five appointments, and Mouse looked ecstatic. Kat was happy, but didn't have the glow about her that infused Doris and Mouse. DI Marsden, taking the afternoon off to attend the opening, had confirmed that still nothing had been heard of Leon's whereabouts, but they wouldn't stop looking.

Kat missed the Leon that she had known, but definitely didn't want the Leon that she now knew, to return.

Enid Silvers linked her arm through her husband's and looked at all the people milling around. 'I'm so proud of her. She was devastated when Leon left, I know she was, but look how she's holding herself together. I remember saying I wanted to have grandchildren, but really, it's a good job they didn't, isn't it?'

Victor squeezed her arm. 'She'll meet somebody else, there's plenty of time.'

By seven o'clock, they were locking up. All the leaflets had been handed out, and the next day the serious side of the business would begin.

They had decided to eat at Kat's after the opening, and as they entered the kitchen, all three collapsed onto the chairs, exhausted by the long day.

'Shall I dig some beef burgers out of the freezer. I've plenty of bread cakes in,' Kat said.

'Fine by me,' Mouse said.

'And me,' said Doris. 'I'll do the onions.'

Kat went through to the garage and rummaging sounds could be heard coming from the depths of the big freezer. She returned with a box of burgers and a chicken. 'I'll defrost this and have it tomorrow, I think,' she said. 'You're both welcome to join me.'

'You have to put the chicken back, Kat,' Doris said.

'Why? It's ages since I cooked a full chicken.'

'Don't ask questions, young lady. Just put the damned chicken back. I'm in charge of your freezer supplies.'

Kat stared at Doris. 'What's wrong with this chicken? Why can't we eat it?'

Doris grinned. 'It's got a gun and a bullet up its arse.'

'What?'

'I had to get rid of the gun, didn't I, just in case Marsden clicked on I'd shot Leon.'

'So you inserted it in the chicken, and froze it?' Mouse's eyes were huge as she took in what her nan was saying.

'Yes, I thought it was a good idea at the time. Do you think it's safe to get it out now?'

Kat and Mouse looked at each other, both trying not to laugh. Doris said everything in such a matter of fact way, and she had no idea how funny it was, this chicken with a gun up its bum.

'I think it's safe now,' Mouse said, and took the chicken from Kat to inspect the hiding place. 'She's right; there is a gun up its bum,' she said. 'I can feel the end of it. Smart idea, Nan. I never worried about what you'd done with it. What do we do with it now it's re-surfaced?'

'We'll defrost it overnight,' Doris said, 'and I'll have a look at it tomorrow – the gun, not the chicken.'

Mouse moved to the fridge and lifted out a bottle of champagne. She took out three champagne flutes from the cupboard and placed them on the kitchen table.

'Time for our own celebration,' she said, and picked up the bottle, preparing to pop the cork.

'Before we do that…' Kat held up a hand. 'I have something to tell you.'

Mouse stared at her friend. 'I hope this is good, not bad. You heard from Leon?'

'No, I haven't. This is kinda apropos of nothing, in the grand scheme of things. It's a little bit of news for you two to digest, and work out how this is going to impact on the business.'

Mouse groaned. 'Are we going to like this?'

Kat gave a dismissive shrug. 'I don't know. Remember when I had that really sore throat and Neil gave me some antibiotics to help me with it?'

Mouse clapped her hand to her mouth. 'You're ill?'

'Not really. Antibiotics have this strange effect on contraceptive pills. I'm pregnant.'

THE END

Follow Kat and Mouse's next venture in part two of the trilogy.

Acknowledgements

I have two people to thank for allowing me to use their names in the book: Caroline Boldock, who threw a proper wobbly because it had taken me until book number nine to include her, and Sarah Hodgson, a top class fan and beta reader. Thank you so much you two, and Caroline, I'm sorry I turned you into an escort! At least you didn't become a corpse.

I also owe thanks to Kirsty Waller, my youngest daughter. She sets me straight on legal issues, and she teaches me such things as how to roll a joint, what goes in a joint and what a roach is, all fascinating stuff, I'm sure. She also gave me two phrases to use in the book. She was in pain after a boxing injury, and when I rang her to check if she was okay, she said she had taken enough painkillers to floor a baby kangaroo. That definitely was included. The second phrase came via a text message that said, **Mum, I like apropos of nothing. Can you put it in your book?** I did.

This book is the first in a trilogy, and I extend my grateful thanks to Bloodhound Books, my publishers, for commissioning me to write the series. I also want to thank Sarah Hardy, Alexina Golding and Sumaira Wilson, Bloodhound staff members, for their helpfulness at all times.

My editor, Morgen Bailey – I hope you know how much I appreciate your work. Thank you so much for sorting me out. You're a star.

Eyam deserves a mention in these remarks – our beautiful Derbyshire plague village. Everyone should visit Eyam, steeped in a history that is tangible; residents wiped out over a period of around fourteen months because they selflessly gave up their own lives to stop the spread of this dreadful disease. Take a walk around the churchyard, the plague cottages. Everywhere you go you can imagine the despair as the villagers buried their children, their spouses, their parents, leaving others to bury them when their time came. Heartbreaking history.

And last but not least, my readers deserve all my thanks. Your reviews, your personal comments to me, and your support make this author one very happy lady.

Anita Waller
Sheffield UK, August 2018

Printed in Great Britain
by Amazon